THE RISE OF

THE CHEMIST

BOOK TWO OF THE GRANVILLE SERIES

Nathan Parker

I

DEDICATION

Steve

I wish I could have finished it in time, but there's a copy on its way up to you at your new, heavenly address.

Sonny

You are life.

ACKNOWLEDGEMENTS

Thank you to those I love for the inspiration and
encouragement to keep striving for more.

Writing has kept me going this year, through
some of my darkest days yet, as has the warmth
and support of those closest to me.

Thank you to my proof readers, as without
you, this book would not be here.

Thank you to Tony Higginson for the advice and
direction during a year of learning and transition.

Thank you to the wonderful team at Lancashire Book
of the Year. The award ceremony in 2019 provided me
with a platform which I have benefitted from through
untold personal, creative and professional growth. I am
proud to represent our county in the world of writing.

Thank you readers, your validation has
spurred me on to write more.

Thank you finally to Nadina, for listening to me read each
chapter and scene out loud over and over. For investing in
the story as much as I have and for being honest at all times.

CHAPTER ONE

The drop of condensation clung to the rim of the bottle. He watched as it delicately began to tumble, multiplying in size, plummeting effortlessly towards the wooden table below. Its fall had left a clear trail behind on the otherwise frosty brown glass of the Budweiser bottle. As it hit the table it dispersed, vanishing into the damp ring, where there arguably should have been a coaster. At that point Tommy questioned whether college parties really were for him. He'd resorted to watching the finer details of his soon-to-be-warm beer bottle, instead of laughing, dancing and mingling with his fellow party goers.

It was warm in here tonight. Fifty teenagers keen to forget their woes on a Friday night will do that to a two-up two-down terraced house in Granville, Tommy thought. It was Robbie Fisher's party, a kid from his Sociology class at Granville Sixth Form. He knew he'd been invited out of courtesy, as Robbie had been talking at length about it during their lesson yesterday and evidently felt rude not extending the invite his way.
This put him in a predicament.

Did he follow the will of every fibre in his body and avoid the party, hiding at home in his bedroom as he had done so much lately? Or should he be brave and face up to the fact he hardly had any friends and the fresh start he'd hoped for at college, hadn't been feeling all that fresh?

In a moment of madness earlier this evening he'd

thrown caution to the wind, put on his white Oxford shirt, slipped into his brother's old denim jeans and took Robbie up on his invitation and right now, in this moment, he wasn't quite sure why.

He looked around and saw familiar faces from college, some he knew the names of and some he didn't. The pungent scent of cigarettes reminded him of home. The music was loud, so much so he could feel every sound inside his chest, almost as though the thunderous, repetitive bass line had replaced the beat of his heart. It wasn't Tommy's preferred music and he'd have loved nothing more than to have the confidence to jump up and change the track to a classic *Motown* track or something from *Kasabian* or *The Stone Roses* perhaps, however he recognised that he was the minority here, so accepted the fact he'd be listening to rubbish music for the duration of his stay.

He'd been people watching for a while, saying hello to some of his classmates when required, but he'd managed to avoid any further conversation by pretending he was going to the toilet. An uncharacteristic green trickled through his veins as he observed people getting drunk and having fun from afar, and for once he envied them.

He'd watched some strange characters coming and going, people dancing, fighting over what song to play next, taking shots of spirits coming in all sorts of bright radioactive colours, friends sharing heart to hearts, strangers sharing heart to hearts, subtle flirting, in-your-face snogging – pretty much your average Friday night house party in Granville.

He picked up his beer and took a sip, placing it back on top of the water stained ring, which his previous three beers had a hand in creating.

"Tommy, isn't it?" an over exuberant voice bellowed.

A large figure jumped onto the couch next to him, almost sending Tommy flying towards the ceiling. Once he composed himself and settled back into his seat, he turned to notice it was a boy who looked vaguely familiar, but he couldn't quite place him, or remember his name.

Awkward.

"Yeah, Tommy that's right," he replied tentatively, pondering how to get around the fact he didn't know this guy's name.

"It's me, Seb..."

Great, that's that problem sorted.

But Tommy knew his awkward smile was transparent. He couldn't figure out how he might know this person, who clearly knew him. He may as well have had a sign on his forehead which said in bold capital letters – *I don't remember you, sorry!*

"... from the Fresher's Fayre. First week of college, you showed me where Student Services was... because I'd lost my bag and didn't know what lessons I had,"

Bam! It clicked, he'd helped this guy, Seb, out on their first day when he was walking around the Fresher's Fayre. They'd only spoken for a few minutes at the time, so the fact he'd remembered his name was quite impressive.

Seb's presence was intense and a little overly familiar, considering their previous encounter was just a two-minute conversation and a little helping hand around about 3 weeks ago, then it registered with Tommy as to why. His lack of acknowledgement for personal space, wandering eyes and a noticeable slur told him that Seb was well on the way to being hammered.

Tommy reached out and smiled with a touch more conviction. He shook Seb's hand, a gesture which would re-ignite their apparent whirlwind friendship from Fresher's Fayre.

"How's it going, Seb?" Tommy asked.

"I've been hoping to bump into you mate," Seb continued, "I wanted to say you really helped me out that day. I came to the college, new to the area, not knowing anyone or anything. You were the first person I spoke to, you helped me find my bag – and my phone thank god – you made me realise that most folk are nice and friendly and since then I've not looked back. I've made loads of mates, college is amazing, don't you think?"

Seb finished his sentence by raising his bottle of cider, as if honouring Tommy's help and support with a toast, before taking a healthy, celebratory swig straight from the bottle. Tommy drew a gulp from his bottle of *Bud* as he contemplated his answer.

Was college amazing? Really?

That wasn't his experience so far. This guy came to Granville not knowing anyone and here he was, talking about having loads of friends already. Tommy went up to sixth form with lots of people from his school, yet he'd never felt more alone. Before he could answer, Seb continued, oblivious to Tommy's lack of response.

"I'm just loving life at the minute, it's brilliant. Look around us man, loads of girls, good tunes, enough alcohol to sink a dozen ships, times are good. Did you hear about what happened last weekend…?"

Tommy zoned out a minute as Seb continued zealously about the tales of last weekend. He pondered this alien lust for college life and questioned why he didn't feel the same way. It was understandable, he thought, or rather he hoped. Considering all that had happened over the last year, he felt sure that he was bound to feel a little apprehensive about mixing with others.

It was bad enough before, having to deal with the jibes about the fact he was poor, no money, hand me down clothes, drug addict as a mum – and a brother for that matter. But ever since the incident with Smiler and the devastation in finding about his dad's murder, exposing the town's most feared criminal, who just so happened to be daylighting as Granville's saviour and prince, Councillor Jim Carruthers, things had been a tad more difficult.

Tommy thought for a second about the things that rattled around his head daily; never getting to meet his dad felt so final and the fact he was murdered just made it even more challenging to comprehend. Losing Jack was another big blow and one he strangely felt more of an emotional inheritance, than finding out about his dad. Jack was his mentor and friend, a father figure almost and he literally saw his last breath leave his body.

He recognised these were huge life altering events and the fact he was just expected to squash them down and get on with life troubled him. Not forgetting about the traumatic events which led to Smiler's arrest; being tied up and beaten, in fear for his life and having to listen whilst his captor boasted in harrowing detail of how he had groomed and abused his mum when she was just a teenager. This information had scarred him, and he still hadn't been able to discuss it with anyone since, especially his mum. Topple all of that with the fact that Smiler escaped custody and the bonus prize; he was still on the run. Everywhere Tommy went he was the poor kid that had to deal with *all of that.*

The promises his mum had made about going to rehab and getting clean disappeared into the wind along with Smiler. Tommy constantly agonised over the hope and control which momentarily returned to his mum. It teased him with what life could be like, before being ripped from their hands the moment Smiler's assailants drove into the prison wagon, killed those armed guards and broke their master free. Free to reign again and Tommy knew it; he was sure that Smiler was just waiting for the right moment to strike, a feeling that he lugged around with him and it weighed a tonne.

Tommy considered all of this, yet it still didn't complete the picture. Yes, it was awful, he thought. Yes, it was distressing and sometimes he found himself reliving the trauma through vivid flashbacks and nightmares. But he knew deep down it wasn't the sole cause of his new found tendency to isolate himself, his lack of confidence – something he'd always struggled with but lately it was the lowest he'd ever known – and his lack of a sense of self, which was the thing that bugged him the most. This was down to another significant thing, or person rather; Kirsten.

God, I miss her.

"Do you want some of this?" Seb inquired, interrupting his inner reflections, still obliviously unaware that this whole time he hadn't even been listening to him.

Tommy turned to see Seb holding a small zip lock bag with some white powder in it.

"What is it?" Tommy asked, intrigued but by no means tempted.

He'd seen enough substance use in his house to last a few lifetimes, so nothing surprised him when it came to drugs.

"It's a bag of *Charge*, of course," Seb said, with a huge grin.

It was only now that Tommy was drawn to look more closely at Seb and recognised that he must be well under the influence by now. His pupils were wide, eyes bulging ever so slightly. He noticed that Seb had a few beads of sweat bubbling at the surface of his forehead, but not quite well formed enough to fall.

His eyes were drawn to Seb's mouth, which was closed, teeth clenched, jawline pronounced, and he had those little bits of white, congealed saliva at the corners of his lips. Tommy had heard murmurings about this latest drug called *Charge* around college, but this was his first encounter seeing both the drug itself and its effects up close. It looked intense.

"No, I'm ok cheers Seb," Tommy mustered.

Tommy hoped his polite decline would be enough to deter Seb's advances and that he would move on to chat to someone else, somebody who was perhaps a bit more in the mood. There are levels to the drug dance, Tommy knew that. If two people are not on the same level, they just aren't compatible during a conversation or any form of interaction really. He'd found this the hard way. He reminisced about growing up, whether drink or drugs, he often found himself several levels apart from his mum and brother and it was always hard work to try and waltz.

Unfortunately, Seb wasn't giving up on him just yet.

"Mate, you need to get involved," he babbled excitedly, "It's the best thing ever. They call it the perfect party drug you know. Did you know that?"

Seb's chatter was gaining in speed and modulation. He opened the zip lock bag with sublime intricacy. He noted the impressive dexterity in his index fingers and the speed by which he gained access to his supply.

He watched excitement visibly soak Seb's face, as he took out a door key from his jeans pocket. He stuffed the end into the bag and shovelled out a huge pile of white powder. Seb lifted it up in between their faces, it was close enough that Tommy could smell it; a sweet yet metallic odour. The mound of *Charge* was reminiscent of an arctic shelf, sat there on the edge of his key, glistening. Tommy's stomach tightened and his palms became slightly moist.

Seb steadied himself, waiting for what could have only been a couple of seconds, yet it felt like an age to Tommy. Once composed, Seb leaned forward and with a swift, hard sniff, the *Charge* disappeared up his right nostril. He popped his key back in his pocket and shuffled even closer to Tommy on the couch. He shook his head looking mighty impressed with himself.

"No, I didn't know that, Seb..."

Tommy leaned back, attempting to increase his efforts to disengage from the conversation. He needed a way out, but he was too polite to walk off, or at least he thought he was. This guy was off his head, but at the same time his demeanour was warm and friendly. Plus, he was the only person who had gone above and beyond to see past his reluctance and strike up a conversation tonight. His mind was torn.

Should I stay, or should I go?

"Yep. That's what they're all saying..."

He wondered who *they* were.

"...it keeps you going all night like cocaine, it gives you that fuzzy feeling in your stomach like ecstasy and it makes you feel like you can forget all your troubles, like you wanna dance, like you could walk up to anyone and start a conversation,"

"I've noticed," Tommy said dryly, to which Seb cackled and slapped Tommy on the back endearingly.

It felt quite nice to make somebody laugh again. As strange as this situation was, a slight fondness towards Seb was creeping in, a fondness that he wasn't expecting.

"You know, ever since that Smiley bloke or whatever he was called got nicked and then escaped..."

Smiley bloke? Tommy froze for a slight moment.

"...although from what I've heard he wasn't all that smiley..."

A sense of liberation suddenly rushed through Tommy's body that almost made his cheeks tingle. He realised that as Seb was new to the area, he didn't really know the story of Smiler and better still, he didn't know how Tommy was connected. He wondered if he'd finally managed to find somebody in Granville that didn't see him as Tommy, the poor kid with all those troubles linked to Smiler. Instead, he was just Tommy, a kid from college.

Copious amounts of white powder and 100mph conversation aside, Tommy started to think Seb seemed like a pretty stand-up guy. Perhaps he was a little lost in the popularity rat race of teenage life - which in fairness was symptomatic of living in Granville for many - but stand-up all the same.

Seb continued, "...people have been saying that gear has been a bit harder to get hold of, you know? But then some scientist dude has come along and created this super drug, and everyone is absolutely buzzin' – look around."

Seb smiled and gestured towards the hordes of party goers dancing under a ceiling of sweat, as if to show off a collection of Monet paintings. Tommy scanned the room and saw something that was perhaps a little more akin Picasso. He saw lots of swaying, stumbling and gurning, but he couldn't argue with Seb on the basis that everyone looked as though they didn't have a care in the world. He wondered what that felt like.

"Seriously man, it's so cheap too," Seb thrust the baggy in front of Tommy, "Three grams that had in it, guess how much? Go on, have a guess,"

"I've no idea," Tommy said.

"Fifty quid! Unbelievable isn't it? I got it off my mate in the year above, Finn, he's over..." Seb tailed off and looked around the room pointing at pretty much everybody and nobody all at the same time, "ah, I can't see him, he's probably chatting up some girls upstairs, " Seb gushed, "that's cool. More *Charge* for me and you, eh?" Seb's cackle returned.

"I'm ok, thanks though,"

"Tommy, the sooner you realise that *Charge* is the way to go, the sooner you'll unclench and start enjoying college life. Everybody's doing it and sooner or later you will be too my friend." Seb said with a wry smile, almost philosophically.

Time to go.

Tommy turned towards the wooden coffee table on his seat and shuffled towards the edge, priming himself for a swift exit. He reached for his beer and took a sip. He looked away from Seb towards the kitchen, which led to the back door. He took another sip of his beer and plotted his escape.

Quarter of a beer to go and I'm out of here.

He noticed Seb had sat back in his seat and momentarily stopped his nattering.

Peace at last.

CHAPTER TWO

Tommy nursed his bottle of beer, gauging a polite amount of time before he could finish it and depart. His mind wandered back to Kirsten. He wished she was here, if she was, he had no doubt that he'd be having a much more enjoyable time. In fact, if Kirsten was here, they would have probably left some time ago as the party was – in her words – rhubarb. Which he had learned pretty quickly to be her word for terrible.

He thought about how they'd drifted apart and questioned whether he was to blame. If he wasn't ready to take their friendship a step further was that really his fault? On the other hand, should he have been honest with her from the start about how he felt during the Smiler aftermath, instead of pushing her away?

If only he'd said something sooner, before she went off to that stupid summer camp at the Derry Bridge University. It wasn't stupid really, he knew that. He was proud of her; not that that would mean anything to her now. It just hasn't been the same since she returned. He wished he could go back a few months and fix it. What he'd give for another evening at the Junction pub watching her work and sneaking a drink or two whilst she was on her break.

The music in the room suddenly took a random turn towards the better, with an indie disco classic blasting out of the speakers, chosen by a girl from the year above, who obviously wasn't as concerned with being banished from the in crowd as he was: *She Moves in Her Own Way – The Kooks*. The song was fitting, as even more fond memories of Kirsten washed over him. He noticed his face crack into a wry smile as he thought about her. Then he remembered the present situation; they go to the same college, but it feels like they're worlds apart. It will be two months tomorrow since the last time they spoke, and he missed her like crazy.

Tommy snapped back into the room, unnerved by a shaking feeling on the couch. He turned and quickly realised that Seb was in trouble.

He was shaking uncontrollably, and his mouth appeared to be frothy.

"Seb! Seb!" Tommy yelled.

Seb was unresponsive. The shaking became more pronounced and Tommy realised he was having some kind of seizure. Seb's whole body fell into spasm and his eyes rolled back into his head. Tommy could see the whites of Seb's eyes and scarlet blood began to trickle from his nose, before the involuntary shaking became that violent that it abruptly flipped him off the couch and onto the floor, where the seizure continued.

A girl standing close to the couch screamed. It pierced the atmosphere and drew the attention of other party goers.

"Phone an ambulance!" Tommy shouted to her, but her jaw was open, and she was barely moving, disturbed and unable to take her eyes off Seb and his thrashing.

"I'll phone one, what should I say?" The girl's friend stepped in nervously and pulled out a mobile phone. She began dialling.

"Tell them he's having a seizure and he's not answering me when I shout him. Tell them he's got blood coming from his nose too."

Tommy was panicking but his instincts kicked in. He pushed the couch and coffee table out of the way and cleared a space. He must have remembered some of the advice he was given on that first aid workshop at the boxing club last year.

Some party goers gravitated towards the living room to get a look at what was going on, some in shock, others looked like they were too wasted to even realise what was happening. Tommy saw some of the party goers heading straight for the door. He assumed they would have put two and two together and made four; recognising that paramedics coming to a house party, increased the likelihood that the police would too. They obviously didn't fancy their chances with all the drink and drugs lying around and Tommy would have bet his one and only pound that Finn was amongst those fleeing.

Some mate he was.

Tommy watched on, helpless and in disbelief as Seb wriggled around the floor unconscious, before slowly coming to a standstill. Tommy bent down, crouching over to put him in the recovery position and as he did, he saw that his face was covered in sick and white froth. His skin looked clammy and the pink glow from his rather chubby cheeks had turned a worryingly blueish hue.

Tommy placed his hands over his face as he crashed onto the couch. The burst of adrenaline made him feel queasy. He noticed his fingers were trembling yet numb and his heart was thumping hard.

What the hell had just happened?

The music had been turned off, quite when this happened Tommy wasn't sure. His mind must have switched off to all the noise the moment he recognised his newfound friend was in a whole world of trouble. As bizarre as it was, he was the only friend Tommy had managed to make in the three weeks he'd attended Granville Sixth Form.

CHAPTER THREE

Tommy stared at the sparse notice board in front of him in the waiting room at the Intensive Care Unit, Granville St. James' Hospital, attempting to piece together how he'd got there.

He remembered that the paramedics had looked pissed off because nobody was forthcoming with information at the party. Tommy knew it wouldn't have been the first time they'd been greeted with a wall of silence by the people of Granville.

From an early age, people were scared into withdrawal at the sign of anything with a siren. It's what had enabled regimes such as Smiler's to operate untouched for so long. The criminals of Granville worked on the basis of intimidation and they succeeded with most, particularly the young, the impressionable and the vulnerable. Their threats filtered down to the school playgrounds across the town; talk and bad things will happen.

Tommy recalled all eyes turning unanimously towards him outside Robbie Fisher's house; some scared, some expectant, some struggling to see straight.

It had suddenly felt as though Seb was his responsibility. He'd reluctantly obliged and bundled himself into the back of the ambulance, with a no-nonsense paramedic slamming the door behind him.

Talk about wrong place at the wrong time.

After that the journey had been a blur; sirens, lights,

shouting, machines beeping, panic, paramedics asking lots of questions and losing patience with Tommy's vagueness – he'd not even known Seb's surname. He also had to deal with a crescendo of guilt for telling the paramedics there were drugs involved.

What else am I supposed to do?

He now sat in the waiting room, his bum sore from the blue plastic chairs. His fingers twisted and ripped at the paper cup in his hand, which he'd drained of bad coffee a few minutes earlier. He'd managed to persuade himself that this could be a question of life or death and the thought of getting Seb into trouble, or the risk of being branded a grass, had to be put to one side.

Although he longed to be elsewhere, in a way he was glad he'd accompanied Seb to the hospital. Whilst they weren't friends as such, or not in his mind anyway, a peculiar attachment had formed within Tommy's conscience. Strangely, he was sure that Seb would have done the same for him.

Right now, Seb was on his own and he wasn't in a good way; he was still unresponsive, unconscious and on a life support machine surrounded by nurses and doctors all with the same look on their faces.

The noise from the machines had settled to an unnerving and steady beep. Tommy looked through the meshed glass on the ICU doors and caught a glimpse of Seb. He looked pale and had a tube in his mouth, lines into his arms and a couple of machines next to his bed that Tommy presumed were keeping him alive for now, based on what the Doctor had said earlier.

An aching throb of sadness moved through his body towards the pit of his stomach, building with every glance he caught of Seb. He had been unable to tell the medical staff Seb's surname as he didn't know it, so as yet, nobody had been able to track down his nearest and dearest.

He wasn't sure what to do with himself now, the nurses and doctors, akin to the paramedics, had been short and to the point with their questions. He'd sensed a disapproving brow form at the news Seb had taken some white powder. Tommy had attempted to explain that he himself hadn't taken anything, but he couldn't help but feel that judgement had been served. Being judged was second nature to Tommy, he'd grown up on the receiving end of folk saying what he could and couldn't do, what he should and shouldn't look like, talk like, act like, all based on where he lived and what his family were like, so right now, he didn't really care; his mind was firmly fixed on Seb's health and whether he was going to be ok.

He noticed he was restless; tapping his feet, cracking his knuckles. The back of his shirt had started to feel damp. Sweat beads had congregated at the small of his back, after trickling down his spine.

It's so warm in here.

He took a seat again, a different one this time with a view of a vending machine and a lifeless pale green wall, although he didn't hold out much hope that it would be any more comfortable. He waited.

How long should I stay?

Tommy checked his watch again, it was 02:16; he'd been here for nearly two hours. Still no parents or loved ones for Seb. The doctors and nurses were bypassing him now, as though he'd served his purpose. He was picking up a slight air of panic and uncertainty with every doctor that passed through, so he decided that until somebody told him otherwise, he wasn't going anywhere.

Not that he had anywhere he needed to be. His mum would be obliterated by now in a heroin induced coma of warm, carefree fuzziness. His brother, Derek, might be concerned though, he should send him a text message.

Tommy pulled out his mobile phone. It was dated, he'd picked it up from *Cash Convertors* a few months ago; it did what he needed it to though. It made phone calls, sent text messages and, unlike his old one, he could even download music to this one. He remembered feeling so chuffed when he bought it.

He had used his first wage packet from the weekend job he'd acquired over the summer holidays down at the Old Mill café in town. Now that winter was here, he alternated Saturdays and Sundays with another guy, Charlie and only having one shift per weekend, had really taken a hit to his disposable cash. He wasn't sure why Charlie even needed the job, he always seemed to have loads of money and all the latest gadgets.

Battery ran out – bollocks.

In times gone by, he wouldn't have bothered texting anyone, but things had been different with Derek lately. Tommy believed the one good thing to come from the shocking revelation of their dad's murder and the challenging times that followed, was that he and his older brother had become close once again.

Derek had surprisingly taken the opposite road to their mum, following the events of the past year. Tommy enjoyed the new sense of pride he was experiencing with each step forward Derek took. He'd enjoyed watching on as his brother curbed his drug use dramatically and had started spending his time more productively; he was even volunteering at the local Community Centre, noting their dad as his new found inspiration, which had made Tommy smile inside. He still liked a drink, but as far as Tommy knew, Derek was off the drugs, looking healthy and looking out for his younger brother a little more than he used to.

"Tommy Dawson, I didn't expect to see you here young man," a voice sounded from across the waiting room which shook Tommy from his thoughts.

Tommy turned to see who the voice belonged to.

"Hello, Detective," Tommy said.

The man walking towards Tommy was Detective Kelvin Brightwell, a face he hadn't seen for several months.

Following Smiler's escape from custody, Detective Brightwell paid Tommy, his mum and Derek a visit at home to assure them that he and his colleagues in blue were doing everything in their power to catch up with Smiler and put him away - obviously everything in their power, wasn't quite enough. At the time he'd left his card in case of emergency but thankfully, Tommy had never had to use it.

"Please, call me Brightwell,"

"You here about Seb?" Tommy asked, sheepishly.

He sensed this was going to be difficult but hoped the prior encounters with Detective Brightwell would stand him in good stead.

"Yep," the Detective began, "unfortunately Tommy, that's exactly why I'm here. Emergency response to a teen collapsing at a Granville house party brings with it a little bit of interest from us bobbies. Are you good friends with this young man? Seb was it?"

"Not particularly," Tommy said.

Brightwell took an exaggerated look at his wristwatch. Tommy noted the brown leather strap and the large face and presumed it was an expensive one.

"It's 02:26 and you're sat in a hospital, on your own, waiting to see how somebody you're *not* friends with, is doing?"

Brightwell's words were sceptical, and Tommy could see why.

"It's a bit of a strange one,"

"Go on," Brightwell encouraged, pulling out his notepad and pen.

"Well we first met a few weeks ago, first week of college. We only spoke for a few minutes.
I helped him find student services – he'd lost his bag,"

"Ok, so what happened tonight then?"

"Anyway, he comes up to me tonight at this party and gets all friendly – I'd forgotten his name to begin with – but we got reacquainted for a few minutes. I was about to leave the party, then he goes and starts having a big fit right next to me,"

Brightwell looked up from his notepad and held eye contact for a few seconds. He looked dissatisfied with Tommy's brief description of the evening. His stomach churned. He knew he'd not done anything wrong, but this hospital and the impending interrogation from Brightwell was making him a little hot under the collar.

"Tommy, there's a lad in there fighting for his life," Brightwell animated, "you're the only one who knows who this kid is and what the hell happened to him, so forgive me for being forward, but I'm going to need a little bit more to go off that that,"

Brightwell had upped the ante and Tommy could feel his words playing a solo on his conscience.

"Ok, ok! He offered me this white powder, *Charge* he said it was called – I didn't have any, I swear,"
Brightwell looked up at the ceiling in despair, grasping at his wavering composure, before he responded.

"I know you didn't," Brightwell said with a heavy sigh. Tommy was relieved yet a little perplexed at how Brightwell could be so sure. It was the fifth time he'd said those words tonight, yet it was the first time that he recognised genuine faith from the person on the receiving end.

"So yeah, I guess he had some of that stuff and it sent him doolally," Tommy concluded. "Quiet spell before the fit?" Brightwell probed.

"Pardon?" Tommy quizzed, taken aback by the random question.

"Was there a quiet spell before he went into fitting?"

"Yeah, there was actually,"

"Frothing at the mouth?"

"Yeah,"

"Blood from the nose?"

"Erm, yeah definitely,"

Tommy was wondering how on earth the detective knew this information.

"This is not good. This is not good at all,"

He flipped his notepad closed and slipped it into the pocket of his black and white hound tooth jacket. He had kind eyes, but the life seemed to drain away from them in an instant. He rubbed his stubbly chin firmly with the tips of his thumb and index finger simultaneously, backwards and forwards from the centre, up the jawline and back again. He appeared to be lost in thought.

"He's going to be ok, isn't he?" asked Tommy.

"Right now I can't be sure, but a full recovery isn't looking likely."

CHAPTER FOUR

Tommy sunk back into his seat. His mouth fell open softly and hung there as he tried to process what Brightwell had just said. He wanted to ask him how he could be so sure and how did he know the things he knew about what happened, and yet he couldn't clutch at a single word. His brain scrambled looking for logic, but he came up short.

Brightwell continued,

"Over the past four months we've had nine deaths in situations almost identical to this one. Nine! That's nine sets of parents I've had to go home and talk to, to tell them their little bundles of joy won't be coming home because they were stupid and took a drug that they knew absolutely nothing about."

Brightwell was incensed. His words carried a harshness and desperation of a man carrying the weight of the world upon his shoulders.

"Nine deaths? That's crazy," said Tommy, "but how come we've not heard about it on the news or in the Granville Gazette?"

"You really think the powers that be within Granville's elite want word getting out that the town is amidst *another* drug crisis after the horror, shame and embarrassment that followed the Smiler outrage? The town's most well respected councillor being uncovered as the town's most feared criminal, drug lord and child abuser, well it didn't do public relations for the council and their chums much good let's just say that,"

"But people need to know, it could stop more incidents like this one," Tommy pleaded, perhaps naïvely.

"Look, the last thing they want is yet another scandal getting out there, so if you were wondering whether the town had learned from its mistakes with Cllr Carruthers, or should I say Smiler... It hasn't, they're still brushing teenage deaths under the carpet in favour of bullshit promo stories for local businesses and reporting a fake rise in tourism revenue and employment,"

"What the hell is this stuff?" Tommy asked.

"They're calling it *Charge* on the streets. It's a legal substance that, under the laws of the current system, we can't get on top of."

"How can it be legal if it's a drug?"

"There's been legal highs before, all over the country, but none like this; this is lethal, Tommy. It's synthetic, which means it's manmade and to be quite honest with you, at this stage the timescales are too convenient for me to rule out Smiler as the person still pulling the strings from afar. He's still got resources, money and contacts to orchestrate something like this. But on top of that, he's got greed and a lust for power and destruction over this town to *want* to. If you ask me, it stinks of him."

Brightwell paused for reflection.

Tommy's palms began to sweat at the prospect of Smiler being closer to Granville than he'd hoped. He'd had nightmares of the day he'd have to face up to the reality that he was still out there and may one day return to take back what was his and avenge those who had crossed him. Tommy wasn't sure what to say, so he waited with bated breath, before the detective carried on.

"Its core compound is called Ethylphenidate. It's a stimulant, like cocaine, but they're boshing it with another chemical known as MDAI, a sister chemical of the MDMA family. So basically some whizz kid has thrown together this drug by switching up the chemical compounds, so that it isn't covered in any laws right now."

"Ok, that kind of makes sense, I guess," Tommy said, still trying to work out what all of this meant.

"It's cheap and kicks like a mule, keeps people up all night and makes them fall in love like the pills of the early nineties – just the kind of meal the people of Granville love to dine out on. We can't trace it, we can't stop it and we can't arrest people to try and gain leverage because, as it stands, its legal. It's a game of cat and mouse, except I no longer know who is playing the cat and who is playing the mouse,"
Brightwell's will deflated with an exaggerated sigh, slumping into the plastic chair next to Tommy.

"Our lab coats did some tests on some seized product recently," Brightwell added. "They concluded that the dosage for this so-called *Charge*, you know what a person should take in one hit... should be the size of the head of a match,"

Tommy's eyes widened as unwelcomed dread suddenly filled his gullet. He recalled the amount that Seb had taken right in front of him, and that was just the amount he knew of; he'd suspected Seb was already under the influence by that point.

Brightwell continued, "and these stupid, naïve kids are whacking god knows how much up their noses thinking they're invincible and *that* -" Brightwell paused and pointed purposefully through the window towards Seb laying helpless in the ICU bed, "- that is the result."

They both gazed over towards the ICU. Seb was motionless, as still as the night, as the nurse tended to him, checking his charts against the machinery.

"Is there anything else you can tell me about the night, Tommy? Anything at all that can help me stop this madness,"

Tommy began to fidget; he was uncomfortable. He knew he had more information that might help. But he was reluctant. He had always tried to do the right thing, but something was holding him back. He wondered if it was perhaps fear of being sucked into another whirlwind of mess, but deep down he knew he had to tell Brightwell what he knew.

"Well, there are a couple of things that I picked up on," Tommy said tentatively, "Seb referred to a scientist dude as the person who had come along and made the drug, he told me people were calling it the perfect party drug or something like that."

"Scientist dude... That's interesting," Brightwell pondered, "we've had people refer to somebody known as the Chemist. That's all we've managed to gather in terms of intel', a few whispers of what I'm assuming is some kind of alias. Thanks Tommy, that supports what we know already, which makes the intel' stronger, I suppose."

Brightwell smiled. It was forced and Tommy could sense his disappointment with the lack of leads. Tommy thought about leaving it there.

But what about Finn?

Tommy considered himself a streetwise kid, wise beyond his 17 years and certainly somebody who didn't go looking for trouble in this horrible town of his, even though one would never have to look too far if they wished to find it. Well, that was up until the back end of last year, when he walked into the middle of the biggest scandal the town had ever seen. If he could cope with that, he could help Brightwell out with some info that could potentially stop these senseless and tragic overdoses.

Oh well, here goes.

"There is one more thing," Tommy began, Brightwell bolted upright after dropping his head into his hands.

"Go on Tommy, I'm listening,"

"Seb told me who he got the gear off,"

Brightwell nodded, reaching for his pad and pen without breaking eye contact.

Tommy continued, "He said it was off a lad, called Finn?"

Brightwell slapped his notepad off his knee and jumped to his feet. He brushed his hands forcefully across his forehead and through his hair. He was pissed off.

"I knew it, I bloody well knew it!" Brightwell exclaimed, overly animated, almost delirious as he spat out an ironic chuckle. "I knew those sons of bitches would have something to do with this,"

"You know who this Finn is then?" Tommy asked, already knowing the answer of course.

"Do I ever, Tommy. Finn O'Cleary, youngest son of The O'Cleary family. A family full of wrong'uns, the main culprit being the father, Stephen. He's a right piece of work and just the kind of scum bag who could serve as a willing middleman for Smiler and get this *Charge* shite all over the town like an air-born virus,"

"Who in their right mind would want to be associated with Smiler, after the disgusting things he did to all those kids?"

"Listen Tommy, in the underworld they have different rules to you and I, different morals. There's an old saying; when the tide is up, it raises all boats," Brightwell mused. "So, if Smiler's stock can continue to go up, Stephen O'Cleary will want to get his grubby fingers slap bang in the middle of that pie. And he's obviously got his sons doing some of his dirty work. I bet he's got this Chemist fella on the books, or Smiler has and O'Cleary is his distributer. This is just the breakthrough I needed, I'm going to nail that son of a bitch once and for all."

Tommy wasn't too sure which son of a bitch Brightwell was referring to and he noted his mood had suddenly shifted significantly; the pacing around, the swearing, the frantic scribbling on his notepad, chuckling to himself like a man possessed.

Following the mention of this O'Cleary family, he'd transformed from deflated and beat, to incensed and almost wired; attempting to piece a jigsaw together without all of the pieces. Tommy wondered whether this excitement was really over a new lead, or whether there was previous with the O'Clearys.

Brightwell snapped back into the room.

"Ok Tommy, listen. We need to get close to these guys, I need you to get in there with them. They're your age, they go to your college, there's going to be parties-"

"Woah, hang on a minute!" Tommy cried, sensing which path Brightwell was ready to drag him down. "I'm not getting involved in this, I've had enough of all this criminal underworld bullshit. This is no longer my battle, I'm seventeen for god sake. I just want a quiet life,"

"It's never going to be quiet with Smiler still out there and you know it. He's got one of the biggest scum bags in Granville running his operation now and I need to end it."

Brightwell's words were disconcerting, his demeanour intense and his gaze transfixed; it suddenly seemed as though the space was closing in around Tommy. He took a step to the side and broke eye contact with Brightwell, only to catch a glimpse of Seb through the meshed glass to the right, which compounded his dread. He gathered his thoughts for a second.

"How on earth do you expect me to get close to Finn? I don't even know who he is. I'm hardly Mr Popular over at sixth form in case you hadn't heard and besides he's supposedly in the year above,"

"His sister isn't,"

"Wait, who's his sister?"

"His sister is a year younger than Finn and I'm betting she goes to your college too. You see, this family like to pretend they're all prim and proper now and they live in a nice area of town, in a big house and their kids go to college yadda yadda yadda, but behind the scenes the dirt is still as thick as it always has been in the O'Cleary household."

Brightwell had drifted again into his own world. He seemed to be scorned.

"Ok, so who is his sister?"

"She's called Darcy, Darcy O'Cleary."

Tommy noticed a familiar and overwhelming inferiority consume him, flooding right to his fingertips. Everybody said college would be different, but he still carried around the same complex.

"I know one Darcy," Tommy said sombrely, "and she's the most popular girl in lower sixth,"

"Perfect." Brightwell exclaimed, as if oblivious to Tommy's self-doubt.

"What do you mean, perfect? I'm not getting involved, I told you! I'm certainly not making a fool of myself trying to get friendly with the most popular girl in college and her family, who you haven't particularly sold to me all that well to be honest,"

There was a brief moment of silence. Brightwell looked to be scanning his mind for another card to play to try and convince Tommy to help him.

"That's it," Tommy spoke before he had the chance, "I've told you what I know, it's up to you now detective. I'm sorry, I truly am. But I can't do this, I'm just the not the guy you need me to be."

Tommy sensed it was time to leave now. He sympathised for Seb; a mixed bag of empathy, guilt and fear perhaps, but he was tired and shaken up and he was desperate to get away from this mess, before he was hauled into the centre of it. He wasn't leaving Seb alone now, which was his biggest concern earlier. Detective Brightwell would find out who his loved ones were and make sure they came to wait for him to wake up.

If he woke up.

Brightwell pulled out another one of his business cards and handed it to Tommy.

"If you change your mind, call me. Call me on my mobile number, my personal one is on there so you can get hold of me straight away at any time. It's never too late to be who you might have been, Tommy."

"Detective," Tommy shouted as Brightwell began to walk away, "How were you so sure I hadn't taken any of this *Charge* stuff?"

Brightwell stopped in his tracks and paused, before turning to look over his shoulder at Tommy.

"Because you'd be in that bed next to him."

Detective Brightwell paced the final few steps towards the ICU ward, his shoes clapping on the shiny floor as he strode. He pushed through the double doors, leaving Tommy in the waiting room, alone again.

CHAPTER FIVE

The common room was busy this Monday break time, but Tommy managed to find a seat over by one of the vending machines in the far corner. It was a cluster of four purple chairs and only one was taken. A Chinese kid from upper sixth was tapping away at lightning speed on his laptop and with his bulky headphones clamped to his ears, Tommy assumed he wouldn't mind if he took the seat opposite him.

The chairs were known as the 'comfy' chairs, but in truth they weren't all that comfy; old man time was certainly baring down on them. They were the kind of chairs where a swift smack with the palm of your hand would send a cloud of dust whirling into the sky.

In keeping with the rest of the town, Granville Sixth Form was underfunded, undervalued and under the spotlight when it came to local and national expectations. Poor results had led to even less funding and hence the vicious circle that drowned the vast majority of the town was now creeping up to the neck of the college, and right now nobody seemed to be forthcoming with a life jacket.

Tommy nestled into his chair, reached into his bag and pulled out a *Chomp* chocolate bar. He loved a little chocolate fix, but he was thrifty with his money – born out of necessity than choice – so a 20p *Chomp* was about as far as he took his confectionary spending. It just so happened that today, the *Chomp* was also his breakfast.

He took a bite and pulled away, leaving a line of stringy caramel trailing. Tommy smiled to himself, reminiscing about the type of thing Jack would say about trivial things such as chocolate bars, *"In my day they were twice the size and half the price, they have your bloody pants down nowadays these big bloody companies!"* he'd say, or words to that effect.

He missed Jack, especially after the weekend he'd had. An arm round the shoulder and some words of wisdom wouldn't go amiss right now from his old boxing coach.

Whilst it was a little more nippy than usual this morning, especially given the Indian summer they were having in the north west of England this year, Tommy had perceived a rather unusually frosty welcome when he arrived at college. He couldn't decide if it had been a bad case of paranoia after a sleepless weekend, or whether everybody really was shooting wary looks and raised eyebrows his way.

He guessed it was probably somewhere in the middle. Tommy knew the whole shenanigans with Seb at Robbie Fisher's party on Friday night will have spread like wildfire, so he half expected it to be hot news around the place. But still, it's never easy to deal with a tribe of sixteen and seventeen year olds gawping at you. He gazed at the masses, helplessly wondering how many other victims this so-called Chemist and his latest designer drug would devour in the coming weeks and months.

He'd considered not coming into college this morning, as his mind was elsewhere – mainly thinking about how poor Seb was doing in the hospital. Tommy could neither shake this from his mind, nor the thought of the penetrating conversation he'd had with Brightwell at the hospital about Granville's criminal underworld. He found himself on the cusp of scandal *again*, and it worried him.

The one question that circled Tommy's mind repeatedly throughout the whole weekend was *why me?* He just wanted to escape, a feeling he'd carried with him for as long as he could remember, but this time it was different. It always used to be an urge to leave in the hope of finding something more, but now it was like a need to flee in fear for his safety.

He found himself on troublesome terrain, yet again.

One thing he had learned over the years though, was that running from problems didn't do anything other than exasperate them, ultimately amplifying the inevitable difficulties that would be waiting there, patiently. He had his mum to thank for that life lesson. Theresa was a shining example of what can happen if you forfeit control and power to your fears or problems. Over the years he had watched his mother recoil into a painfully thin shadow of her former self; resentful, ashamed and self-destructive. As soon as he'd reached the age of consciousness, Tommy had told himself that he would never follow in the same footsteps. So today, despite his burning desire to run and hide, he'd thrown on his navy-blue wind runner jacket, with the Nike logo half peeled off, and set out to see what the day would throw at him.

Thankfully, by the time morning break had come around, the weekly hustle and bustle of college life had taken its course and things seemed to be back to normal-ish, which is to say he could move around the place pretty much unnoticed. He took another bite of his *Chomp*, working the sticky caramel chocolate between his teeth as he scanned the common room.

The space was open plan and the far side, opposite to where Tommy was currently sat, doubled up as a canteen. He spotted a hair net full of grey curls bobbing through the crowds. It belonged to the chief of the catering staff, Mrs Finnegan. She was a favourite amongst the students as she made the best sausage toasties, which unsurprisingly were particularly popular with anyone carrying around a hangover and strangely also often, but not always, wearing sunglasses indoors.

He saw Alec, a boy from his English Language class, with his long bristly beard that made him look at least thirty-five, playing his guitar with friends sat around willing him on. He saw girls putting on their make-up, perhaps to impress somebody, or possibly just to feel good and look the part. He saw Colleen Summerbee, an old friend from primary school, laughing and joking with some of her fellow basketball teammates, tossing the ball to each other with Mr Lowry glaring over from the faculty brew station.

College life seemed like such a thrill for most people; people willing to take risks, make friends, grow their hair, shave their hair, skip lessons, roll in late, take a class on something they know nothing about, join a team or a club, chasing their dreams or living them right this very instance. But it was yet to take Tommy in its grasp.

He pondered whether he'd been too shy, too reserved, too cautious up to now or whether in truth he simply had too much baggage. But either way, aside from a few glances this morning attributed to some weekend gossip, he was a ghost in this college and he was filled with a bizarre mixture of envy and apathy towards those who looked and passed through him.

He thought about what Brightwell had asked of him – to get close to Darcy O'Cleary – and spat out an ironic chuckle, which caught a bemused look from the boy opposite him on his laptop, who paused his typing momentarily. Tommy offered an awkward smile and scratched his head. He was about to get up and leave when he saw her; Kirsten.

Gliding through the common room with her friend, she looked majestic. A clang of anxiety filled Tommy's stomach like a hot meal. His breath quickened and his lips were pursed. He longed to approach her, but hesitation was getting the better of him, barricading his internal pathways, leaving him trapped in a world of apprehension.

Too much time had passed, hadn't it?

Her deep brown, ringlet curls bobbed ever so gently as she walked. Her warm, tawny skin appeared smooth and her figure hugged her clothes in all the right places. It was as though the summer had transformed her from girl to woman. Tommy noticed he wasn't the only one watching as she passed, with many a wandering eye, mostly boys but some girls too, awestruck by her glowing presence. Then he saw the thing he missed the most: her smile. He didn't know what her friend had said that was so funny and he didn't really care, but he wanted to thank her for saying it, because it brought out a spark in Kirsten that nobody could match.

I've got to do something!

Tommy had seen enough, he had to act. He had to make things right with Kirsten. He thought through in an instant what he needed to do; *get up calmly and naturally, walk over and say hello, ask her if you can talk to her for a minute, apologise, tell her you miss her, ask to see her after college to catch up. Simple but effective.*

Tommy braced himself, took a deep breath and for a reason unbeknown to him nodded to the random boy sat opposite, who now just looked confused. He stood up and went to make his move.

Like a prize-winning racehorse falling at the first fence of the Grand National, Tommy's simple but effective plan was in tatters after the first step. He managed to knock a cup of cold coffee over by his chair that he'd previously not seen. Upon taking his next step, he slipped a little on the spilled brown liquid which had raced off to form a rather sizeable pool on the shiny common room floor. He just about kept his balance through wide legs, a few squeaks and a little arm wafting, but the kerfuffle had caught the eye of Kirsten. She stopped and looked over through the crowd, who had since jumped to their feet to stampede to their next lesson. As their eyes met for a second, Tommy's heart thumped against his rib cage and time seemed to be delayed. Kirsten held her gaze as she repositioned her bag on her shoulder and offered a fraction of a smile, before striding away, up a couple of steps and through the double doors towards the main corridor.

Tommy had not felt this way for months; suddenly he was alive. Kirsten's stare seemed to speak to him and, despite his calamitous effort, he took hope from the willing smile she sent his way. He smirked to himself as he made his way over to apologise to Mrs Finnegan and ask for some napkins to clear up the mess he'd made.

He mopped the cold coffee up and headed towards the bin to discard the sodden napkins, flicking his fingers outwards to rid his hands of any excess. He checked the time and realised he was late for his GCSE Maths lesson with Miss Cartwright. He liked Miss Cartwright and so far, the feeling had appeared to be mutual. He remembered the first lesson he had with her; he'd been deflated at having to re-sit his GCSE Maths qualification at college, he worried it made him look and feel dumb and Miss Cartwright had picked up on it straight away. She'd asked him to stay behind after the lesson and they talked it through. Since then, she'd been nothing but helpful and supportive and her lessons were pretty cool too. He felt bad that he was late and although most kids at Granville Sixth were late to their lessons, he knew it was disrespectful, especially towards a teacher who had gone out of her way to help him.

Clicking his heels, he picked up the pace, barging through the same double doors that he'd watched Kirsten depart through a few minutes previously. He couldn't help but smile to himself again. However brief an encounter it was with Kirsten, if you could even call it an encounter, he was buoyed by it and excited. It had given him exactly what he needed; a sign of encouragement and the confidence to take that first step in making things right with his best friend.

CHAPTER SIX

Tommy had braced himself for a rocket-type telling off when entering Miss Cartwright's lesson late, sixteen minutes late to be precise. He knew that because she greeted him with a familiar smile, whilst challenging him on his tardiness – *'Morning, Tommy. Why are you sixteen minutes late to my lesson?'*

He couldn't tell if she was mad, or disappointed, or not really that bothered at all. The smile and pleasant tone threw him a little bit. Not because it was different, in fact the opposite – it was the same friendly welcome as always. He wondered if she was doing that thing where people say things through a smile but in truth they're actually pissed off; passive aggressive, or something like that.

But the rocket never came. He explained that he was sorry, and he was late due to cleaning up after his embarrassing altercation with a cup of cold coffee. Miss Cartwright thanked him for keeping the college community clean and tidy, which triggered laughter from his classmates, but Tommy thought her gratitude could have been sincere.

He then went and sat down, removed his jacket and reached into his bag for his note pad and pen. Miss Cartwright was finishing off the equation on the whiteboard at the front of the class, marker pen squeaking as she wrote. Just as Tommy started to relax, popping the biro lid off and was ready to learn, then the follow up remark came.

"You won't mind staying behind the extra sixteen minutes at lunch-time will you?" Miss Cartwright turned to face the room, pausing as the classroom fell silent and all eyes turned towards him, "we just need to catch up on a few things."

Miss Cartwright finished her comment yet again with that familiar, pleasant expression, which left Tommy pondering whether she was in fact annoyed or not. His gut told him she wasn't, but he'd been wrong about stuff like this before, so he decided he'd keep his guard up until he could be sure. Sixteen minutes was no big deal to make up and besides in the three weeks he'd been here, Miss Cartwright had shown him nothing but kindness, so by that logic, he had no reason to worry.

Her smile seemed extra warm today. Perhaps it was the bright, red lipstick she wore that accentuated her pearly, white teeth. Or maybe Tommy was opening up to the fact that not all people are to be mistrusted and if somebody like a teacher is kind and helpful, it might be because she's actually a nice person and good at her job.

He watched her for a few moments. She was attractive, there was no denying that. Some of the other lads in his class had made inappropriate comments on just how attractive they found her. Tommy had kept his teenage hormones in check however and remained respectful. Anyhow, he wasn't feeling the same way as the other boys. He liked his teacher, he respected her as a person, as a woman and as his tutor. He guessed it was possibly because positive female role models hadn't really existed in his life all that much. So, when one seemed to be looking out for him, he found it comforting in a nurturing way, as opposed to fantasising over intimate desires like the rest of the class.

One comment did make him chuckle though, when little Stevie Jones – or Jaffa as he was known due to his bright ginger hair – said that Miss Cartwright was like an ice-cold bottle of Coca-Cola straight from the fridge and resigned all other women to mere warm, post-mix pop. It's bizarre what goes through teenage boys' brains, he remembered thinking, as well as wondering what on earth Miss Cartwright would make of all this secret-crush-philosophy. Miss Cartwright may have been Jaffa's goddess, but to Tommy she was a kind, understanding teacher who was his gateway to a Maths GCSE.

A flash thought of Seb crept into his mind. *Poor Seb.*

He wondered how he was doing. Tommy hoped for improvements but judging by Detective Brightwell's diagnostic, he wasn't banking on it.

I must go and see him after college.

Tommy had a habit of daydreaming, allowing his thoughts to flood his mind, jumping from one topic to the next, almost in the same way dreams do. But when you were in a classroom full of people and already in the teacher's firing line, day dreaming was a dangerous pastime. He shook his head, bringing his thoughts back into the classroom and tried to concentrate for the remainder of his time with Miss Cartwright this morning, ensuring it would only be sixteen minutes that he would owe at the end of today's double lesson.

The lesson passed with little drama. Tommy found himself in familiar territory with algebra though, which is to say he found it frustratingly difficult to process and comprehend.

Why does x have to get involved and confuse things?

The rest of the class dispersed for their lunch and Tommy began his sixteen-minute sentence. He helped Miss Cartwright tidy up around the classroom and they made general chit-chat, before she suddenly stopped and slammed her hands rather firmly on the table, causing Tommy to jump.

"Do you want to make something of yourself, Tommy?" she said, with a slight aggression that most definitely wasn't passive.

"Erm, yeah. Yes, I do," Tommy stumbled, "I can't help it if I don't understand Maths, Miss!"

"I'm not talking about that Tommy. Maths is Maths, and if we try our best, we can almost certainly get you where you need to be. It's your whole mentality that worries me, you're drifting. You come to college, you float through the day, you don't really care if you speak to people or make friends, you go home and you come back and do the whole thing again. There is so much more to college life than this, Tommy. Or do you want to end up like the rest of the wide boys that seem to be so common around here? Happy dawdling along yet doomed to be inevitably sucked into the black hole of Granville's vice-ridden swamp," she paused. "Well, we know where that gets you, don't we? I heard about your little ordeal over the weekend,"

Wow, kick me where it hurts, Miss!

He was taken aback by how much his teacher seemed to have picked up on his college life but also, and perhaps more importantly, how bothered she seemed about the choices he made. It felt nice to have somebody who was actually taking an interest in his future, if a little strange and vaguely resembling a courtroom onslaught.

He could only assume her last comment was referring to the incident with Seb. It seemed a little raw, but he could see her point; nice kids making poor choices didn't end well.

"To be honest, Miss, I've been worried about it myself. Like, am I missing something? Everyone seems to be getting so much from the whole college experience and I just feel like I want the ground to swallow me up?"

Tommy surprised himself at how easily he opened up and how honest he was being, but in truth, he couldn't see the point in trying to blag Miss Cartwright who had clearly, and shrewdly, analysed the way he was conducting himself at college with ease and in no time at all.

"What is it you want from life?" Miss Cartwright said, returning to her more usual, softer self, but by no means easing up on the depth of interrogation.

The shock tactic had worked, Tommy didn't know she had that in her arsenal. He pondered the question for a few moments.

"I want to get out of this town. I want to get away and never have to think about coming back. I want to travel. I want to start over, meet people on my own terms, get an interesting job and then maybe start my own family when the time is right,"

At that moment he realised he couldn't do things as

he currently envisaged – move away and start his own family when the time was right. As moving away meant leaving behind the only person he currently would ever want to start a family with; Kirsten.

"So do it!" Miss Cartwright exclaimed, "Ok I agree, kids can come later, wayyy later... But the rest all starts with opening yourself up a little, be prepared to take some chances, gain some new experiences, meet some new people, open up a little, because right now you seem a little reluctant. You need to take responsibility for breaking the mould that has been set for you, as nobody else will do it for you,"

Miss Cartwright spoke a lot of sense. Why have I been so reluctant?

She continued, "I know you've had a rough time these last few months, years or whatever. But don't let that define you, or worse, condemn you. If you don't want people to treat you like a victim, then don't be one,"

Her words cut through all kinds of bullshit that Tommy had been kidding himself with, it was almost as though she had a secret line to his inner most personal thoughts.

"You're right Miss. I guess I just feel really low on confidence and a bit insecure. I've lost my best friend recently, she won't talk to me. It just feels like everyone I care about either dies, leaves or is-"

He stopped.

He was on the cusp of precarious ground, almost rolling into explaining the situation with his mum; *man, Miss Cartwright was good.*

Fortunately for him, old habits die hard and college was still education. Education equals duty of care. And his experience told him that heroin addicted mothers don't usually mix with a teacher's duty of care all that well.

"Ok. So, we're in agreement," Miss Cartwright said, thankfully moving the conversation on, "you're going to try and at least loosen up a little bit, broaden your horizons and have some fun – appropriate fun of course. And if you do that bit, I will worry about how you and algebra can start to get along, is that a deal?"

He waited a few seconds, before offering out his hand the old-fashioned way.

"Deal."

Miss Cartwright laughed and took his hand, shaking it firmly to indicate that she was in charge here. Tommy laughed and it felt good. He may have only opened up ever so slightly, but it felt liberating.

"Now if we're serious about this Maths stuff we need to be honest with each other about where you're at," she hesitated. "It's not exactly where we need to be, in fact it's far from it, lots of work to do. Why don't we make an extended appointment at next week's Parent's Progress Review? We can tell mum how we're getting on and what we plan to do?"

Woah!

Tommy scrambled around in his mind, frantically searching for the hand break – no scratch that, he was looking to put this conversation into reverse. There was no way he could let anyone from college anywhere near his mum.

In the blink of an eye, he'd plunged into deep water. With all his might he wrestled to compose himself and play it icy cool, unflustered, but assertive enough to absolutely nip this idea in the proverbial bud. Embarrassment alone was enough of a motivator, but couple that with people knowing his business at college – all the meetings that would follow; Social Care, the Police, Family Support, this service, that service – *no thanks!*

"I think we'll be ok Miss, let's keep it in between us for now. I can pass the message on to my mum and keep her updated on my progress. I think she's working next week so won't be able to make progress night," he forced a smirk which had more edges than a pentagon.

Work... My mum... And pigs might shoot lightning out of their arses!

He waited a few seconds, before reaching for his jacket.

Miss Cartwright watched on, analysing. He worried his forced smirk had shown a crack of vulnerability in his usual discreet and inconspicuous routine, which had kept teachers at bay for the last five years or so.

Man, Miss Cartwright was good.

"Well ok then, if you say so. But know this young man," there was that infectious smirk again, "I'm going to be on you like a hawk, pushing you every day until Maths becomes part of you. In the near future that might mean extra lessons at lunch time or after college, *or*, it might mean having to meet your lovely mum at some point so we can make sure that we're all on the same page when it comes to you and passing your Maths GCSE."

Tommy nodded in agreement and offered a smile. How could he not? Miss Cartwright's approach was so supportive and nice. He'd escaped unscathed, for now, with no arrangements to meet mum, that was the main thing. He could cross that path if or when he was faced with it. He'd almost always wriggled out of his school life colliding with his home life in the past, he was sure he wouldn't have any difficulty doing it again.

Miss Cartwright might have been good, but she wasn't *that* good.

"Come and see me tomorrow for some mock exam papers and we'll go from there. And don't worry about the best friend situation," Miss Cartwright added, "things like that have a way of working out – if it's meant to be, it'll be."

A sense of comfort showered him, following her closing remark; it deposited another shovelful of hope on top of the pile which began to form at break time this morning. He left Miss Cartwright's class with haste, checking the clock on the way out. He'd missed out on twenty-two minutes of his lunchtime – *so much for sixteen*. He was in so much of a hurry, he heard the person he almost bumped into before he saw them.

"Hi Tommy,"

He stopped in his tracks. The voice flooded Tommy with nerves, excitement, joy and relief all rolled into one big torpedo of emotion, jetting around every single capillary in his body.

"Oh, hi Kirsten," Tommy mustered, suddenly finding it difficult to hold eye contact.

She looked beautiful, yet timid. Tommy wondered if it was coincidence him bumping into her, or whether had she been waiting for him outside his classroom. His stomach tightened, dousing him with a potent cocktail of delight and dread.

"Hey," Kirsten said tentatively. She spoke softly, clutching her bag to her midriff with both arms wrapped around it, her back leaning against the wall. Protective stance, he noted. "How are you?" she added.

"I'm great thanks yeah," *That's a lie,* Tommy told himself, before adding, "erm, how are you?"

"Well, I've been better, to be honest," Kirsten sighed.

He detected a slight hollowness in her voice and nervousness within her eyes. She looked down at her feet and twiddled her fingers. It was difficult to see her this way; he felt a gust of guilt and apprehension, anticipating what was coming next.

She continued, "I, erm, I've been waiting out here for you actually. I wanted to come over before at break time in the canteen, but, well you know the bell went and everything, but then all lesson I've not stopped thinking about you,"

Tommy recognised that Kirsten wasn't holding back, and he felt a little sheepish having flippantly exaggerated his mood by saying he was great a few seconds earlier. He wasn't great, far from it. He'd been nothing but miserable for two months at least, because he missed the person stood in front of him right now.

Now is your chance!

"I lied Kirsten, I'm sorry. I'm not great. In fact I'm far from it. I've been properly down in the dumps lately – and the main reason is because, well... I've missed you so much,"

He reached out and touched Kirsten's arm gently, a gesture to which Kirsten offered a slightly embarrassed grin and an endearing nudge in return.

"Well, I've missed you too. That's kind of why I came

to see you, so thanks for stealing my thunder, yeah?"

They laughed. It filled the air around them and injected light into their faces, flooding the dull corridor within which they stood. Tommy had missed that sound and by the look on Kirsten's face, so had she.

"Did you like the dance I did for you at break time? I call it the spilled-coffee jive," Tommy said, the laughter continued.

He had missed being able to joke about himself to Kirsten, who was perhaps the only person in the world he felt like he could do that with.

"Oh, that was for my benefit was it?" she said, sarcastically. "There was me thinking you were putting on a show for the rest of the common room,"

The mood was so light. An instant buzz warmed Tommy, almost as if their friendship was the remedy to his recent emptiness. He hated to bring a sombreness to the occasion when things had just got moving again, but he was overcome by a need to say what was on his mind.

"Listen for a second please Kirst', I'm so sorry... for all of this," she turned to face him, still clutching her bag as though it was a shield protecting her, "I don't even know what happened really, but I don't want to make excuses, I should have made more of an effort to communicate with you. I guess I was scared and yeah, well, yeah that was probably it. I'm sorry."

Tommy's words hung in the air for what felt like a decade. Kirsten deliberated, pinching her lips together slowly as if in deep thought. She maintained eye contact though, which he thought seemed promising.

I've missed those eyes.

Once her thinking was done, a deceptive five or six second period having passed, with Tommy waiting in the wings. Kirsten eased the grip on her bag and finally brought it away from her midriff, tucking the strap back over her shoulder, arguably where it belonged.

"I know you are," she said, playfully pushing Tommy ever so slightly off balance and revealing a glimpse of forgiveness. "Come on, I'm starving, what are we doing for lunch?"

They turned and walked down the corridor together, following the smell of food towards the canteen. Whilst Tommy was aware it would take more than an apology and a few giggles to get things back to where they were, he was lifted by the past few minutes. There were flashes of their friendship as it once was, the friendship which made him feel as though he could face anything and anyone.

CHAPTER SEVEN

Despite making his way to the St. James' Hospital with the daunting prospect of visiting Seb ahead of him, Tommy's mind was almost completely fixed on Kirsten. He tried to refrain from smiling as he walked, reminding himself where he was heading and what was likely to be waiting for him when he got there, but his heart was rejoicing at reconnecting with his friend and his brain seemed determined to follow suit.

He couldn't wait to call her later once he'd left the hospital. Since departing college this afternoon, he'd typed out three versions of a text message, each time he'd deleted before sending to Kirsten's number, his nerve failing him at the final moments. Whilst they'd chatted over lunch, he wanted to ask about making plans to meet up, but he'd refrained, cautious not to overwhelm her at this delicate stage, having spent so much time apart.

He was always so sure he was the kind of person who wouldn't partake in the politics and tactical play that came with relationships; how long to wait until texting back, whether to play it cool, how many rings to leave it before answering the call and so on, but the opportunity to figure this all out right now excited him. Not that he wanted to play games, gosh he'd learnt from his previous mistakes and spent what felt like a lifetime nursing the harsh bite on his backside, after messing up the last time. He was mindful that he might only get one shot at this and he didn't want to mess it up.

He had his focus firmly fixed on Kirsten, the pleasant ache in his chest only serving as confirmation that he desperately didn't want to lose her again. Furthermore, like the dense growth of evergreen ivy, a yearning for their relationship to become more than just friends was blossoming eagerly. He just hoped there was the possibility that she might still desire the same.

He picked up the pace, noticing he only had a forty-five-minute window left of visiting time, with the big hill on Finley Drive still to climb. He kicked through the autumnal leaves that were beginning to gather around the pavements of Granville's more plush areas and hurried with his ascent.

Reaching the summit of Finley Drive with his breath a little heavy, he shuffled across the pedestrian crossing without waiting for the green man to beep permission. He hopped the wall and scampered between the cars on the car park towards the main entrance.

St. James' Hospital had an impressive front, with huge glass panels either side of a large revolving door, which swallowed up local residents and spat them back out twenty-four hours per day. The sign for St James' was quirky; it was designed by a local artist and a group of sick kids earlier this year. He remembered hearing about the initiative on the radio at the time; one of those schemes to try and involve the community in the development of services or something. It was nice, it added a personal touch and reminded folk of the hope that could be found even in the depths of despair.

As he approached though, it wasn't unwavering hope that welcomed him. It was a confusing sight, which quickened his heart rate, prompted a sudden surge of unnerving restlessness and created a confused facial expression that almost tied his eyebrows into a knot.

Pushing through the revolving doors almost by force, the foyer appeared to be amidst some kind of mass evacuation; Tommy wondered if there was a fire drill, or an equivalent, but there was no accompanying alarm sounding to indicate that this was the case. He fought through the hustle and bustle of the crowd, scrambling towards the corridor which took him to where he needed to go.

As he wrestled against the current of people, he sensed the atmosphere had cranked up a notch, an air of distress lingering, causing a sour taste in his mouth. There were doctors and nurses tripping over one another, he even spotted a couple of policemen marching with purpose, dashing towards the red flashing light above none other than the Intensive Care Unit.

His eyes were fixed upon the door, he bobbed and weaved trying to get a look at what might be going on. People were bundling into him as if he wasn't there. He spotted a nurse and went to call out to her, only for a man in a black hooded jumper to barge into him before he had chance. It almost knocked him off his feet and disorientated him for a split second. The man's hood was pulled down so Tommy couldn't even get a look at his face, let alone ask him what his problem was. He noticed a luminous crow type of emblem on the upper shoulder blade area, a brand he'd never seen before.

The guy must have been in one heck of a hurry, as he bulldozed through him like a prop forward for the infamous All Blacks. Despite the bafflement, Tommy just about maintained enough focus to watch the man continue to elbow his way through the crowds, before fading into just another head amidst the flowing traffic of people. Flabbergasted, he dusted himself down and scurried over to the nurse who looked to be heading towards the ICU doors.

"Excuse me," Tommy shouted.

The nurse turned her head a fraction in slight acknowledgement, but continued to punch in the code to get into the ICU.

"You can't be here, sir," she said, sternly.

Her face appeared to be pre-occupied, as though she didn't have the time to even look at Tommy, let alone answer his inevitable question that would follow. He noticed her fringe was damp and she seemed a little dishevelled.

"What's happening? My friend is in there!"

"Sir, I need to ask you to leave, please make your way out of the hospital, we've had an incident which requires all hands-on deck. Visiting hours have ceased for the afternoon."

Before Tommy could respond, the nurse was through the door of the ICU, slamming it shut, as if the verbal message wasn't clear enough. Tommy tried to peer through the glass panelling, but the curtains were drawn. With little other choice, he turned aimlessly and joined the remaining visitors, guided by clerical staff and porters, as they made their way towards the main foyer once more.

The pit of Tommy's stomach burned with uncertainty. He reached the revolving doors and pushed through them, almost forgetting to step out when he felt the outside breeze on his face. He stood on the pavement in front of the entrance staring at the sign, which was supposed to offer so much hope, trying to digest what on earth could be going on in there. His mind whirled.

Was it Seb? Of course it was, knowing how Lady Luck follows me around. Oh, please say it's not!

With little idea of what to do, Tommy was readying himself to make a move and head home, he couldn't wait to speak to Kirsten and tell her all about this ordeal, the whole lot of it, starting from Friday's incident to the craziness he'd just stumbled into here at the hospital.

He placed his hands in his pocket and felt something that he wasn't expecting. A mobile phone was in his left jacket pocket, a mobile phone that wasn't his. He checked it over, although there wasn't much to check. It was a small black one, a ten-pound phone they called it at school, or the more streetwise kids would call it a dealer's phone. It was one of the cheap supermarket phones that come with a pay-and-go sim card. Tommy remembered hearing that they were untraceable as, unlike smart phones or those with a monthly contract, these were disposable, hence the link to drug dealers. As he inspected it, he suddenly felt it vibrate; *bzzz bzzz, bzzz bzzz.*

Squinting at the screen, he saw that the phone had received a text message. He looked around the immediate area but could only see a scatter graph of random people minding their own business; making their way to their cars, talking to each other at the bus stop, or talking on the phone to their loved ones. The one thing that probably united them was that they all looked as confused as Tommy was about what was happening inside the hospital.

The lampposts which surrounded the hospital were beginning to flicker on in no particular order, as dusk began to extend its reach across the clouds. An orange stripe burned away at the horizon as another day disappeared beyond the Granville skyline and Tommy suddenly felt a familiar chill dance across the back of his neck.

He pressed the Menu button, swiftly followed by the star key to unlock this strange phone that had appeared in his possession. He hesitated, wondering whether he should be nosey or just hand it in at reception. He held it up ever so slightly and rather unconvincingly in truth, in the hope somebody may jump out of the crowd and claim it as their own; for the incident to go down as just a bizarre misunderstanding. But nobody came forth.

It's not like I found it on the floor – it was in my bleedin' pocket! Maybe the text message might tell me who the phone belongs to...
Tommy paused and took another long, hard look around the front of the hospital, but nobody seemed to even notice he was there.

He opened the text message.

16:46

> *"Me and you have got*
> *unfinished business, Tommy.*
> *I'm coming for you!"*

Tommy felt himself choke on thin air. He frantically scanned around once again, but each time he did more people had left the area outside the hospital, leaving fewer and fewer people to scour between. The nurse was right, he should leave. He backed up to the wall and read it again.
What the hell?

Carefully retracing his footsteps inside his head, right the way back to his journey to college this morning, he attempted to figure out where the phone had come from. Tommy thought about his lessons. Miss Cartwright's lesson was a none starter, as he didn't leave his jacket anywhere other than the back of his seat and in his other classes he'd not even taken his jacket off – the central heating was a tad temperamental at Granville Sixth, often leaving the classrooms colder than it was outdoors. He thought about the bustling corridors and it was blurry. But he was able to jump forward in his mind to his departure through the college gates. He recalled putting his hands inside his jacket pockets, as he walked out of Granville Sixth and past the busy bus stop to make his way to the hospital; the only thing in his pockets at that time was a ten pence piece. He remembered it clearly as it triggered a smile, with the realisation that the ten pence discovery put him halfway towards tomorrow's *Chomp* bar.

BAM! It hit him like a freight train straight from hell and Tommy once again looked up and searched the vicinity to see who was around, eyes darting, as his biological responses caught up with his surroundings, aligning with the hospital hysteria.

The man in the hooded jumper!

Despite the hectic corridors outside the ICU, Tommy had felt something wasn't right at the time. He'd been quick to blame it on the mass exodus, believing the bloke to be rude or maybe upset, it was the ICU after all. But the man had seemed overly eager to push into him – a slight bump and an apology may have been conceivable as an accident, but this guy had *wanted* to bump into him.

It seemed so clear upon reflection and now, with the phone in his hand and the threatening text message to boot, he knew why – he just didn't know who. His first thought was obvious, but he wasn't sure this was Smiler's style, although who could be sure of anything that crazy bastard wouldn't do?

All of the surrounding streetlamps were glowing to their full potential now. The inconsistency of yellows and ambers and oranges painted an ombré type shading across the concrete path, which led to the car park. Tommy knew he had to make a run for it, he just hoped the hooded man wasn't holed up somewhere in the encompassing area, watching him, waiting for him to give up his safe haven outside the hospital, advancing into the shadowy, vulnerable streets where he could be approached from any which way.

Tommy plunged his hand into his pocket and pulled out his own phone. He opened his messages and without thinking about what to say, or whether he should use any flirty banter, or how many kisses he should put at the end, he typed out a text message to Kirsten and hit send within the space of ten seconds.

16:50

"Kirsten, are you home?
In a spot of bother and need to talk!"

He slid both phones back inside his pocket and took one last look around, craning his neck to nervously check around corners, before scurrying into the car park. He bounced on the balls of his feet and was direct with his movement. The blustering wind tickled his ears, as his head turned almost three-hundred-and-sixty degrees at light speed, checking every angle possible, his eyes struggling to keep up. He tried to remain calm and focussed, despite detecting the change in his breath, which was now fast and shallow.

Reaching the far side of the car park unscathed, Tommy hopped the car park wall once more and, sticking to the well-lit pathways, headed back down Finley Drive towards Kirsten's house.

CHAPTER EIGHT

Tommy shut the door behind him and rested his back against it, his head following suit softly. He closed his eyes and focussed on calming his breath, trying to make sense of the events which had occurred.

Unfortunately for him, nobody answered the door at Kirsten's house and he'd yet to receive a response to his text message. Not wanting to be stuck on the streets as a potential sitting duck, he headed for the next best place; home.

Ironically home was the place he had always felt lost and unsafe; often the last place he wanted to be. He recollected times where he'd stayed away for days on end, just to avoid what – or who – might be waiting here for him. Times he'd cried himself to sleep, or lay in bed unable to sleep, frozen with fear trying to decipher the catalogue of noises from downstairs.

Of course he'd gotten by, even if only just. The unpredictable environment throughout his childhood unsurprisingly had enabled him to develop an inoculated tolerance to his mum's drug use and alcoholic rampages, the mystery guests who would come and go at all hours and the general unknown entities that may be there to greet him each day when he arrived home; he'd simply learnt to cope. But it had never truly felt like the safe haven that perhaps a home should.

Since Smiler things had changed. Since he now knew a little more about what was behind the invisible scars that imprisoned his mum, he no longer saw rage and hostility, he saw confusion and sadness. This didn't mean his mum's drug use was any easier to deal with, it just meant he'd found an inner strength to see past the behaviour and recognise the trapped person beyond it.

The familiar sound of his brother's voice pulled him from his thoughts.

"How's it going, bro'?" said Derek.

He appeared to be on his way out the house as he hooked the frayed straps of his rucksack over his shoulders and walked towards Tommy at the front door, leaving the tobacco stained living room behind him. Tommy glanced over his brother's shoulder to see there was the usual sight of a mound of cigarette butts in the ashtray that was almost stuck to the coffee table and the standard accompaniment of a half drunken bottle of cheap vodka that tasted more like white spirit than anything else. To be fair to Derek, this wasn't so much his doing lately, it was Mum's.

"Not bad, thanks," Tommy said, reluctant to share the details of the incident that had just occurred at the hospital.

Derek had taken the traumatic revelations about their dad and Smiler in his stride, finding an internal drive that neither of them knew he had. It had fired his brother on a positive trajectory, and he didn't want to mess with that with half an ambiguous story about text messages and hooded figures.

Tommy continued, "Where are you going?"

"I'm off to the Community Centre for my volunteering," Derek beamed.

Tommy didn't think in all his years on this planet that he would ever see his brother functioning in the way that he was currently. Sure, there was still progress to be made, but who doesn't have things to work on? The important thing was that he was thinking and behaving like somebody who wanted to play an active role in his own life, as opposed to a passive bystander.

"Nice one, mate. Hope it goes well," he said.

"I'm sure it will," Derek predicted. "Oh, and be careful, Mum's upstairs and it isn't pretty. Catch you later, little brother!"

And with that Derek scooted out the front door with a spring in his step.

"Mum!" Tommy called, wondering but almost certainly knowing what was waiting for him.

He heard groans before any words were audible. They came from upstairs and they were unmistakably from his mum. He climbed a couple of steps and directed his call up the dimly lit, enclosed staircase, gripping the banister ever so slightly.

"Mum! It's me, are you ok?"

Theresa appeared suddenly at the top of the stairs and Tommy jumped ever so slightly, retreating back down to the bottom of the staircase by the front door. She'd been drinking for sure and Tommy was willing to bet that wasn't the only thing she'd consumed that afternoon.

Her hair was matted and through the gloom he could barely see her cloudy, sunken eyes. She was slumped over as though she carried the weight of the world on her back. Her dressing gown hung loosely around her shoulders and her nighty swamped her frail frame.

"What?" she said, emotionless.

"Jesus, Mum! You scared the life out of me then. I was just letting you know I was home, that's all,"

"Well now I know," she responded, sarcasm tumbling out of her mouth, despite her dishevelment.

Tommy watched on as his mum swayed at the top of the stairs, attempting to light a cigarette before she'd even managed to place it in her mouth.

"You've just missed Derek," Tommy said, attempting small talk in the hope that the next few minutes could pass civilly.

He gazed up the narrow staircase and wondered whether he was going to need to catch his mum in the following moments, as she flirted with the edge of the landing.

"Huh, well that's just fantastic isn't it? I never see him anymore now that he's started that stupid volunteering," she said, scorned, "I don't know why he bothers; he's going around thinking he can be this new man. Ha! People will never see past what we really are."

Here we go, this should be fun.

"Don't be like that, Mum. Derek's doing great. Maybe you should try and get out and about a bit more, you know, try and connect with people?"

"What do you know about it, hey? *Mr Smart Arse*, thinking you know it all. Well you know what, you don't know shit about what I need and what I don't need,"

"Ok mum, sorry I spoke."

Tommy was resigned, he knew there was no way he would get anywhere when his mum was in this kind of mood; he'd found that the resentful routine with a twist of bitterness was almost impossible to overthrow. He'd been there, done that and had to rewash the t-shirt countless times. She was pissed off that Derek, her emotional crutch in life and partner in crime, was outgrowing the four walls which had confined them for so long, and Tommy was the prime target to feel the heat of the backlash.

There was a time when he would have toyed with self-pity in this situation, longing to be able to unburden himself of his worries, but simply unable to, due to the barrage of self-consumed nonsense which his mum frequently poured all over him. But not now. He'd figured out that his mum was unable to offer him that comforting sounding board and safety net; his problems were his alone and he'd finally accepted that.

Fortunately, amidst the swaying and the ranting, she had slowly begun to make her way down the stairs safely, albeit in rather unconventional style as she hugged the walls, sliding down each step precariously.

"Are you? Are you sorry you spoke?" she demanded, following him into the front room as he attempted to walk away, her cigarette – now lit – flailing through the air, "because all I can see is you and Derek in your little perfect world trying to make everything perfect and you know what? Nothing is perfect Thomas, nothing!"

Before Tommy could respond to her derisive and rather random scalding, there was a firm knock at the door. It startled them both, triggering a cease fire on the exchange of words. It was an unspoken rule in their house akin to a pack of wolves; external threat was danger and the pack should always stick together, regardless of whether the pack were bickering or not. She toddled off to the kitchen and flicked her head towards the door with misguided pretension, indicating that the visitor was Tommy's issue to deal with and that was that.

CHAPTER NINE

A further knock at the door followed immediately, even louder this time. His mum didn't flinch as she took a long drag of her cigarette and turned to stare vacantly out of the back window in the kitchen. Tommy found that with all the drugs his mum had taken over the years, a certain numbness consumed her from time to time; this was one of those situations. With a roll of his eyes, Tommy dragged himself towards the front door and opened it. He was startled by who was standing there.

"Evening, Tommy," Detective Brightwell sighed solemnly, his shoulders tense as speckles of rain splashed silently around him.

"Evening, Detective," said Tommy poking his head out into the street and pulling the door tight to his back, "what can I do for you?"

"I told you, please, call me Brightwell. Is it ok for me to come inside?"

Tommy hesitated. He attempted to call upon one of his failsafe excuses – my mum's unwell, we've got family over, there's a burst pipe and the plumber is trying to fix it – but he came up empty. His tongue lay dormant in his time of need, a time in which he needed to keep a policeman from entering his home, not just out of embarrassment but for fear of what he might find; one look at his mum in this state would leave Brightwell's suspicious senses tingling, he had no doubt.

Brightwell spoke again, probably sensing Tommy's uncertainty, "or you could come out to my car and we could talk?"

Thank god.

"Yes, let's do that. My mum's just having a snooze on the couch you see," mumbled Tommy, charged with relief and yet simultaneous apprehension as to what this surprise visit would deliver.

He skipped through the fine rain across the uneven pavement towards Brightwell's car, a silver Vauxhall Astra. Tommy couldn't see what year but judging by the pockets of rust near the wheel arch, it didn't look brand new. Brightwell pointed over towards the passenger side for Tommy, as he whipped open his own door and dived in.

The doors slammed shut simultaneously and Tommy shuddered, the short encounter with the autumn rain sent a chill to his core.

"What's going on?" Tommy quizzed.

"Your friend is dead, Tommy."

Brightwell was dead pan and deadly serious. The words jabbed Tommy in the stomach as he scrambled around for some words to respond with. Death wasn't the kind of subject you could skirt around, and Brightwell didn't seem to want to try.

"Seb?"

He knew it was a silly question. Of course it was Seb, but right now he needed more time to process what this all meant.

"Yes, Seb," said Brightwell, "he died earlier in the hospital, quite suddenly. By the time the nurses and doctors figured out what was going on, it was too late."

"Earlier, at the hospital..." Tommy's speech was staggered as his tongue yet again seemed to go to sleep, "I was there... there was a mass panic, I thought, I mean I assumed it would be serious... But I just never really allowed myself to think of this scenario,"

He struggled to grasp this information and felt vacant, as though this wasn't real. Despite not really knowing who Seb was a week ago, he felt so invested in this situation. His mind also scattered to the other nameless people who had encountered the same fate at the hands of this unpredictable and deadly *Charge*.

Brightwell continued, facing out through a rain splashed windscreen, "I've got my own ideas about whether he died of his own accord, or whether he was given a helping hand-"

"Wait! What do you mean helping hand?" Tommy interrupted.

"That takes the body count to ten, Tommy. Awful right? But nobody has survived to tell the tale? Do you not see? If Seb wakes up and starts talking, that doesn't look good for our friend Finn, this mysterious Chemist fella and his *Charge* from the Scumbag Brigade,"

"Are you saying somebody went into the ICU ward at the hospital and finished Seb off?"

"I'm saying I don't know what happened, but Seb not waking up is pretty shit for us and it's worked out, yet again, that nobody knows a damn thing about where we go from here," Brightwell paused, before turning to face Tommy, "except, maybe you?"

"No way!" Tommy protested, "No. way. I can't get involved, I just can't. Something happened tonight that quite frankly has scared the life out of me,"

"Tonight? Tell me, I can help whatever it is," Brightwell said, earnestly.

Tommy thought for a few seconds, granting himself time to discover some composure more than anything. He took a deep breath before launching into his recollections from the hospital.

"Basically, a bloke bumped into me at the hospital when all that madness was going on. I thought nothing of it at the time other than that he was rude and a bit of a tosser. Then I get outside and put my hands in my pocket and there's a mobile phone in there – not mine either. Had to be the geezer who bumped into me, yeah? I open it up and there's a text message addressed to me personally on this phone talking about unfinished business. I looked around but couldn't see anyone. So, I darted. I wasn't hanging around to see if this person wanted to reacquaint there and then if you know what I mean?"

"Show me," Brightwell ordered, "this could be the link we need."

"Never mind the link you need – what about me? Yet again I'm being dragged into something that is way, way bigger than me. Granted, last time you could argue I was asking for it by poking around looking for any trace of my dad. But this time, I want nothing to do with it."

Tommy reluctantly passed the phone to Brightwell, who was undeterred by his plea.

"Have you tried calling the number who sent this message?" Brightwell asked as his eyes quickly scanned over the threatening text message.

"Have I hell! I was afraid of who might answer,"

"Do you think it's something to do with Smiler?" said Brightwell.

"How should I know? You're supposed to be the Detective around here," Tommy paused for a second, sensing his tone may have been on the wrong side of sarcastic, encroaching on the boundaries of being disrespectful and, whilst frustrated, he didn't think Detective Brightwell deserved that. He spoke again, "But yes, something tells me it does. I got that same sick feeling I've felt before and it shook me up as soon as I read it,"

Tommy noticed Brightwell put the phone up to his ear.

"What are you doing?" he exclaimed.

"Phoning the number and seeing who it is," said Brightwell, boldly, "if they think we're going to be messed around by cryptic bullshit then they've got another thing coming."

"Who on earth do you suppose *they* are?" Tommy quizzed, baffled by Brightwell's gung-ho tactics.

"Smiler. The Chemist. The O'Clearys. All three of them. Whoever." Brightwell's words had fire in them. He seemed determined to solve this puzzle, even if it meant forcing some of the pieces together. "Straight to voicemail. Who else have you told?"

"Nobody, yet," Tommy said, "but I was going to tell Kirsten?"

"That pretty little girlfriend of yours?"

"Yes. Well, no. She's not my girlfriend."

"Don't bother,"

"Why?" questioned Tommy, his face perplexed.

"Do you really want to drag her into this mess again? If she's not been contacted, why risk putting a target on her back?"

Tommy stopped and looked out of the window. He was so fixed on getting things back on good terms with Kirsten, he'd not even thought about the risk he might pose. He'd battled long and hard with his own thoughts some months back, after feeling responsible for putting Kirsten through the traumatic events last time around, as well as harbouring the guilt for Jack's death. He guessed it was probably part of the reason he put some distance between himself and Kirsten, as he was fresh out of any other ideas as to why he would even contemplate, on any kind of conscious level, pushing away such a beautiful, kind and sweet girl who had told him that she loved him.

"I'd not even thought that far ahead," Tommy mumbled, almost not wanting to say it too loudly, as that would mean admitting it. "I swore to myself if I ever got the chance to rekindle things with Kirsten, I would grab it with both hands and slap a big chain and padlock on it. How can I do that if I'm lying to her? Our whole friendship was based on supporting each other through the tough times – or rather she supported me. It doesn't seem fair... What am I going to do?"

"Look, whilst teenage romance isn't usually my area of expertise, I feel your pain Tommy, I do," Brightwell consoled, "But right now, we need to keep this on a need to know basis and frankly, I don't think Kirsten *needs* to know. It's not technically lying; it's omitting the truth..."

"Oh thanks, spoken like a true policeman there, Detective Brightwell?"

They both sniggered, which offered a welcome break to the tension.

"All I'm saying is, to keep her safe, just keep her away. And in the meantime, my view is that attack is the best form of defence. So, let's not wait around for some mysterious text threats to become a reality and lets go and catch this so called Chemist fella and the rest of the monsters who are killing kids with ropey drugs and put an end to this once and for all. It's a straightforward plan; we know that bastard Stephen O'Cleary is involved, we know the *Charge* is coming from an alias called the Chemist and we know that Granville parties are a hot bed for this shit. So, it all starts with you contacting Darcy O'Cleary, get yourself involved in the action and we'll take it from there. We just need some solid intel to link the story together and tie it all to O'Cleary and bingo!"

Brightwell became transfixed, his eyes had glazed over once again at the mention of Stephen O'Cleary, which Tommy felt was peculiar seeing as he was under the impression Smiler was the overall menace here.

Brightwell passed the mystery phone back to Tommy.

"Keep this on, in case they try to make contact again. If they do, call me straight away,"

Tommy tentatively took the phone back and put it in his coat pocket.

"I'll be with you every step of the way, now what do you say?" Brightwell added, hopefully.

Tommy reflected for few moments on Brightwell's rallying call. He had spoken sense, at times, at least he thought he did. Tommy wasn't sure what his history was with the O'Clearys, but it was becoming more and more apparent that it wasn't a fond one. He couldn't shift the heavy feeling in his gut; it almost throbbed. He wasn't sure if it was the whole *Charge*-Chemist-O'Cleary escapade that he was slowly but surely being suckered into, like yet another black hole appearing in the middle of Granville. Or whether it was the prospect of potentially hiding things from Kirsten. Something didn't feel right, and he'd always trusted his gut.

"I really don't know, Detective. I just want all of this to go away."

Before Tommy could continue, he felt his phone – his actual phone – buzz in his trouser pocket. He reached in and pulled it out. The screen revealed he'd received a text message, from Kirsten.

CHAPTER TEN

"One minute!"

Despite coming from the other side of the front door, Tommy recognised the muffled voice as Kirsten's. He had finally plucked up the courage to knock on the door, after standing outside in her front garden for several minutes wondering how he was going to play this. He puzzled over how he would explain the panicked text message he'd sent following the incident at the hospital. He agonised how he would even begin to 'omit the truth' – as Brightwell so eloquently put it – to his best friend, who had always been so truthful to him. And mostly, he longed to be close to Kirsten as they had been previously, closer even, but he feared for her safety should trouble find its way to him again, as it had done before.

The rain had eased off slightly and the cool air felt just about bearable, otherwise he might have been forced to knock on her front door sooner. Maybe less time to think would have been easier, maybe he was overcomplicating it. One thing was for sure though, he had less than one minute until he had to face the music.

The door swung open and he felt a gust of warm air spill out from the hallway towards him, contrasting against the night's chill. Kirsten greeted him with a surprised yet joyous look.

"Hey, I didn't expect to see you," she smiled, "I text you back, did you get my message?"

"Hi," he waved awkwardly, "yeah, I got your message. I thought it'd be easier if I came to your house. Don't really want to be at home right now – mum stuff, you know?"

"Oh, is that what you meant by your message?" Kirsten asked, "That you were in a spot of bother with your mum?"

Tommy couldn't believe that the conversation had opened up for him like this so quickly. The thought that technically he *had* had a little run in with his mum softened the slight guilt he was feeling around the deception which was about to follow. He needed a way round this problem, and he would be foolish to turn down this opportunity, wouldn't he? And besides, as Brightwell said, it was all to keep her safe.

Starting with technicalities, this isn't going to end well.

"Yeah, you know how she gets Kirst'. Tanked up all afternoon, lonely and frustrated, just waiting to take it out on somebody."

Woah! Slow down, finding this 'omitting the truth' a little too easy.

He'd noticed his voice and face had subconsciously slipped into being prime for sympathy; puppy dog eyes he'd heard it referred to. Inside he was kicking himself at the depths he had already gone to in misleading Kirsten, inside just a few minutes. *Pathetic!*

"Ah I'm sorry to hear that, I know it bums you out when she does that," said Kirsten.

She stepped out of the house and down the two front steps to where Tommy was standing. He scanned her face, *still as beautiful as ever*. She shuffled over a few more inches, not quite managing to make eye contact, he assumed it was the time spent apart that made her apprehensive. Tommy stepped back a fraction, only to feel the cold moisture, which clung to the green, leafy bush behind him, trickle onto his neck.

Her arms slowly came away from her side, her hands tucked in her sleeves ever so slightly as she gripped the cuffs of her baby blue hoody. She stepped in and slotted her arms underneath his, before wrapping them gently around his back. She pulled him close, laying her head gently on his chest, and gave him something he hadn't experienced in months: a hug.

"Everything will be fine, it will all work out in the end – always does," she added, optimistically.

Whilst Tommy's mind was still coming to terms with the dilemma of keeping Kirsten in the dark about current events, inside the rest of his body felt fuzzy and began to dance. He could smell the mango and passionfruit hair products that she always used, it reminded him so much of her. They rocked slightly as they remained in their embrace. The gentle rocking gradually became more exaggerated until they both burst out laughing and broke free.

He noticed that Kirsten held her tender grasp on his waist a little longer than anticipated. As she stepped away, he saw that her hands had broken free from the cuffs of her sleeves.

"Thanks, Kirsten," Tommy said, softly.

She smiled and turned back towards the house. Tommy spotted she only had some tiny slippers on her feet, she must have been freezing.

"You coming in then, Mr Dawson? Or do you need a formal invite these days?"

Tommy's heart fluttered slightly as he offered up a nervous giggle. Kirsten smiled, recognising that her comment put her one-nil up in the banter stakes. Tommy had to think quickly to draw level.

"Well that all depends," he said, "on whether your mum is home? You do know her cooking is the main reason I come around to visit, don't you?"

1 – 1.

Kirsten burst out laughing and playfully nudged him in the arm.

"You cheeky so and so," she said, shaking her head, "and are there any other reasons you may come around to visit?"

Kirsten's eyes were piercing, it felt almost as if they

were reaching inside and triggering an alarm; intruder has breached the perimeter. At that moment, he realised how much he'd missed her and, perhaps more poignantly, just how much he cared about her.

She seemed to be growing in confidence by the minute, whilst in turn he became more relaxed; it was as though they were in sync, both becoming more self-assured in each other's company again as they reconnected.

He smirked, "There may well be,"

Kirsten held out her hand for him to grab hold of, as if not leaving it to chance as to whether he would follow her inside.

"Come on, let's go inside, my mum will be dying to see you,"

"What's she cooking?" he jested cheekily, as Kirsten pulled him towards her, up the two steps and inside the house, before pushing him over the threshold eagerly, closing the door behind her.

He looked around and soaked in what was before him. He was back in his happy place; a place he felt safe and loved. It was as if he'd never been away. Whilst it had only been a few months, as he made his way over this evening he'd convinced himself that it had been a lifetime and considering he would have usually visited four times a week, a thought suddenly consumed him as to whether Kirsten's mum would have something to say about his apparent disappearing act.

Kirsten took his jacket and hung it on the tall, wooden coat stand in the hallway. Despite the town crumbling around them, the Cole residence was always sparkling clean. They had maintained some of the classic features of their house, with patterned, porcelain tiles blanketing the floor and original coving flanking the high ceilings, whilst also adding modern touches along the way. It was a wider entrance than most of the houses had in Granville, especially when consideration was given to the fact his own version of a hallway at home was a half-metre squared space to wipe your feet.

Kirsten walked down the hallway towards the kitchen/diner. His eyes wandered as he noticed her walk turn into a bit of a strut and he wondered if she knew he'd be watching her.

As he followed her lead, his stomach began to clench, a feeling that he was used to out there in the unpredictable Granville terrain, but not here. Here he never felt uneasy, until now and the prospect of Mrs Cole being upset with him. Before he could overanalyse what Kirsten's mum may say or think about his lack of appearances lately, he heard her jolly voice booming from the kitchen.

"Oh that is wonderful," she exclaimed. "Where is he? Get him in here so I can give his cheeks a good squeeze,"

Tommy smiled as he shuffled into the dining room, relieved.

"Hi, Mrs Cole,"

She didn't say anything at first, simply flung her arms around his shoulders and hugged him. Tommy felt the authenticity of her grasp down to his marrow; she was happy to see him.

"Tommy! How many times – its Judy. Now, before you say anything and tell me all about college and what you've been up to," Kirsten's mum's voice was pitchy with excitement, "let's get the important stuff out the way. For supper, it's nothing fancy, I've got some Chicken Kievs that have just gone in the oven. I'm putting you one in, no questions asked, ok?"

"Great, thanks,"

"Secondly, we've got to do something about that hair, Tommy love. You look like you've been sleeping in a barn,"

"Mum!" Kirsten screeched, slapping her mum spiritedly on the arm.

Tommy laughed, glancing in the framed mirror, which hung above the fire place, "Wow, you're right, I have let myself go a little, haven't I?"

"You look just fine, Tommy," Kirsten cooed.

"Course he does," Judy said, "but a little hair cut won't

do him any harm so we can see a bit more of that handsome face, isn't that right Kirsten?"

Tommy felt himself blushing, whilst also noticing a tinge of pink surface in Kirsten's cheeks too.

Judy continued, "now, you sit yourself in that chair and I'll get my scissors. Kirsten, why don't you make Tommy a nice cuppa'?"

He sat down in the chair as instructed and a grin decorated his face. He appreciated Judy not making it awkward and asking where he'd been or what had gone on. When a thought slowly crept up on him. In order for that to happen, perhaps Kirsten had protected his name by not divulging the inner workings of their brief spell apart. Maybe she hadn't told her mum that Tommy had freaked out and distanced himself. That would be such a Kirsten thing to do. A clang of anxiety hit him suddenly in the solar plexus.

How can I 'omit the truth' with somebody so caring and loyal?

CHAPTER ELEVEN

That night Tommy didn't sleep much. Or the night after. Or the night after. He was left haunted by a melting pot of chaotic, uncoherent visions; Brightwell, Finn O'Cleary, Seb, the Chemist – a figure with no face, the hooded man from the hospital, Kirsten, Derek, his mum and of course his old foe; Smiler, ever lurking in the shadows inside his head.

A relentless whirl of thoughts consumed his mind leaving his body rigid and tense. His teeth were in a constant clench, his tongue ached from pressing up against the roof of his mouth and his eyes twitched nervously with every attempt he took to close them. He lay there in bed each night desperately seeking answers, only to find more and more versions of how the situation played out.

He feared for his own safety and sanity should he be drawn further into this Chemist saga with Brightwell and the O'Clearys; he'd already had the mysterious phone and threatening text message situation and he didn't particularly share Brightwell's enthusiasm for finding out whether they were empty threats or otherwise.

How in the world would he even get close to the O'Clearys anyway? Through Darcy O'Cleary? Yeah right. She was the most popular girl in college. Besides, he wasn't a 'grass'; he knew the unwritten rules of the Granville streets. But he had also just experienced something tragic with Seb that he couldn't bear to stand by and watch happen again: a needless teenage death.

Clearly not everybody who consumed *Charge* was dying. Maybe if people knew how to take it safely, if there was such a way, then that would help cease the deaths and keep him from compromising his ethical issue around becoming a 'grass'. But who in Granville would have the guts to back a harm reduction campaign amidst all this secret scandal? Nobody, that's who. It would mean going public and admitting it's actually happening for a start. Plus, it was madness to think a person such as himself could influence anything, let alone the town's drug policies.

This was one of a thousand possible versions of the story his mind had raced to create over the last few nights. They ranged from him helping Brightwell and being successful, to him helping Brightwell and winding up beaten black and blue by Finn O'Cleary, or worse, another hostile encounter with Smiler. In each version of the story however, there was one common thread; the people close to him got hurt; his mum, Derek and Kirsten – and that's what sucked the most.

He ached at this thought, as these last few days had finally been going well with Kirsten. They had hung out one evening, just walking around but it was nice to spend time together again laughing and flirting innocently. They'd spent a little time together in college, but Tommy was mindful not to force it and encroach on her new friendships. They'd even made plans to spend tomorrow night together, like the Friday nights of old, except now he was only one year off the legal drinking age, which was more often than not seen as old enough in this town.

Whichever path he took with regards to Brightwell and the developing Chemist chronicle, hiding things from Kirsten wasn't going to end well.

As he meandered through the corridors at college this Thursday afternoon, his brain wilfully keeping him upright after several nights of poor sleep, Tommy felt a sense of injustice towards Seb and the other unknown souls who, according to Brightwell, had also lost their lives to *Charge* and the Chemist.

Earlier that morning there had been an assembly to share the awful news that Seb had been taken from them far too soon, with a flaky explanation being given around him 'falling ill after having too much to drink' coupled with a cheap and patronising shot to all the students present around the dangers of drinking alcohol. No mention of *Charge*, not even a murmur.

There were some tears from those who had bonded with him and some from those who take sad news hard. Tommy supposed that the most shocking, if slightly self-consumed, thing was that Seb was the same age as them and it could have been any one of the people sat in that assembly hall.

The sense of injustice further enraged Tommy when he heard not moments after the assembly, hordes of dizzy students scramble to make plans to honour Seb by getting wasted this weekend, with references to house parties and scoring bags of *Charge* for the ride.

"Let's see Seb off in style, it's what he would have wanted," one of the overly eager year 13 students had rallied, whilst putting his arms around two of the more emotional students.

Tommy was furious yet pitiful that an outgoing, caring young man such as Seb would be 'honoured' by booze, synthetic drugs and potentially prompting somebody to meet the same fate. Whilst his relationship with Seb was brief, he was pretty sure he deserved more than that.

People had to know how dangerous Charge was.

As he made his way towards the library to spend his free period pretending to do work when in fact engrossed in yet more sleep starved, frightening thoughts about Granville's criminal activity, he was woken from his trance by Miss Cartwright.

"Tommy, I still need to see you for those mock exams,"

she claimed playfully, as they crossed on the corridor.

"Oh, shoot! Sorry, Miss, I've had a hectic week, I'll come and see you tomorrow,"

She rolled her eyes, "And when do you not have a hectic week, hey?"

"Ha," Tommy forced, "I guess you're right,"

"I could always come to your home and sit at your dining table with your mum and we can both watch you do them instead?"

She flirted with the blurred line between jest and seriousness, which made Tommy shudder slightly.

"Erm, we haven't got a dining table?"

Miss Cartwright stopped and smirked, before turning back to face him, "Come and see me tomorrow and let's get them done; the quicker we do them, the quicker we'll know what we need to improve on,"

"Sure thing, Miss" he agreed. She was trying to help, and he had to admit that she was persistent. He respected that, however alien it felt to him.

"How's that fun side of yours coming along anyway? Have you met some new friends yet, or checked out any of the different clubs here at college, like the art club for instance? I hear that's rocking,"

"Miss, I'm not being funny, but the only artist names I know, are Michelangelo, Leonardo, Donatello and Raphael," he quipped, dryly.

Chuckling, Miss Cartwright back peddled a few paces before turning to walk off down the corridor.

"Very good Tommy, very good," she echoed down the hall. "You, of course, are referring to our pizza-eating, sewer-dwelling, crime-fighting, half-shelled ninja turtle friends, I take it?"

"The very same."

He stood and admired his gag for a few moments, proud of his quick wit and pleased that Miss Cartwright was

also a fan of The Teenage Mutant Ninja Turtles, before turning blindly to walk off himself. As he turned, he suddenly felt
a big bump colliding with somebody, knocking books and bags
all over the floor.

Darcy O'Cleary!

CHAPTER TWELVE

"I am so sorry," she said, a quick response that surprised Tommy and left him even more tongue tied than he already was.

Here was the most popular girl in college apologising to him after *he* bumped into *her*. This was not what he expected at all. As he struggled to find words, he opted instead to kneel down and help collect the books which had scattered across the corridor.

"It's ok, I think it was actually my fault," he began, "it's funny because-"

"Tommy isn't it?" she said, interrupting his imminent ramble.

Surprise number two; she knew who he was.

This was unbelievable. All this time Tommy had been drifting through college believing he was completely invisible, flying beneath the radar, like a depressed ghost skulking around in the background, when in truth, even a girl like Darcy O'Cleary knew who he was.

He picked up the final book and they both rose to their feet, eyes meeting at the top. Darcy adjusted the strap of her bag, nestling it more comfortably onto her shoulder and offered a cute, endearing smile. Her dark brown eyes contrasted against her pale complexion, which was framed with hickory coloured, poker-straight hair, finished off by a fringe that hovered with precision just millimetres above her eyebrows. She was attractive and in this slightly intimate moment, there was no escaping that fact. Tommy felt uneasy and wrestled to keep the quiver from his voice.

"Yeah, Tommy, that's me. I mean, that's my name."

God I am awful at this.

She giggled, "Ok, well I'm Darcy,"

She extended her hand out as an invitation to shake and formalise their introduction, to which Tommy obliged, despite a slight tremor in tow.

"I know," he said, eyes widening a little at his revelation, "I mean, everybody does, right?"

Her hands were soft, yet somewhat cold. She was so pleasant and friendly; not what he envisaged when Brightwell had told him the back story of the family, but Tommy of all people understood the common misconception which comes with tarring all family members with the same brush, so perhaps he was wrong to pre-judge.

"I guess so, although I'll let you into a secret," Darcy said, leaning in ever so slightly and lowering her voice, "not many people *really* know me, most of them are full of shit,"

This girl continued to surprise him.

"Ha!" he guffawed, "I can relate to that,"

They both huffed out light-hearted laughter as he passed her the last book, which she placed in her designer bag.

"I'm sure you can," she paused, as if pondering a thought for a moment, "Tommy, how would you like to come to a party tomorrow night? It's the 21st birthday of one of my older brothers, Seamus. It's at *The Grove* down on Horrocks Street..."

He almost fell over in astonishment. How on earth had this happened? He instinctively put his hand in his pocket and nipped the skin on his thighs, it must have been some kind of mechanism to maintain his composure he assumed, as he'd never done anything like it before.

She continued, "...I know it's a bit random, but believe it or not, I don't meet many genuine people. I've seen you around college and, well, let's just say I've got a good feeling about you. No pressure. So, what do you say?"

Oh God help me!

"Sure, why not? Sounds like fun," he said.

"Just don't let that good feeling I've got about you be wrong, ok?"

Her face had straightened and the shift in tone stunned him. He scrambled to sense if she was kidding or in fact serious. He suddenly felt transparent, as if she could see through his pretence and had latched onto his potential hidden agenda with Brightwell. He stammered a little.

His bizarre involvement with Granville's underworld this past year had added a layer of complexity to his character which unsettled him. Gone were the days where he was blissfully ignorant to the illegal goings-on in the town and he could just focus on himself, Kirsten, his mum and Derek, whilst keeping the teachers at school happy enough so that they wouldn't think to visit his house.

These days, he constantly felt as though everybody was hiding a secretive, sinister side, which evidently now included himself. He was starting to lose who he was. He missed just being Tommy; genuine, what you see is what you get. No skeletons in the closet, no arch nemesis, no secret, dangerous tasks to undertake.

Gradually a chink appeared in Darcy's armour. Her eyes lightened and the left side of her mouth lifted, cracking a mischievous smirk. He was relieved, whilst realising he'd have to think twice before entering a game of poker with this one.

"I'm kidding!" she gushed, "So that's that then. Oh, it starts at eight,"

"See you there," he said smiling, noticing a trivial flutter inside his chest.

Darcy nodded and began to slowly walk off towards the main entrance, flashing a rather conspicuous grin herself.

What about Kirsten, dummy!?

So here he was, the first significant hurdle in the

moral tussle between Kirsten's friendship, and Brightwell's undercover mission. His thoughts moved so quickly that his mind could barely keep up. In the blink of an eye he'd weighed up his several options.

He had an opportunity handed to him on a plate to pursue Brightwell's scheme and find out more information on the O'Clearys, the Chemist and *Charge*, but what would he tell Kirsten? They'd made plans for tomorrow and besides, he *wanted* to see her.

Did he really want to go messing around with the O'Clearys and risk losing Kirsten again? After all, they didn't sound like the forgiving type if he were to get into hot water and besides, Darcy actually seemed quite nice, so he wasn't convinced at present that he wanted to be the guy who waded in and messed with her family.

Perhaps if he went to check out the party *with* Kirsten, he could subtly get enough information on the *Charge* supplies to keep Brightwell happy. Surely then he could pull the plug on this whole cloak and dagger type operation that he was being primed for and concentrate on rekindling things with Kirsten. Plus, Miss Cartwright did say he needed to have more fun so a party would make for a good starting point.

Oh what the hell, it's only a party, how much could possibly go wrong?

"Darcy!" he shouted up the corridor, "Can I bring a friend?"

She stopped and turned willingly.

"Bring who you like," she said with a smile, "nice haircut by the way."

CHAPTER THIRTEEN

"So, she just asked you to go to this party? Just like that?" Derek asked intriguingly. He lay back on his bed and took another drag of his cigarette.

"Yeah, well, it was really strange. She was," Tommy paused, pulling his head out of Derek's wardrobe for a moment to face him, "I'm not sure how to explain it. She was really familiar, as though she knew me – like knew my name and said she had a good feeling about me or something,"

"Woah, sounds like somebody wants to be Mrs Tommy Dawson," Derek teased.

"Don't be daft, Derek. Look at me, I'm rifling through my older brother's wardrobe for a hand-me-down shirt to wear tonight and I've got barely got enough money in my pocket for some beers tonight, as if she'd be interested in me,"

Tommy dived back into the wardrobe, frantically rummaging through Derek's clothes.

Contrary to his decline in self-care and self-interest over the last few years – with the exception of recent months of course – Derek was always quite trendy when he was younger and in keeping with his ritualistic traits, he'd kept most of his clothes. Quite why, Tommy wasn't sure, as it seemed that Derek had kept the same two t-shirts on a continuous rota for the last couple of years. The upside was that now Tommy was of a similar size to Derek, he had a selection of outfits at his disposal, without spending what little money he had from his winter wage at the Old Mill.

"And where does Kirsten fit in to all of this?" Derek quizzed, reaching over to the ashtray on his bedside table, tapping his cigarette gently three times, as he always did, to offload the excess ash.

Tommy paused and stopped his pursuit for tonight's fashion statement for a moment. His heart sunk and his head dropped, as his hands clung to two clothes hangers, a sight which he was in no doubt was symbolic of his current situation. He desperately wanted to share what was going on in his head.

"Derek," Tommy said, solemnly, "I need to talk to you,"

Derek bolted up right and swung his legs off the bed to sit up straight. He extinguished the remainder of his cigarette immediately with three swift prods into the ashtray.

"Sure bro', fire away."

Tommy proceeded to tell Derek the details of Seb, the Chemist and the *Charge* related deaths in Granville, Detective Brightwell and his plan, The O'Clearys and their assumed involvement and probably most significantly how he was in a pickle over putting Kirsten in danger by dragging her through it all – again. He purposefully left some details out, such as the phone and text message he had received and any gut feelings he had about Smiler being in and around this situation; he didn't want to upset Derek's current positive mind-set with references to the man who held so much fear and control over their family.

"That's a lot to be carrying around Tommy, are you sure you're ok?" Derek asked.

"I'm not sure no, I'm torn, you know? I want Kirsten and I to get back to how we were, or more, presuming she wants the same of course. But I also feel an obligation to Seb and anyone else who is at risk of losing their life because of this *Charge* stuff,"

"Why does Brightwell think you're the one who has

to do this?"

This was the question he really didn't want Derek to ask. Brightwell knew about the run in with the hooded man at the hospital and the threatening text message. He knew that there was a high probability it was linked to Smiler and the only way to end this was to wade into the eye of the storm, or so Brightwell believed. Tommy didn't quite share his eagerness but recognised the logic all the same.

Tommy had to think fast.

"Erm, something to do with me being there when Seb died and that kind of stuff," he mumbled, turning back to the wardrobe once more in an attempt to avoid any follow up.

Derek seemed satisfied with Tommy's response, as he shuffled back onto his bed and took out another cigarette from his deck. He took a sip from his pint glass of cider; Friday night's supply of two lots of two-litre bottles of the supermarket's own brand *Strong Arm* sitting alongside, before lighting up and laying back to the position he was before.

"Look, Tommy. If you want my advice, I say you see tonight's party as a date with Kirsten. You two go and enjoy yourselves; she is your primary focus by the sounds of it, so make the most of tonight. I've heard of this *Charge* stuff from a few mates and whilst it sounds nasty, it's not actually your problem. So, screw Brightwell and screw the O'Clearys. I know Stephen junior, the oldest of the O'Cleary brothers, from back in the day. He slapped me around once or twice for not paying a few debts for some of my, well you know, my extra-curricular activities shall we say. He's not a nice fella, but that's the world I lived in and the world they battle daily to reign. I'm sure Seamus and Finn are being inducted into the family business in just the same way. Be careful with this Darcy girl, she's obviously taken a shine to you and if I were you, I'd keep both eyes on Kirsten. But you know what, Darcy may well be a nice kid who is trying to break free from a family reputation, does that sound familiar at all, little brother?"

Derek's words were actually quite shrewd and considering how jumbled the situation felt inside Tommy's head, he had managed to simplify it in a rather profound manner – a juxtaposition which contrasted those astute words with the image of his chain-smoking, cider-guzzling brother.

Tommy wondered if Derek would offer the same advice if he knew of the threat he had received about unfinished business. But he was right in one sense; tonight was a party, he should make the most of spending time with Kirsten and forget about the other noise.

"I suppose that makes sense," he eventually said, nodding in agreement.

"Are you working tomorrow?" Derek asked.

A wry smile crept across his face, "No, Charlie is in all day tomorrow. I'm in on Sunday. Nice lie in for me in the morning."

He had finally whittled his outfit choice down to two, pulling out a long-sleeved burgundy polo shirt and a lumberjack style checked shirt. He held them up for Derek's thoughts, who suggested the polo shirt and Tommy was inclined to agree with him.

"So, what's the plan then, Tommy?" enquired Derek.

"I'm picking Kirsten up at 8pm from her house and we're going to walk into town to *The Grove*, probably arriving about eight-thirty I reckon,"

He then stretched to reach for his brother's glass of cider and stole another gulp.

"Hey, you cheeky bugger, get your own glass; I've told you five times,"

They both laughed. Derek snatched back the glass and topped it up to replenish his loss and then some.

"Pour me one then please, bro', a bit of Dutch courage will probably do me good,"

Tommy was happy that he could now revel in these kinds of moments with his brother, having gone so long without them. Messing around and being silly together was something he and his brother had always enjoyed doing as small children, but Derek's drastic tumble down the rabbit hole to nowhere-land put a huge strain on their relationship. Whilst Derek and their mum had hidden from their problems and responsibilities in a drug induced paradox, Tommy was left to face them head on in a daily fight for survival. Naturally, they drifted apart quite significantly.

But recent months had seen them draw closer than ever with Derek's newfound approach to life. Silly games of 'mattress wrestlemania' and 'kerby' from their childhood had now turned into silly conversations about life and more importantly, an actual interest in one another, which proved as the catalyst for that close bond they held as youngsters, once again returning.

Despite this, Tommy often felt guilty for not truly believing it was going to last, that he will wake up one morning and Derek will have returned to the shady side of the street. Old habits of checking his brother's eyes whenever he entered the room, for instance, were seemingly hard to shift.

But right here and now, they were brothers in a way that brothers should be; close and supportive.

Just as Tommy straightened up his newly claimed polo shirt, pulling the cuffs of the sleeves into place, his phone buzzed in his pocket. He reached in and pulled it out; Brightwell was calling.

"Detective Brightwell, what do I owe the pleasure?" Tommy said, noticing that the few stolen swigs of cider had already began to take their toll.

"Anything to report?" Brightwell asked, sternly from the other end of the phone.

Despite the twinge of worry which now stirred inside, he tried to think about Derek's advice before responding; *focus on Kirsten, screw the rest.*

"Well, not really. It's only been a few days," he said.

"What about this party tonight? I need you there, Tommy,"

How did he know?

81

"Oh yeah, I forgot about that. I did get invited to it actually, is that tonight? I might see if I can get down there,"

He spotted Derek with a bemused look on his face, perhaps puzzled as to what Brightwell was requesting and why Tommy was taking this course of action and in truth, he shared that same uncertainty. He was getting himself tangled up over a simple question, imagine the mess he'd be in if he found himself behind enemy lines with the O'Cleary family.

"Tommy, I know you're worried and I know I'm asking a lot. But this is big, bigger than both of us. I need your eyes in there. If we don't get this squashed, who knows what might happen to you, or your family. Can I count on you?"

Tommy stalled. He didn't need the perspiration which had suddenly formed on his forehead to tell him that he was flustered by this direct approach. He felt the pressure crank up abruptly and the unfair expectation which Brightwell seemed to have of him resonated once more, despite Derek's best efforts to allay his sense of responsibility as the saviour of Granville.

He kept Brightwell waiting for a response as his eyes darted around his brother's bedroom in search of some divine inspiration, but all he could see was a collection of items which summed up a twenty-four year old recovering heroin addict, still living with his mum; posters on the walls, doodles on the wallpaper, which he had done whilst locked in his room going *cold turkey*, broken cd cases, a pile of dirty washing in the corner, a luminous coloured bong which sat on a shelf alongside a ninja star – amongst several other sophisticated 'ornaments' from Wacky Joe's. There was also a photo frame with a picture of the three of them – him, his brother and his mum. But what he didn't find was a creative stimulus that might get him out of this predicament.

"I'll see what I can do," Tommy said, resigned.

"Good lad. I'll be in touch."

CHAPTER FOURTEEN

The walk towards the town centre was brisk, mainly born out of a desire to stay warm on this chilly November evening. There had been a peculiar eeriness on the outskirts of town, with only the faint sound of solitary, belated fireworks exploding in the distance, despite *bonfire night* occurring over a week ago. Whilst they could hear the fireworks, visibility was restricted by thick, onyx clouds, adding an unnecessary edge.

Tommy wasn't sure if it was his paranoia that told him something seemed at odds tonight, or whether something really was brewing in the air.

On the stroll over to Kirsten's house around fifteen minutes prior, Tommy had Brightwell's pressing phone call buzzing around his mind; *why was he pushing this so much?*

Fortunately, he soon became occupied by other thoughts when Kirsten greeted him at her door. It's often said that girls are fashionably late when a night out on the town is concerned, however as with most female stereotypes, he believed Kirsten had a knack of breaking the mould.

He'd wrapped his knuckles on the door a couple times, expecting Mrs Cole to answer and invite him in. But within seconds, it was Kirsten herself who opened the door, clutching her bag; right on time and ready to go.

She radiated natural beauty that almost made him

gasp for breath. Her face was glowing with what could have only been a subtle touch of make-up, so subtle that he wasn't even sure she had any on, but for catching a glimpse of her blusher brush as she zipped up her purse. She wore a white, off-the-shoulder top, a black leather skirt and black ankle boots. She oozed class and as usual, Tommy felt that old tingle of inferiority and self-doubt creep in.

After whipping her coat off the coat stand, slipping it on over her shoulders and shouting a quick goodbye up the stairs to her mum, Kirsten had stepped out of the house and they began their journey to *The Grove*. Tommy attempted to compliment Kirsten on her appearance this evening and, whilst in reality it was a bumbling mess, she seemed to be grateful of the gesture all the same.

It didn't take long for the cold to set in. His teeth chattered together in the chill as he marvelled at Kirsten's ability to cope with the wintery temperature. Whilst he was appreciative of how dreamy her legs looked, he couldn't help but feel they would be freezing right now, exposed to the current elements. As they'd reached the top of her street, Kirsten nestled her chin into her black, faux-fur coat and subtly hooked her arm under his, pulling him in ever so slightly closer.

Along the way they exchanged pleasantries and stories from their respective days, making each other laugh as was typical with anytime they spent together. He told a tale about his mum losing her slippers after putting them in the oven and Kirsten giggled her way through a story about her psychology teacher, *Mr Richard Head*, or *Dick Head* as he will now – and forever more – be known as, even though he profusely insisted it was pronounced *Heed*.

Kirsten had queried how the invite to tonight's party had come around, but to his relief, she didn't feel the need to press the issue following his basic explanation around Darcy's invite. The gentle enthusiasm in her voice, told Tommy she was excited to get out and enjoy herself. The glisten in her eyes, told him she too had enjoyed a couple of alcoholic aperitifs at home, which put him at ease a little following his cider indulgence with Derek.

The desire to tell Kirsten about everything, from the *Charge* to Brightwell to the whole story behind going to this party tonight, flared up in his tummy yet again, but instead he opted for more crazy anecdotes from home, this time he told the one from earlier in the week when his mum tried to tell him that the man next door was a benefits spy working for the government – whatever one of those were.

The atmosphere began to pick up as they reached the corner of Horrocks Street, home to *The Grove*, Granville's premier Irish pub. It was the street known as the *gatekeeper*, containing three drinking establishments which paved the way towards the rest of the town's bittersweet night life.

Tommy recalled seeing an article published by *The Granville Gazette* last month which reported a jaw-dropping statistic, claiming that the town was host to a licensed premises for every eighty-two residents – *and people wondered why folk turn to drink and drugs*.

Much like the fireworks, the eeriness which clouded the outskirts of town, had fizzled away as scantily clad girls – and boys – walked the streets, giddy and hopeful, in search of the Elysium which Friday nights so often promised around these parts.

"Please swear to me that if you ever see me in an outfit like that, Tommy, you will slap me in the face and send me home," Kirsten said boldly.

It revealed a glimpse of her mildly ostentatious side, which didn't come out all that often; granted her comment was in reference to a forty-year old woman donning a pink PVC boob tube and florescent cycling shorts, in November no less. Tommy chuckled and did his best to make a *meow* sound, accompanied by a *claws-out* gesture, which made Kirsten snort with laughter, as they made the final few paces towards the front of tonight's party venue.

As they approached, his senses were overloaded with

stimulus; bright colours, loud noises and his nose detecting a range of different scents, from stale ale and cigarettes, to cheap perfume and of course, the unmistakeable smell of the food being cooked up at the *Turkish Kebab House* on the corner.

The Grove was a larger than life place, epitomised by its neon green sign and accompanying slogan; *nobody leaves sober.* It was the kind of establishment which preferred familiar faces, where folk could ask for their 'usual' and the bar tender wouldn't need a reminder. Tommy recognised the timeless tones of *Thin Lizzy* currently blasting through the door each time it swung open.

Naturally, it was a home away from home for many of the Irish and Celtic community in Granville, but it was by no means an exclusive admission. One family who did have a strong connection with this place though: The O'Clearys. Tommy hoped that his personal invite from Darcy herself would be enough to steer away any potential unwanted attention from some of the more territorial folk who frequented *The Grove.*

As he and Kirsten both braced themselves to pass the ultimate test, the make or break moment of the night; entry past the doorman without proof of age required, they were stopped in their tracks by an unexpected sight.

The single door next to *The Grove* opened, with a crack of light spilling out onto the street. A female figure bundled her way out of the doorway and onto Horrocks Street, before flicking off the light and closing the door behind her. She turned around and they spotted that it was none other than Miss Cartwright.

"Woah! Hey, Miss, I didn't expect to see you here tonight, what are you up to?" Tommy quizzed, cheerfully.

Miss Cartwright turned to face the pair of them, sporting a pair of rosy cheeks, looking rather flustered. She had casual clothes on, gym wear if he had to label it, and a black sports holdall over her shoulder.

"Hi, Tommy. Hello Kirsten," she said, nodding politely, "you caught me, guilty as charged. I've just finished my *Zumba* class upstairs, excuse the red face and sweaty clothes,"

She turned back to the door and locked it, popping the keys in her bag. Tommy looked up to spot the windows of a dance studio on the floor above.

"That's cool, Miss. I didn't have you down for *Zumba*, I would have guessed mixed martial arts, if anything," Tommy said, goofily sniggering.

"Ok, Tommy," Kirsten intervened, pushing him towards the door of *The Grove*, "let's leave Miss Cartwright to go and enjoy her weekend. Nice seeing you, Miss,"

Tommy saw Kirsten offer a supportive smile to Miss Cartwright, some kind of girl code he presumed, and he wondered if his comment made him look like a bit of a dick.

"Well you two have fun," Miss Cartwright said, "and don't do anything I wouldn't do,"

Tommy and Kirsten laughed simultaneously.

"We won't," they both said, in sync.

"And Tommy," Miss Cartwright added, "you know where to find me if you ever want me to teach you some of those *Zumba* moves, they can be just as deadly as mixed martial arts I'll have you know."

Miss Cartwright winked before turning up Horrocks Street and off into the night.

"I did not expect to see her tonight," Tommy said, seizing the opportunity to have something to be talking about upon approach to *The Grove* entrance.

The doorman's beady eye weighed the pair of them up as he kept one ear in tune with his walky-talky, which crackled repeatedly. In his, albeit limited, experience, Tommy had found it was always better to appear confident through conversation with the person you are with, than to arrive in silence.

"Me neither," Kirsten responded, a dynamic plan of how to overcome the doorman's prowess formulating between the pair via telepathy, "I like her though, she's nice,"

"Oh yeah, me too, she's helped me out a truck load already," he said with conviction, before cocking his head towards the doorman and nodding, ensuring he made solid eye contact.

His final comment proved to be enough, as the doorman reached over and pulled the door open towards him to allow them entry, even wishing them a good evening as they passed.

They were in.

CHAPTER FIFTEEN

An hour or so had passed and Tommy and Kirsten had loosened up with some light-hearted chatter and a few drinks; bottled lager and Bacardi-Diet Coke respectively. Tommy found himself at the bar again ready to order another round, whilst Kirsten had excused herself to nip to the ladies' room, which was downstairs. They'd agreed to have one more drink up here before heading down to the function room where the party was being held, hopefully avoiding the fearful possibility of arriving too early to an empty room, which of course is not ideal when one doesn't really know the person whose party it is.

The Grove had a strange layout, it was reminiscent of the Tardis; it didn't look much from the outside, but the place seemed to expand at will once you entered. The front doors opened to the ground level bar area, which was pretty standard; tables, chairs, a couple of booths by the window, a curved bar stacked with plenty of choice towards the back.

It continued like a maze downstairs, which had two rooms; the function room and a sports lounge, with access to the toilets and couple of fruit machines which stood tall and bright on the sticky, tiled floor of the lower ground foyer. The sports lounge housed a snooker table, a large TV on the wall and, judging by what Tommy saw through the glass panels of the doors when passing to go to the gent's toilets earlier, it had a much quieter, members-only kind of ambience.

Tommy looked around as he waited his turn at the bar;

it was busy, bordering on rowdy, so he didn't want to be stepping on anybody's toes, neither figuratively nor literally. Irish memorabilia covered the walls; from green, white and orange flags, replica *U2* and *The Cranberries* records, vintage *Jameson* and *Guinness* advertisement posters and autographed sports equipment from icons such as *Steve Collins* and *Roy Keane.*

Above the bar, he spotted another bumper sticker type slogan, which read; *We're here for a good time, not a long time, so let's dance!*

Upon reading it he stifled an ironic laugh. He found it frustrating to see such catch phrases at large, when living in a place like Granville, and how many people were drawn in, adopting it as their life motto. He believed his generation, and arguably most generations, didn't have the option of either a good time or a long time, as they were denied both.

The older he got, the more he could see that political puppeteers had masterminded a rigged system, so those that were most deprived remained exactly where they wanted them to be. His fellow Granvillians were consequently left scrapping for survival, lucky to even make it past the age of forty, with any concept of a good time – beyond the temporary and bittersweet buzz of drugs or the escapism of alcohol – was just a distant ideology, an unachievable reality that was paraded in front of their eyes, yet out of touch, by the media. On the other hand, he wondered how many would even opt for a long time given the choice, if their current circumstances were the conditions that they were subjected to. Round here, it sometimes felt like a race towards death to escape their incarceration.

As he stepped off his internal political soap box and back into the room, he noticed that the music had been a steady flow of traditional Irish music with some pop, rock and soul dotted in, which he was more than happy with. Regardless of its reputation, he got a nice feel from this place. Sure, people seemed aggressively happy, greeting one another with bone crushing slaps on the back and a slur of expletives and insults, but he would settle for that, it was kind of endearing.

Just as the barmaid hovered over to take his order, having finally spotted him on his tiptoes between two grizzly blokes, he felt a tap on his shoulder.

"Hey there, handsome,"

Tommy span round, losing his turn at the bar in the process, to see Darcy standing there. She wore a short, sequinned dress, high heels and mischievous guile in her eyes.

"Hi, Darcy," he paused, recognising this wasn't always his strongest trait, "you look... nice,"

She smiled, "Thanks, not so bad yourself,"

She leant in and gave him a hug, which he found a little uncomfortable. Yet again she seemed to be overly familiar, given they hadn't spoken more than twice.

"This is a great place," he said, "I'm just getting a drink for me and my friend, Kirsten, then we're going to head down to the party,"

He stepped away from Darcy's grasp and placed one hand on the wooden bar top, eager not to lose his position in the queue again.

"Yes, I noticed who you were with. You know, when I said you could bring a friend, I didn't think you meant a girl, especially somebody as stunning as that,"

Darcy smirked to show her jesting was meant with no malice, but he was sure he could still detect the essence of jealousy that was sprinkled within her words.

What was she up to?

Danger was summoning his morality to tango, as his eyes scooted around to check out the vicinity; he wasn't used to this kind of forward behaviour. He offered an awkward laugh, before turning to order his drinks from the returning and now rather impatient looking barmaid.

"Hey, Darcy, you'll never guess who we bumped into outside?" he said, scrambling for neutral conversation, once he'd placed his order.

"Who?" she said.

"Miss Cartwright, from college. Is that weird or what?"

She chuckled, "Not as weird as you think, she rents the studio upstairs from my dad. She does dance classes or something up there,"

The barmaid asked if he wanted a small or large measure of Bacardi, to which he turned to nod and gesture with his index finger and thumb to indicate a large.

"So, are you having a good time?" Tommy uttered spinning back to face her. His words were barely audible above the latest song selection inspired by the emerald isle, prompting several regulars to jump their feet in a raucous: *Teenage Kicks – The Undertones.*

Darcy took a purposeful sip through the straw which sat in her drink; vodka and lemonade if he had to guess. She made sure to maintain eye contact with him as she sampled, to which he twitched, struggling to return the favour. She appeared to be conjuring up her next move, when she swiftly stepped in close, almost pressing herself against his body. She pulled at his arm, bringing his ear down towards her mouth.

"Not yet," she whispered sensually, "but make sure you come and find me in a little while and hopefully that will all change,"

Tommy's eyes widened; her comments almost floored him, like a knockout blow from the pride of Ireland herself, *Katie Taylor*. Before he could respond, she had turned and sashayed away through the crowd, like an illusion. Dazed, he shook his head to try and awake from this bizarre moment.

Was she for real?

He handed a ten-pound note to the barmaid and collected his change, barely keeping his hand still enough to receive the coins. He turned back around, drinks in hand, and almost jumped out of his skin to see Kirsten standing there.

"Jesus, Kirst', you scared the shit out of me then!"

Kirsten giggled and took her Bacardi and Diet Coke from him, before he dropped it.

"Charming!" she exclaimed, "Hey, easy on the blasphemy in here Tommy, we don't want to be pissin' people off, if you feel me?"

"Oh yeah, I feel you alright," he said, still processing the peculiar conversation that had just taken place.

"Why are you so jumpy anyway? Although I must say, it was rather enjoyable, maybe I should see if I can get a copy of the CCTV, I'd like to watch a rerun of your face just then. Good job I'd just been for a wee isn't it,"

They laughed, before Kirsten's face suddenly expressed a hint of embarrassment, perhaps the thought of oversharing her toilet routine had got to her. Tommy didn't mind, she was real; it's what he loved most about her.

"Well, I've just had a really strange and rather intense conversation with," he paused and leaned in to speak a little more subtly in Kirsten's ear, "Darcy O'Cleary,"

"Oh, I wondered who the hotty was chatting you up, I could only see the back of her head whispering sweet nothings into your ear," she joked.

"Well, that's just it, it kind of was like that and it's freaked me out to be honest,"

Kirsten tittered, "And why wouldn't she? You're a catch, Dawson,"

"Don't tease, Kirsten," he said, "I don't know what I'm going to do; she seems a bit cuckoo,"

"I'm not teasing," she said, somewhat resolute, before lightly adding, "oh will you just relax, you'll be fine. You're with me,"

She grabbed his hand and pulled him away from the bar towards the stairs. Electricity permeated his skin, infusing his body with a warm, uncertain, aching sensation.

"Come on, let's hit the party," Kirsten added, "it sounds like it's getting lively down there, and I'm itching to dance."

If only you knew the half of it.

CHAPTER SIXTEEN

Tommy sat on his stool, with one arm leaning against the bar, watching the room. He'd spent the last few minutes peeling away the label on his bottle of beer thinking, over-thinking perhaps.

The party, up until a point, had been great. He and Kirsten had danced and laughed and danced some more; he'd forgotten about his worries for a short while and lived content in a little bubble, perfectly sized for two, gazing into one another's eyes.

Unfortunately, Tommy knew all too well that bubbles have a knack of bursting. So, when taking a trip to the gent's toilets and coming face-to-face with Finn O'Cleary, who was heading into the private barracks which the cubicles pro-vided, he was brought crashing back down to earth by the harsh realisation of what he was on the cusp of being dragged into. Although the encounter was muted – Tommy doubted Finn would even know who he was – his intimidating persona and a look on his face that spelled trouble, meant that Tommy was having difficulty seeing an easy way out.

When he returned to the party, it was as though some-body had wiped away the rainbows and the gloss, as he no-ticed rough edges that were previously invisible from within his protective bubble with Kirsten. He saw the vomit in the corner, he saw the hordes of party-goers gurning, presumably from hits of *Charge*, talking at one another with no clue as to what the other one was saying. He saw tension and unpredictability. He saw a dingy room filled with people, ninety-nine percent of whom he didn't want to talk to. He saw a microcosm of Granville.

And now here he sat, on the outskirts once again. He watched Kirsten as she gloriously performed care-free dance routines and enthusiastically yelled the words to every song with some of her friends from her psychology class, oblivious to the fermenting danger which consumed him at present.

Her confidence prompted him to smile through the guilt-ridden pain that festered within. He wanted so badly to tell her everything. He needed her right now, but he knew that he was being selfish for that. It didn't sit right with him that Brightwell was the only person he could turn to; the pressure being applied by his detective acquaintance suffocated him in truth.

He yearned to rekindle the gung-ho, partner-in-crime, if-you-go-I-go kind of closeness he once shared with Kirsten. The kind of closeness that D'artagnan and his Musketeers would have been envious of. The kind of closeness that enabled them to bring down the almighty Smiler. But that would not be fair on Kirsten, this was his problem to solve.

Out of the corner of his eye, Tommy spotted a sparkly dress inbound, hastily rushing towards him, thrusting him back into the room from the depths of his thoughts. He braced himself.

"Come on you," Darcy said with a noticeable slur, "let's go for a chat,"

"Huh?" Tommy gasped, "What do you mean?"

Darcy gripped his arm, yanking him from his stool and out of the function room doors in no time at all.

"I've hardly seen you all night, I want to get to know you a bit more," she said.

"I should really stay in there, my friend, she's-"

"Don't worry I'm not stealing you forever just yet, just

five minutes, that's all,"

His pleas were futile. Darcy was deceivingly strong and pretty damn determined to get him away from the party for some alone time, to get to know one another. Whilst Tommy was a tad alarmed by the current goings on, stumbling into the downstairs foyer, in a somewhat perverse manner, he actually felt flattered that somebody with Darcy's social clout seemed so interested in him.

He was concerned leaving Kirsten and what this looked like to the unknowing onlooker, but he knew that he wasn't in any position to be making a scene right now. He just needed to ride the storm, be polite and get back to his beloved friend in five short minutes and who knows, along the way he may find something out about how Seb came to meet his tragic fate.

"Let's go in here," Darcy said, indicating the sports lounge would be the chosen destination for their third encounter, by bundling him through the doors.

The sports lounge was a stark contrast to the bustling function room, it was spotless for a start, with polished tables, hoovered carpets and gleaming brass hand rails attached to the bar; it was clear that the member's area took top spot on the priority list at *The Grove*.

There was a quieter atmosphere in here; that was the first the thing that made him feel uneasy. The second; spotting two of the O'Cleary brothers propping up the bar.

"Here she is, my darling little sister," the older looking one heckled, Tommy presumed that was Seamus, the birthday boy.

"Hi boys," Darcy chimed, still dragging Tommy behind her like a rag doll.

"You caught us, we've snuck in here for a quiet drink. Come over here and join your brothers," Seamus cackled, "and tell us who your friend is,"

For all Tommy had heard, his first impressions of Seamus were rather pleasant, but he was fully aware of just how deceiving first impressions can be.

"This is my friend, Tommy," she said, gushing. "Tommy, these are my brothers, Seamus and Finn,"

"Nice to meet you Tommy," Seamus said, offering out a firm hand, "and you can call me Shay."

Tommy shook it precariously and nodded. He turned to Finn expecting to follow the same routine, however the response was more of a disapproving grunt than anything else. Tommy swallowed hard, retracting his hand sheepishly.

Shay was broad and quite imposing, a look which was softened by his fleshy cheeks and a huge, friendly grin. He had curly black hair, slicked back with styling mousse. Finn was the opposite, slim build, a scrawny, angular looking face with deep auburn coloured hair and patches of matching facial growth.

"I'll have a bottle of WKD please, Shay," Darcy said, excitably.

Shay turned to the bar and shouted, "Colin, get my sister a bottle of WKD and whatever her boyfriend wants. And get me twenty *Lambert and Butler* whilst you're at it. You can stick it on my tab,"

"Oh, a lager please, thanks. We're just friends though by the way," Tommy said, hesitantly, which failed to provoke a response from anyone.

Colin, the barman, got to work on the drinks, leaving the other patrons that had been waiting patiently to wait a little longer. Nobody protested though, suggesting the gentleman's agreement of waiting your turn at the bar didn't apply to the O'Clearys and nobody felt compelled enough to argue. What also became apparent to Tommy upon Shay's request, was that selling cigarettes illegally over the bar was just business as usual around here.

Tommy could feel himself fidgeting. He put his hand in his pocket, then took it out. Whatever he did, he didn't feel comfortable, leaving him conscious of every minute movement he made. He met eyes with Finn once more and offered half of a smile, which was countered with a glare that would give small children nightmares; he seemed wired, on high alert almost. Having seen Finn occupy the cubicle in the gents' toilets, he took an educated guess that he was probably under the influence of the already infamous *Charge*.

He found himself swallowing hard, again.

Shay passed over his pint of lager as requested, and Tommy thanked him for it. He felt his eyes involuntarily twitching nervously towards Finn at every moment, trying to depict whether his hostile mood was a general thing or directed specifically towards him.

Shay then reached over the back of Tommy's head and latched a vice grip onto his neck, startling him enough to spill a splash of frothy lager down his shirt front.

"Now then, Tommy, let me explain a little bit about how we go about our family business," Shay began, almost philosophically, "anybody who is alright by our sister, is alright by us, isn't that right, Finn?"

Despite Shay's rather jolly approach, Finn still had difficulty cracking a smile, managing a mere eye-roll in response.

He added, "Ignore him, he's a moody swine," Finn's body language transformed instantly towards a more confrontational stance following Shay's bait, but the older of the two just laughed it off before continuing, "If you're going to be spending time with our family, we need to initiate you properly, you seem like a decent lad to me," he turned to Darcy, "he's not quite as good looking as us though is he, Darc'?"

This prompted laughter all around, even a brief exhalation from Finn, so Tommy felt obliged to humour them.

Shay was about to continue his lesson on family integration or whatever it was he was intending, when he was stopped in his tracks. A scruffy looking lad approached. He must have only been twenty-five, but his appearance sentenced him to another twenty years on top of that. His face was gaunt and pale, he seemed shifty and almost unconscious to the fact he had walked into the middle of a conversation. He fiddled with his baseball cap before speaking.

"Can I get some *Charge* from you boys?"

His voice was hoarse, weathered even. Tommy's eyes immediately snapped towards Shay, then Finn, then back to Shay. He could see shock rapidly turn into rage, particularly with Finn, who became as animated as he had seen so far.

Before a moment could pass, Finn stepped forward in a flash and slapped the bloke with a violent yet clinical open palm to the cheek. The velocity of the strike threw his head away from his body, no doubt straining his neck. It knocked his hat to the floor and forced him to stagger backwards several paces, before spilling onto a table. When he looked up, he seemed stunned. He touched his face, which sported a raw, pink handprint.

Just from observing, Tommy could almost feel the blow down to his shoes. It sent a nervous shudder rocketing up his spine all the way up behind his ears. He felt his legs wobble as he placed his hand on the back of a chair to steady himself, not wanting to seem too unnerved by the brutality which seemed so ordinary to everyone else in the room.

Finn shook his hand by his side, before speaking for the first time since Tommy had entered the sports lounge.

"Mitch, don't you dare stumble up in our faces and talk about that to us, in here, in front of our family and friends,"

Finn was pointing aggressively as he spoke, but bizarrely gestured towards Tommy when referencing *friends*, something that took him by surprise given the frosty reception he'd had.

The intruder, Mitch, mustered enough breath to respond, "Finn, please mate, I'm sorry, I didn't mean no offence, I just need a fix, you know? I'm rattling,"

Finn's breathing was short and fast, so much so Tommy could hear each exhalation surge from his nose; he half expected fire to burst from his nostrils any moment. Fortunately, Shay stepped forward with seemingly a slightly cooler head. He firmly cupped Mitch around the back of his neck and turned him towards the far side of the room.

"You know the drill, Mitch," Shay said pointing over towards a table of lads who seemed to have taken an interest in the current kafuffle, "never under any circumstances do you come to us direct, understand? Or do I need to remind you how Vinnie Fleckney got his nickname *Van Gough*?"

Mitch shook his head furiously. There was genuine panic in his expression at this point. Tommy had never heard of Vinnie *Van Gough*, but he didn't need his Maths GCSE to figure out that something unfortunate had happened to one of his ears and he didn't have a difficult time figuring out who sanctioned such a punishment, or why.

Shay continued, "Now, if you need some gear, you go and see Ryan *The Hat* about finances and *Tortoise* Pete for the Chemist's latest produce; you never come direct to us, ok?"

"Thank you, Shay. I'm sorry. Thank you," Mitch said, frantically trying to shake both Shay's hands at once. Tommy thought all that was missing was him dropping to his knees and kissing his master's shoes.

This was insane.

"That's your last fucking warning!" Finn bellowed, as Mitch scurried away, almost rat-like, towards Ryan *The Hat* – who Tommy presumed was the chubby looking lad wearing a tweed flat cap – and *Tortoise* Pete – who Tommy couldn't quite pick out just yet, but he presumed his nickname corresponded with the pace at which he got things done.

"Calm down, little brother," Shay said, gesturing with his hands.

"It really pisses me off, Shay," Finn snapped, "its sloppy; that's how people get found out and come unstuck,"

Tommy couldn't believe what he was hearing. Brightwell's manic hypothesis was actually dead accurate; The O'Cleary network were in cahoots with The Chemist in supplying Granville with *Charge*, as clear as day.

He was trying his hardest to listen without drawing

attention to himself, so he missed some of the following exchange between the two brothers, as they lowered their voice to continue their discussion on the incident that had just passed.

He sipped his lager and looked up at the TV screen. There was a boxing fight that was being televised, so he hoped it seemed as though he was more interested in that than what the hell was happening in this place. He didn't dare look at Darcy, for fear of what might come out of her mouth. Within the space of ten minutes he'd been referred to as her boyfriend and part of the family.

These guys were nuts!

Tommy was drawn from watching the boxing on the TV by Shay's voice.

"Listen, Tommy, my sincere apologies that you had to see that, it's never pretty when business intrudes into family time. I've got to leave now, I've got to go back in the other room and show my face, say thank you to a few people, you know? But hey, we want you to come to the football with us tomorrow, we'll see about that initiation, yeah? Granville vs Blackchester Albion at home; it's going to be a huge game. We've got the tickets – no arguments, you're coming, ok? Finn will sort the arrangements out with you."

Quick, think of an excuse!

Shay embraced Tommy and kissed him on the cheek, akin to the inappropriate gangster films Tommy had watched with Derek when they were younger, before departing from the sports lounge.

Damn it, why couldn't I be working tomorrow instead of Sunday?

Finn barged past Tommy, knocking him off balance as he collided with his shoulder. He turned back, blazing, "Meet us here tomorrow at 1pm. Don't be late, ok?"

Tommy's palms were moist, his body rigid to the core as he stood rooted to the spot. Finn seemed disappointed to say the least at his inclusion in tomorrow's football plans. He wanted to break it to him; he wasn't overly ecstatic about it either.

How on earth had it got to this? What am I going to do?

"Well, that seemed to go well, didn't it?" Darcy said, finishing off the remainder of her bubble-gum alcopop.

"If you say so," Tommy sighed. He hesitated moment-arily before adding, "Darcy, that was crazy. I mean, I've got sweat dripping down my back kind of crazy. Do you think I really have to go to the football tomorrow?"

Tommy held his breath, hoping for some kind of get out clause.

"If my brothers ask people to do something, they gen-erally do it. But if they invite somebody to join them for the football, they *always* do it. But it's up to you,"

Regardless of Darcy claiming it was up to him, he was beginning to feel like that was a little farfetched and that really, he had no choice in the matter. He could feel a mild panic bubbling inside of him already, but was thankful for the eight or so beers he'd had this evening, as the bravery juice seemed to be mellowing out his thoughts and suppressing his angsts, particularly the prospect of going to the football with the O'Cleary brothers tomorrow. He knew that the morning would tell a different story though.

"Can I ask you something?" he said.

"Sure,"

"Are you ok with all of that? The violence? The associ-ation with you know, *other things*?"

"Tommy, listen, I'm not like my family. They do what they do. I love them, but I've got different plans. As far as I'm concerned, the less I know, the better. I'm used to their ways, but it doesn't mean I agree or condone it. I want more for my-self. I don't know, it might not make any sense,"

In a moment of utter clarity, Darcy made complete sense. He could totally relate to what she was saying: family is family, but it doesn't mean we are all the same. The irrational, intense and overly familiar behaviour that made him feel so edgy earlier had subsided and out shone this cool, calm and collected girl. Tommy now had no problem detecting why she was so popular at college and it was based on her own merit, not just her surname.

"No, it makes perfect sense," he assured, readjusting his prior judgement somewhat.

"I said I had a good feeling about you, didn't I?" she toyed, a subtle grin forming across her face, "Come on, let's get you back to your friend,"

"Oh shit, Kirsten!"

He dashed back into the function room and looked around agitatedly. Amidst the madness that Shay's 21stbirthday party had become, he couldn't find Kirsten. He asked a girl he recognised from college to go into the ladies' toilets and ask if there was a Kirsten in there, but there wasn't. He flew up the stairs and out of the front doors to check outside where the smokers were huddling. He frantically scanned up and down the street. His eyes darted across to the taxi rank, he would have been able to spot her curls from fifty yards away, but there was no sign of her.

It was 00:21am and Kirsten had gone.

CHAPTER
SEVENTEEN

It took a few minutes for his mind to clear, having woken up with a thumping headache and blurred vision. He sat up in bed and peered around his room, awaiting the rush of memories from the previous night to come forth and help him piece together what had happened. His hand had a slight tremble as he struggled to raise the glass of water up to his lips from his bedside table, an attempt to remedy his dry mouth.

A hangover, great.

As he drained the glass, gulping down the remaining water, broken images flooded his mind, prompting more questions and anxiety, rather than providing any answers or comfort.

Where did Kirsten go?

What happened with Darcy?

Did I really get invited to the football with the O'Cleary brothers?

He scrambled around his bed and under his pillow in search of his phone. He vaguely remembered trying to call Kirsten and sending her a text message to see where she had gone to. Part of him hoped she had gone on to another bar with her psychology classmates and enjoyed herself. But part of him also felt disappointed that they didn't finish the night in the same spirit which they started it. Every part of him hoped she had got home safe.

He eventually found his phone in his shoe. He unlocked it, squinting as the light which illuminated the screen burned his eyes. He thought about opening his curtains to let some day light in, but right now, even a simple task such as that seemed beyond the levels of effort that he was able to exert.

Text message from Brightwell:

07:14

"Call me asap, Tommy. Cheers, B"

He couldn't begin to stir up enough motivation to contact Brightwell right now, although he had to hand it to the detective, his hunch was right on the money. He'd shared his feeling about the O'Clearys and the Chemist collaborating on the current deadly scheme that was haunting Granville and judging by last night's antics, it looks like that feeling was spot on.

He suddenly had a wave of dread wash over him, recognising that today he found himself at a desperate crossroads. If he attended the football with Shay and Finn – not that there seemed to be any 'if' about it – he was stepping over a line. He became acutely aware that any following information he shared with Brightwell, once apparently befriending the O'Clearys, put him very much in the category of a *grass*.

As much as he told himself it was justice for Seb and to stop anymore senseless deaths, he couldn't escape the danger which the label of being a snitch brought with it, especially when dealing with violent thugs such as the O'Clearys. There was also the added bonus of potentially eradicating any vague scent of Smiler lurking in the shadows, keeping him and his loved ones safe. But still, the fear of being tarnished an informer was unequivocal.

He attempted to disperse these thoughts to the back

of his mind for now by continuing to scroll through his phone.

Text message conversation with Kirsten from last night:

00:21

"Kirsten, where are you? x"

00:38

"Hey Kirst, hope you're ok?
Couldn't find you anywhere? x"

01:07

"Don't worry, I'm home safe.
Talk tomorrow."

He read it again, detecting a reserved undertone from Kirsten's response; something didn't feel right. It was shorter than her usual friendly manner and he couldn't ignore the lack of x's at the end, as she was always a two-kiss minimum kind of person when signing off her text messages.

He strained his eyes trying to extract more information from the seven words she had sent as they stared back at him ominously from the screen. This was the problem he found with text messages; it was easy to misinterpret what the other person was saying.

He toyed with the idea that it could have been short because it was late and she was tired, but his gut told him there was more to it. His gut told him that she left because he had disappeared with Darcy O'Cleary. And his gut couldn't blame her.

What was I thinking?

Recognising he was merely delaying the inevitable of what today had in store by laying in his bed worrying, he decided to get up and take a shower. He hoped following this he would feel a little fresher ahead of contacting Brightwell and Kirsten and not forgetting his jolly boys outing to the football later with his new acquaintances.

He pulled his blue jumper over his head and gave his hair another ruffle with the towel. The shower had certainly woken him up. His plan for a warm, soothing experience had been squashed immediately, after quickly realising that there was no hot water and he would have to settle for an icy cold, jittery and fleeting encounter instead. His mum had obviously used the ten pounds he gave her yesterday for the heating as personal expenses instead. He assumed heroin, as he recalled the unmistakeable vinegary musk still lingering in the air when he got home last night.

He'd spent the last twenty minutes reflecting on his current situation and determining his course of action. He'd decided not to bother contacting Brightwell; if it was urgent, he was sure he would try and contact again. Besides, he'd not figured out what he was going to share with him yet. This whole thing crippled him with worry, he had to tread carefully. Brightwell had become a little forceful, obsessed almost, and that only amplified his reluctance to rush in and make a mistake, leaving himself vulnerable. The last thing he needed was to get stuck in between some existing war between Brightwell and the O'Clearys.

He'd accepted his fate with regards to attending the football. Disrespecting Finn and Shay O'Cleary by refusing their invitation and complimentary match ticket would not stand him in good stead. Judging by last night's run-in with Mitch, they didn't take too kindly to people not playing by their rules. He'd visualised it in his mind; he would simply go to the game, play nice and get the hell out of there at the earliest and safest opportunity.

In an ideal world he would have liked to have called to see Kirsten today to straighten out last night's crossed wires and find out what happened. He was ready to take whatever steps were required to smooth things over if – or rather when

– necessary. However, she had already told him last night that she had a shift today at her Uncle Bill's pub, the Junction, where she'd worked for a couple of years now. He was pushed for time as it was, so a diversion across town to see Kirsten would leave him way late and, as Finn so elegantly warned him last night, that was not an option. So, a phone call on the way to *The Grove* would hopefully suffice.

Following one last glance in his bedroom mirror and a premature attempt at squeezing a pimple on his chin, he departed ready to take on the challenges ahead. His headache had subsided slightly, but he felt it would be wise to gulp down one more glass of water. He headed to the bathroom with his glass in hand to attend to his hydration levels.

Upon passing his mum's bedroom door, he noticed it was closed, which usually meant that she was still inside. He gave her door a light knock. There was no sound coming from within and his knock appeared to fall on deaf ears. It was 12:32pm and his mum was either conked out, or something much worse.

He'd harboured this feeling for almost his entire life. The fear of walking in to find her beyond reparation was something he lived with each time he crossed the threshold of his home. Each time he had picked her up off the floor and taken her to bed. Each time he had phoned for an ambulance. And right here, right now. He questioned whether it was normal that a son should have to fear death greeting them when carrying out the simple gesture of saying goodbye to his mother. But he also recognised there was nothing normal about his house, his family and his life.

His abdominal region rapidly turned to concrete, solidifying by the second, as he gently pushed open her door. He craned his neck into the darkness and saw the silhouette of her lying there, motionless. He cleared his throat, detecting his own apprehension.

"Mum, I'm going out for the day," he mustered, waiting on pins.

Then he heard it, his mum's infamous grunt. The

sound that smashed the abdominal concrete to pieces and replaced it with elation. His mum rolled over in her bed and lazily flickered her hand, which he knew all too well translated to *go away*.

He withdrew his head from inside his mum's bedroom and closed the door, leaving it how he found it, but safe in the knowledge that she was alive, for at least today anyway. He was fully aware that his mum grunting at him from her bed past noon on a Saturday was no reason for celebration, but he felt relieved all the same and a strange comfort came over him.

He headed for the stairs when he heard a vibration coming from his own bedroom that sounded like a text message. He realised he must have left his phone in there, so quickly darted back in.

Upon reaching his bedside table, he was left perplexed, noticing that his phone was actually already in his pocket. Then it dawned upon him. A clang of nervousness plummeted into to the pit of his stomach. He carefully opened his top drawer and lifted out the mystery phone from the hospital, which he had kept switched on in case there was further contact, just as Brightwell had instructed. He quickly understood that it was indeed this phone that was the source of the vibrating sound. He unlocked the screen and saw the flashing notification; one new text message. He held his breath and pressed open.

12:34pm

"I hope you had a nice time
last night with
your new friends, Tommy.
I'm watching you ☺ "

109

CHAPTER EIGHTEEN

He found himself in an unusual situation, almost as if the world was distorted. On one hand, he felt haunted by a weight of worry. It was beginning to claw its way slowly up the back of his neck engulfing his crown.

The reference to *new friends* in the anonymous text message concerned him on two fronts; he wondered how the sender knew he had been acquainted with the O'Clearys last night and why they felt compelled to reference it with such backhanded nicety. One thing that seemed certain however, was that the message being signed off with a smiley face, he presumed, told him everything he needed to know about who the sender was. Smiler.

He had no doubt that being watched would be a creepy experience in any circumstance, but being watched by the devil himself presented him with a complex version of fear that he couldn't ignore any longer. That, plus the added development of Kirsten's phone ringing out on all three of the occasions he tried to call her whilst walking to *The Grove* to meet Shay and Finn, meant that he had unfinished business on his mind which bothered him; it was the uncertainty which bugged him more than anything, although he felt there wasn't anything uncertain about Kirsten blanking his calls; she was pissed off.

Yet on the other hand, the three shots of tequila he was forced to drink upon arrival at *The Grove* in some kind of pre-match ritual, plus the none-stop chatter and hyperactive comradery he'd been surrounded by when striding down towards the football ground meant that his worries were bizarrely buffered somehow.

He felt hazy, bordering on an out of body type experience, as he bumbled his way down the pavement, being held upright by the masses of lively, boisterous football fans all taking their weekly pilgrimage.

He'd never experienced anything like this; he'd never been one of *the lads,* he'd never commanded respect because of the company he kept and clearly, he'd never been to the rival match between Granville and Blackchester Albion.

"You've picked the wrong day to come to a Granville match wearing a blue jumper," Shay jibed.

His plump cheeks propped up a pair of black aviator sunglasses and the noticeable slur in his words told Tommy that he had either got an early start on the booze this morning, or he was still going from last night.

"Oh yeah, why's that then?" Tommy asked.

"Because it's their fucking colours, you idiot," scolded Finn, mercilessly.

Finn's frost, which had nipped Tommy the previous evening, hadn't thawed out and other than a nod earlier, this was the first time he had made any attempt to communicate. He could barely see Finn's eyes due to the *Aquascutum* cap, which was pulled down purposefully, but there was no mistaking the tired, gaunt features which made up the rest of his countenance.

"Here, take my scarf," Shay said, "get some yellow and black colour on you, that will see you right,"

"Do you not need it?" Tommy asked innocently, as he took the scarf and wrapped it around his neck, ensuring he wore it in a suitable fashion.

Shay took a strong draw of his cigarette.

"Don't worry, ain't nobody gonna be thinking that I'm a blues fan," he said, exhaling a cloud of smoke, which masked his face momentarily.

There was a touch of steel that became apparent in his voice and when Tommy turned around, he could see why; they were approaching the stadium.

Whilst Tommy wasn't the biggest Granville F.C. fan, it didn't take him long to pick up on the buzz around the place. It was intoxicating. He could physically feel his heart rate climbing by the second. It was as though the crowd of fans had suddenly become a fluid wave that had lifted him off the floor ever so slightly.

He knew the O'Clearys and the rest of the gang he was with were dangerous, he had no doubts that they were the people that were not only contributing to Granville's dire circumstances, but also benefitting greatly from it. He knew that Seb died because of a bad batch of drugs sourced via these very people and he knew that even by being with them, he was putting himself in heaps of danger. But right in this very moment, those thoughts fell from his conscience as he experienced a Saturday afternoon journey to the match for the very first time.

"Right lads, we know the score. Get your hats over your eyes, avoid the coppers and let's split up. Usual meeting point at the bar inside turnstile seventeen, yeah?" Shay commanded.

"Junior, you're with me," said Finn, sporting a wry, sinister smile.

Tommy swallowed his trepidation, recognising that the term Junior was meant for him. Despite the mere one year between the two of them, Tommy could see that Finn was exercising his dominance by using prehistoric tactics and establishing him as the cub in the pack.

"Why are we splitting up exactly?" Tommy said quietly to Shay, sensing an apprehension building in response to the thought of being under Finn's guidance, without his arguably more conscientious, older brother.

"Because we're all barred for life," Shay said, dead pan.

A brief moment passed as Tommy figured out what to say in response. He had a few questions he'd like to ask, the one topping the list being – *what on earth for? Fighting, drug-dealing, or worse?* But he didn't feel brave enough to follow through and actually quiz Shay on the issue. Quite frankly he wasn't sure the finer details mattered all that much; he knew that people didn't get barred for life for anything other than serious, violent and hostile activity.

Finally, roaring laughter from Shay, followed by a hefty slap on Tommy's back, enabled the conversation to continue.

"Don't worry, Tommy," he said, "we do this every week, nothing for you to look so worried about,"

Tommy wasn't aware he looked so worried, but he sure as hell felt it. Reluctantly, he shimmied over towards the right side of the road as the gang fanned out into their allocated groups. He stopped a yard or so shy of Finn who was stood with two other lads, both of whom looked to have a few years on him.

Finn passed out the match tickets.

"Right we're going in through turnstile eleven, no talking on the way in and put plenty of distance between one another, do you hear me?"

They all nodded, before he continued.

"Oh, and boys this is Tommy, my kid sister's friend. Tommy, this is Gary and Gary. And before you say anything, yes, it gets confusing so just call them Cockett and Pullit, nicknames my dad gave 'em a few years back,"

He detected the patronising *kid* reference once again; Finn was determined to put him in his place today. He was also taken aback by the nicknames of the two lads he'd been introduced to and wondered what kind of role the two Garys had in the O'Cleary enterprise to be given such names. Something that warranted a reference to the firing of guns, evidently.

"Good to meet you, pal," said Pullit, whilst Cockett offered out an endearing fist bump, to which Tommy obliged.

"Are you packing some of the Chemist's powder?" Finn said quietly to Pullit.

"Does a bear shit in the woods?" Pullit responded, dryly.

"Atta boy," Finn praised, "I've got a few punters waiting on it inside the ground,"

"Ay, I'm ready for a tickle myself never mind anyone else," Pullit jested.

They both cackled.

"See you at the seventeen," said Finn, before tucking his chin into his scarf and marching off into the crowd towards turnstile eleven.

Tommy looked down at his match ticket, then back up at the stadium. The reference to the Chemist and *Charge* had hardened his debut experience of the match, serving as a reminder of who these guys were. That being one of the lads and commanding respect – whatever that meant – came at a price when associating with them. He felt torn. Part of him had relished this new, exciting experience. To not be scrapping against the tide, even for an hour or two, felt liberating. But deep down in a place where his true inner self had the deciding voice, he knew that the O'Clearys were trouble and weren't the kind of folk he wanted to hang around with. The small boy inside of him was screaming for him to turn around and run home to safety. But he had to do this, he had come too far now, he had to continue what he'd started.

He repositioned his scarf in an attempt to gather himself and instil some confidence, before heading off in the same direction as Finn, navigating his way towards turnstile eleven, making sure to leave a safe distance in between as instructed.

CHAPTER NINETEEN

Granville F.C. went into half-time holding a dominant 2-0 lead, with *the Bees* breaking the deadlock early in the game after a delightful strike from their latest signing, Marc McAllister, followed by a superb Lee Murphy free kick not long after.

Tommy was impressed by the dogged football shown by his hometown team, despite the shoestring budget the manager apparently had to purchase players. He also noted the toughness demonstrated to compete in what was clearly a bitter rivalry, something which injected energy into the crowd with every hard-hitting tackle.

The atmosphere had been electric, with the consistent, thunderous boom coming from the bass drum towards the back of the stand and a crescendo of chanting which had brought the hairs on his arms to attention.

He had spent the first half stuck inside a relentless vacuum between Cockett and Pullit, both of whom seemed intent on chattering their way to the interval, leaving his ears reddened and in need of a break. The effects of a pre-match bump of *Charge* had shown visible effects on the pair of them, including wide eyes and fidgeting to accompany their talkativeness.

As soon as the players departed the pitch, the gang rushed to make their way down the steep concrete steps, with Tommy struggling to keep up. He watched on as Shay, Finn and the rest of the boys seemed to walk on air towards the bar and toilet area underneath the stand, with almost every other fan that passed stopping to shake their hand or say hello; these guys were kings around here and royalty didn't have to queue for drinks.

The stadium was a hybrid of old and new. With more modern looking steel from the ground extension of recent years contrasting against the ageing wooden seats from last century. Keeping true to Granville's traditions, the extension was evidently carried out on the cheap, as Tommy noticed that the huge metal stanchions which propped up the stadium roof, were already infected with rust, despite only being installed around five years ago.

As they huddled around their drinks by the assigned meeting point, surrounded by dull, grey breeze blocks to one side and a sea of yellow and black shirts, scarves and hats bustling past on the other Tommy felt his phone buzz in his pocket. He had felt the same sensation several times in the first half but chose to ignore it due to being in such close confines with the company he kept.

He pulled out the phone and flashing before his eyes upon the screen was the contact name: Brightwell.

That must be the third time he's tried to call.

Tommy quickly stuffed his phone back into his pocket before anyone could steal a peak at who it was that was calling him, or so he thought.

"Who was that?" said Finn, his beady eyes burning with intimidation.

"Oh, nobody. Just a mate," Tommy said, coolly, "he can wait,"

Finn nodded in approval, "I like that, footy comes first, isn't that right boys?"

The gang all jeered in agreement before Shay cleared his throat, "A toast. To the times that we won't remember, with the people that we won't forget. Never above you. Never below you. Always right beside you, brothers."

Right on cue, everybody raised their bottles of beer to a stiff

clink, before each taking a generous swig charged with camaraderie and pride. Tommy hesitantly followed suit, whilst
frantically wondering if this was confirmation that he was
now officially part of this deranged brotherhood.

He pondered what this might mean for him long-
term, given his allegiances with Brightwell and their apparent desires to bring down this very same brotherhood and
its interconnected drug-ring, to finally rid Granville of the
Charge infestation that plagued its streets. This would un-
deniably include the O'Clearys and this so-called Chemist
bloke and, of course, there was the additional hope that his
arch nemesis, Smiler, would be dragged out of hiding and into
a police cell along the way.

He wasn't sure yet how Smiler's sordid fingers were jammed
into this sordid pie, but given the nature of this kind of business, coupled with the mysterious threats he'd received, he
could almost taste the nasty concoction that his sworn foe
had conjured up.

There was no retreating now, he knew that he'd pre-
tended for too long and his deceitful actions were well in motion; he was behind O'Cleary lines and they thought he was
one of them. If all was fair in love and war, then Tommy undoubtedly found himself in a precarious position.

He was suddenly awoken from his mild trance.

"Yoo hoo," Shay said, laughing and clicking his fingers
in front of Tommy's eyes, "Earth to Tommy. Are you alright,
mate?"

"Yeah, sorry, just drifted off for a second,"

"Well it can't have been anywhere nice with that
scowl you had all over your face. Anyway listen, come with us,
we need you to keep watch, ok?"

Oh shit! What does this mean?

Tommy followed Shay, Finn and Pullit into the gent's
toilets, like a lamb on its way to slaughter. His shallow breath
and quickening pulse made him question if he'd bitten off

more than he could chew. He realised he'd been naïve, maybe he should have talked to Brightwell about this. Maybe he should have given this undercover task the respect it deserved, instead of thinking he could wing it and use his innocent charm to muddle through, keeping everybody happy as he so often strived for, before making a swift exit scot-free. Now he found himself on a bumpy road with an uncertain destination and no apparent turn-off.

Finn hissed at a few remaining dwellers in the gent's toilets and nodded towards the door, striking enough fear so that one bloke didn't even hang around to do the follow up shake, leaving a trail of excess urine on his jeans. Needless to say, the gent's toilets was soon empty, but for the four of them.

Pullit booted open one of the cubicle doors aggressively and stumbled inside, with Shay and Finn loosely bunching behind him. They made no real effort to disguise their actions and this is when Tommy realised why he was here and what this was about; *Charge.*

Shay then turned to face him.

"Keep a watch on that door, Tommy. Anyone walks in, especially wearing a bright orange steward's jacket, just make some noise so the focus is on you, yeah?"

"What shall I say? Do you have like a code word or something?"

The three of them burst out laughing.

"Code word?" Finn lashed, "This ain't a spy movie, kid. Just start chanting or walk straight over to the geezer and talk to him, or stick the nut on him. We don't care. Just give us some time, ok?"

"Sure, ok,"

Tommy took a deep breath and turned to face the door.

"Right, Pullit, let's have it," said Shay.

Tommy turned his head ever so subtly so he could see over his shoulder but was still able to keep his focus on the exit door. He watched through his peripheral vision as Pullit lifted his foot onto the toilet seat and rustled into his sock, before pulling out a bag of white powder, like an unlawful magician with an unforgiving rabbit.

The bag was huge, like nothing he'd ever seen before.

In the same way that Seb had done that fateful night, Pullit drove a door key into the sack of *Charge* and pulled out a mound, which lay nestled on the end. It hovered there in between the three of them, ominously glistening, enticing them in.

"Listen, go easy on this," Finn urged, "the Chemist told me this is a hot batch, strong as an ox. So, no need to be so generous on the hit, yeah?"

"Whatever you say boss,"

Pullit tapped the key on the side of the bag to reduce the size of the dosage, as Shay licked his lips almost perversely and cleared his nostrils ready to take the first round. Tommy quickly figured out that these guys were aware of the strength, only they were failing to let their punters know.

He turned his head to face the door, not wanting to be caught gawping. He then heard a forceful sniff which made him quiver, with flashes of Seb racing through his conscience.

"Ahh, that stuff is good," yelled Shay, "God bless the Chemist."

As Pullit cordially began the process again with his door key shovelled into the zip-lock bag, Tommy felt a wave of something come over him. He wasn't sure if it was guilt, bravery or sheer foolishness. But before he could weigh up the pros and cons of his new idea, his mouth had already begun to talk.

"So, who is this Chemist fella you guys always go on about?"

"A fucking genius, that's who," Finn barked, "and what's it got to do with you?"

"Sorry, you're right. It's none of my business,"

The three of them nodded, still appearing unsure but

satisfied enough with Tommy's apology. They turned back into the cubicle to continue their half-time customary activity.

Tommy took a deep breath, before continuing, "It's just, I can't help but feel bad for the people who are dying because of this *Charge* stuff, you know?"

Just like that, all their heads spun around and stared at him in unison. He'd over-stepped the mark and he knew it. Pullit appeared to be puzzled, Finn's face was screwed up tight with anger and Shay carried a vacant look, presumably reaping the rewards of his recent hit.

"What did you just say?" Finn snapped. He seemed to be in disbelief that Tommy would be so stupid.

"I tell you what, ignore me, what do I know?" he stammered.

"No, no. The pretty boy has got something to say, so let's hear it,"

"I'd rather not,"

Finn shoved his older brother out of the way and clambered out of the cubicle, banging his fist on the partition aggressively, before pressing his forehead up against Tommy's.

"You come around here talking like that, people are going to start thinking you're a snake," Finn snarled. "A snitch. A grass. And by people, I mean me. I knew it. I had a feeling about this guy, Shay. He comes in out of nowhere and, all of a sudden, he's asking questions. Is that what you are? A snitch? Are you a snitch?"

Finn was so close; Tommy could feel moist saliva splatter against his face as he barked the accusations his way.

Tommy could no longer detect his heart rate. In these kinds of situations, it would normally punch hard against his rib cage, or thud inside his neck or wrists as the adrenaline rushed, but it had disappeared off the charts, almost as if his tightening chest had squeezed it into submission. He muttered and stuttered in an attempt to find a desperate way out of this situation, but he felt naked, exposed for what he had become.

"Leave him alone, he's just a kid," Shay reassured, suddenly floating back into consciousness.

"Ok, ok. Just a kid," Finn sneered, as he backed off slightly, hands in the air, "so what do we say we make this *kid*, join the club for real? Let's find out whether he's a genuine product, or just some pussy who wants to run around and tells tales about the Chemist,"

"What have you got in mind?" Pullit queried, suddenly becoming interested in proceedings.

"Hand me that bag," ordered Finn.

Tommy's reality screeched into slow motion as his unescapable fate dawned upon him. He watched on, frozen, as Finn rummaged his way into the *Charge*, breaking up tiny rocks before formulating a consistent snowy mountain upon the end of the key.

"Here, take this," said Finn. He smirked as he held the key aloft in front of Tommy's face, "Let's see if you put your nose where your mouth is and prove you're not a snitch,"

A silent slithering choke wrapped itself around his airways. He could faintly hear the echo of distant chants, suggesting the match had resumed and any chance Tommy had of a saviour interrupting, was probably now up in the stands with a cup of hot Bovril. One by one he looked at the three guys who showed no sign of letting him off this initiation.

Charge had a pungent diesel scent and now that it lingered so close to him, he could see that there were minute crystallised shards in and amongst the softer white powder. Moisture formulated on his brow and his palms were slick with sweat. He was verging on panic mode; fight, flight or freeze.

"Come on, what are you waiting for?" Shay snarled.

He didn't want to do this. This wasn't him. He'd seen what drugs can do to people. Granted not all people, he knew lots of people who took drugs recreationally and were perfectly functional. But he'd seen the catastrophe that can occur when they took a turn for the worst, when things go beyond control; his mum, Derek, Seb and now these lunatics. But right now, he didn't see a way out. If he refused, the best he could hope for was a good hiding right there and then. And where would that leave him on bringing around justice for Seb, for his mum, for his dad for that matter; he'd come too far to just bail, hadn't he?

What's it gonna' be?

He readied himself reluctantly, when suddenly an idea sprung to mind. He leaned forward, hovering over the key. He pressed his thumb on one side of his nose to close his right nostril, before tilting his head forward and, instead of inhaling, he swiftly exhaled out of his open nostril, blowing the *Charge* off in a million directions all over the floor.

"Oh shit! Sorry lads," Tommy mumbled.

In that instant the door to the toilets swung open and two fluorescently clad stewards waddled through.

"What's going on here, then?" the chubby one said, rubbing his chin as he spoke.

Tommy quickly sprung into life, "We were just talking about Murphy's free-kick, what a belter. Did you see it?"

The stewards looked a little perplexed, perhaps taken off guard by Tommy's confident management of what seemed like closed book situation.

"As a matter of fact, I did," the steward said, still weighing up what was in front of him.

Whilst Finn and Shay primitively puffed their chests out and appeared to be gearing themselves up for a fight, Tommy took matters into his own, more pacifist hands and walked towards the stewards with a friendly smile.

"What do you reckon for the final score then? We were just saying we fancy us to put five past these lot today,"

Silence fell upon the gent's toilets for a brief moment, as the boys and the stewards were locked in a stand-off. A loud crackle on the steward's walky-talky interrupted the near certain clash, with a stress signal being called for trouble with the away fans. The stewards looked at each other, then back towards the four of them.

"Today's your lucky day. Get back up to your seats and keep your heads down."

The stewards departed out of the toilet door with haste. Once the coast was clear, the four of them all collapsed into the walls or onto their haunches with relief. Tommy was shaking, the adrenaline almost knocked him sick. It was either that or the thought that he was just millimetres away from a whopping hit of *Charge* rattling its way around his system.

He made no underestimation of how that could have ended, laying six feet under next to Seb for one. But as he stood there, the colour slowly returning to his face, a small part of him was left bizarrely unsatisfied, inquisitive as to what the effects would have actually felt like. He'd often wondered what was so fantastic about drugs that would drive people towards self-destruction, debt, family breakdown, addiction, or death. He supposed that there were positive and negative effects with anything and that's why people such as the Chemist were so keen to swoop in and take advantage.

He quickly snapped out of that mind-set, reminding himself that a person who doesn't take drugs in Granville was a rarity, so that made him unique and an alternative kind of cool, even if that was sometimes hard to see. He rubbed his eyes and steadied himself for what was next.

"Nice one Tommy, you did your job there, mate," Shay said, slapping him on the back.

"Yeah cheers man, you handled that well, proper diffused it like a boss," Pullit added.

Finn begrudgingly nodded in agreement, before they all made their way out of the toilets and back up to the stands to watch the second half. Tommy had escaped unscathed for now, but the way Finn was gunning for him, he was sure that wouldn't be the last of it.

CHAPTER TWENTY

The match finished with a convincing 4-1 win for the home side and it appeared as though the gang had intentions of celebrating long into the evening, stridently boasting victory against their bitter rivals as they marched back to *The Grove* for post-match merriments.

Tommy felt guilty for using his mum as a falsified excuse to pass on the night's undoubtedly shady antics, but it was the only thing he could think of to get away. He'd already tried mentioning that he had work tomorrow morning, which seemed to only encourage them to get more bladdered. He knew the O'Clearys had a weak spot for family, so they let him off lightly as soon as there was talk about helping his mother at home. They even asked him to pass on their well wishes, a contrasting gesture from their otherwise villainous movements that he found hard to swallow.

He had strained to maintain his composure as he casually strolled out of the bar, even turning to give a final wave goodbye to his newfound frenemies. He kept his cool persona up, mindful not to speed off in a hurry and arise suspicion, until he'd reached the bottom of Horrocks Street and turned out of sight. It was here where he now stood in a shop doorway, slouched over with his hands on his knees, gasping for breath.

He desperately tried to analyse his position and figure out what moves he could make next in this turbulent and terrifying game he found himself playing. But he could only come to one conclusion; he was in way over his head.

Despite his gut sensing something a little off about Brightwell's forceful approach, he decided he needed to reach out to him and be a little more open. He was a policeman after all, and he could no longer keep him at arm's length because of some adolescent fear of becoming a grass and upsetting the unwritten ethos of the Granville street code.

Brightwell had called twice more, once during the second half of the match and once whilst Tommy was leaving the stadium. But yet again, the timing wasn't right for him to answer. He assumed Brightwell wasn't calling to talk about the weather, so couldn't exactly pick up the phone and have a nice chit-chat within ear shot of Shay or Finn.

Now he found himself away from the taught madness and with a little peace and quiet, he pulled out his phone and brought up Brightwell's number. There was hesitation as he went to hit the call button. He noticed that he couldn't focus his thoughts enough to think about what to say or what not to say. His mind was pre-occupied by something which was causing him even more unsettlement than Brightwell or the O'Clearys; he needed to see Kirsten.

He needed to tell her about this mess he was in, all of it. She would have every right to be disappointed, furious even, that he'd hidden all of this from her, but he was ready to shoulder that responsibility in the hope she would come through like she had so many times before. He needed to make it right and begin to patch together the trust that they once shared.

A fine drizzle began to fall as he slipped his phone back into his pocket. He stepped out of the doorway and set off walking towards the Junction pub.

Saturday night had always been a busy night down at the Junction. Even amidst the current depression of Granville's social, economic and cultural ecosystems, the local residents mustered enough energy and spare change to head down to their indigenous watering hole for fun, frolics and an opportunity to escape life's woes; a beacon of solidarity in an otherwise lonely and desperate community.

Tommy passed a huddle of people smoking outside, a vague and unmistakeable aroma of cannabis caught his attention for a split second, which wasn't a particularly unusual scent to detect outside the Junction. He approached the front doors, damp from his twenty-minute encounter with some stop-start rain and spotted that Barry, the doorman, was working his usual Saturday night shift sporting his black leather flat cap and his familiar, care-free grin. He'd always liked Barry, a giant of a man with a heart of gold and an aptitude for getting the job done, with job referring to a no nonsense approach to Uncle Bill's three F's; no fighting, no fondling, no fakes – which applied to counterfeit money and any illegitimate products for sale.

"Good evening Tommy," said Barry, polite as always despite having not seen each other for a few months.

"Evening, Barry. How are you doing?"

"All the better for seeing you my friend. Bit wet out there tonight I see,"

"You can say that again," Tommy said, rolling his eyes.

"Bit wet out there tonight I see,"

Tommy giggled, "I left myself open to that one, didn't I?"

"Sure did. Oh, and by the way," Barry mused, "will you stop growing please? You'll be after my job soon,"

"Wouldn't dream of it."

As per their usual routine, they shook hands followed by a fist bump, before Barry held open the doors and Tommy entered the pub. It was packed to the seams, but his eyes were drawn immediately towards Kirsten standing behind the bar. To his surprise, she was already staring back at him and it wasn't a particularly warm stare either.

He meandered through the bustling pub dwellers, many of whom were already swaying, laughing, singing and dancing. He finally managed to plant one hand on the bar at the end closest to Kirsten, who at that moment had decided to trot down to the other end of the bar and empty the drip trays. Sensing the struggle it would take to wrestle his way to the opposite end of the pub, he opted to set up camp and wait it out where he was, hoping that Kirsten would give in and eventually come and speak to him.

It didn't take long before she marched up towards him, glaring with real menace.

"What do you want?" she scolded.

"I just wondered if we could talk for five minutes? I tried to call today but-"

"I'm busy," she said, making half an attempt to walk off. She stopped, before adding, "I have my break in forty-five minutes. Let's see if you can do me the courtesy of sticking around and not disappearing this time and maybe... maybe we can talk."

Good lord, she was an almighty kind of pissed.

"Sure, could-" Tommy stopped himself.

"What?"

"Nothing. I was going to ask for a drink,"

"Hmm yes, I'm sure you were. But then you realised you could queue up like everybody else."

Kirsten walked off to continue her shift, with an essence of diva trailing behind her. He knew she had every right to be annoyed; what happened last night at the party wasn't fair and he was sure it looked even worse from Kirsten's perspective.

He couldn't help but feel a little defensive from how forceful she was being on the issue though and he wondered if this was what a lover's tiff felt like. He sat back and thought for a second, biting his tongue so not to make the situation worse. It was difficult to suppress the desire to interrupt and begin his apology and declaration of the truth, but something told him she needed this opportunity to vent, he owed her that much. He knew he'd hurt her before, and he presumed this was her way of letting him know that it won't happen again.

Even at work, in a sweaty pub, appearing all flustered with a clammy forehead and her hair tied up in a bunch with only the tips of her curly locks poking free, she was perfect. Simply by looking at her, his body managed to produce a stream of butterflies which flapped incessantly around his midriff, causing him to feel alive.

There was something about her feistiness that was like no other. Other girls would make a lot of noise about a lot of things, but with Kirsten, it felt as though when she spoke it meant something. She had self-respect and principles and he was overwhelmingly proud of his best friend for that.

He managed to get served for a drink by Uncle Bill a few minutes later who offered him a wry smile and a flick of the eyebrows, which all but told Tommy he didn't envy him at having to clamber his way back into his niece's good graces.

He sat back and nursed his glass of coke. He couldn't stomach an alcoholic drink, today's commotion had left him feeling spaced out; the tequila, the football, the confrontation and all of that with a hangover. He thought about the phrase *a hair of the dog* and wondered who first coined it. Right now, he thought about finding that person and asking them what happens when you help yourself to *a hair of the dog* and instead of it making you feel better, the dog jumps up and bites you on the bollocks.

The clock ticked forwards at a snail's pace as he obediently watched on, waiting out the forty-five minutes until judgement time.

CHAPTER
TWENTY-ONE

"Well to be honest, it sounds like there are worse tasks out there, Tommy," Kirsten huffed.

That wasn't the response he had predicted.

After patiently waiting an hour and ten minutes, he had finally managed to get Kirsten to sit down with him at their familiar spot, the quiet table in the corner by the juke box, to talk about all of the goings on from the last few weeks and of course, apologise to her for how the previous evening had played out.

From the get-go, her barricades were rock solid, guarded as if her pride depended on it. He muddled through the details and told her everything, although he struggled a little bit with the chronology. The pressure was intense, as if talking about all of this wasn't hard enough, he had the added booby prize of potentially losing Kirsten for good; even if she forgave him for disappearing at the party, there was still a chance she would flip out at him taking her there in the first place, without informing her of the situation and the risks they faced.

He had told her about Seb and *Charge* and this so-called Chemist, about Brightwell and how assertive he was being in recruiting him to become his mole, about the mysterious phone and text messages and what that meant for the probability of Smiler looming to take revenge, a prospect that visibly distressed her. He went on to inform her about how the O'Clearys fit into all of this; Finn, Shay, their father Stephen and not forgetting of course, Darcy.

By the time he had finished, he let out a mammoth sigh, fatigued and emotional and in need of some unwavering reassurance. But Kirsten evidently had other ideas.

"That's not what I was expecting you to say," he said, bubbling inside. "Did you not hear about how barking mad this whole thing is? Brightwell has got me involved with people who cut chuffing ears off if you don't do as they say, or they give the word and somebody does it for them – and I'm not quite sure which is worse. Smiler is obviously back; he could be watching us right now. This drug that the O'Clearys and this Chemist fella are pushing – which I was nearly forced to take today by the way – has a body count that would make Jack the Ripper twitchy and you think there are worse jobs out there? Please enlighten me,"

She crossed her arms and looked away. He spotted that tears began to form in her eyes, a dam on the cusp of breaking, until she just about regained control and sent them packing. A clang of guilt jabbed him under the rib cage.

"Look, Tommy," she snapped, "I thought we were friends, best friends. Well, maybe more,"

"We are!"

"But friends don't do this. Friends don't lie and sneak around, hiding things from each other. I thought we had a special bond, especially after all the shit we went through together finding out what happened to your dad. How could you not trust me with this?"

"I was trying to protect you, whether you want to believe that or not,"

"Ha! Don't patronise me," she insisted.

"Look, the last thing I wanted was for you to get hauled into this mess and be put at risk because of me – again. I thought if I kept it from you, they would have no reason to come after you if it went south. I'm sorry, sincerely I am. And for what it's worth, I'm telling you now aren't I?"

Silence fell between them. The noise from the rest of the pub seemed muted, as though they were under water, detached from the joyous shenanigans that surrounded them. They exchanged looks, neither brave enough to maintain eye contact for long. In that moment sadness took hold of him; he couldn't bear to lose her, not again.

"I saw you with her, that Darcy girl. I was looking everywhere for you and then I saw you through the glass panel doors into the Sports Lounge. It looked like you were having a real nice time with your new chums. And now you tell me that you've been 'tasked' with 'getting to know her'. Give me a break, do you think I was born yesterday? You're acting like you're some kind of secret agent!"

"Bloody hell, as if this was all my choice? You're making it sound like I wanted this. When all that I really want is-," he stopped himself. He was scared of exposing his true feelings in this delicate situation. "I'm putting myself in danger, big time danger, to try and do the right thing. By Seb, by my dad, by my mum – Jesus Kirsten, you were there, you heard what Smiler did to her when she was a kid. I'm constantly looking over my shoulder. This isn't exactly fun for me, ok?"

"I get all of that, of course I do. But don't pretend there's some kind of noble reason for befriending Darcy O'Cleary, just be honest with me. I think I deserve that at the very least,"

"Yes, Darcy is involved, but not in the way you're implying. Brightwell told me she was my ticket to get on the inside and even that happened by chance, seeing as I don't have a clue what I'm doing. You know me and how awkward I can be, I'm hardly Mr. Smooth Talker am I?"

Kirsten offered a subtle breath of laughter and a shrug of her shoulders, but any hopes of that being a light at the end of the tunnel were quickly extinguished when her scowl reformed.

He continued, as if an uncontrollable reflex to fill the

silent void had taken hold, "I mean, I guess she seems pretty cool and everything, maybe a bit too intense, but I don't like her like that,"

"What's not to like? She's pretty, she's exciting, she's popular-"

"She's not you."

A liberating tingle rushed to the four corners of Tommy's body as he finally had the courage to emancipate his feelings, opening himself up completely to her. In that moment, he didn't care about saying the wrong thing, seeming too forward or even what this meant for their friendship.

Kirsten turned to face him and gently wiped her eyes.

"What do you mean?" she said.

His heart was stuck in his mouth almost preventing him from speaking. He braced himself, clearing the way for words to freefall.

"Well, basically, I mean that I've had these feelings for you for quite a while now and I've been scared and reluctant to tell you. Things kept getting in the way, most of which were probably just in my head. I didn't want to hurt you or ruin what we had, and there's the obvious thing as to whether you feel the same about me. But right now it appears as though we're at a junction – no pun intended – and I don't want to lose you, so it seems as good a time as any to tell you that I think you are amazing and special and beautiful and funny and loyal,"

Her laughter stopped him in his tracks.

Oh, how I've missed that beautiful sight.

"Don't think you can come in here being all cute and romantic and expect me to be all impressed," she joked, reaching over the table and taking his hand softly in hers, "because I'll tell you, Mr Dawson, it's working,"

Relief flooded his body. His heart no longer occupied his mouth, instead it sat in its rightful place, pumping hard and fast. As their hands exchanged electricity, he couldn't recall feeling anything like this before.

They both giggled, child-like almost. Kirsten's cheeks appeared flushed with a scarlet tinge and he was sure that the burning sensation he felt around his face meant that his probably looked the same.

He stammered a little, not wanting to interrupt this perfect moment, "So, erm... that obvious thing I mentioned, I guess I'll just come out and ask, do you feel the same?"

Their eyes locked as his heart crept north towards his mouth once more.

"Sorry to interrupt lover birds," Uncle Bill teased as he waltzed by with stacks of empty glasses, "your break is over Kirst', I need you back in two minutes this place is a pressure cooker tonight,"

"Ok, Bill. Be with you in a sec," she said, before turning back towards Tommy and squeezing his hand a little tighter, "I guess we'll find that out soon enough, won't we? But first thing is first, we need to figure out our plan to get you out of this mess you've got yourself in,"

"*Our* plan?" he said, smirking. "Does that mean that our crime-fighting, dynamic duo is back in business?"

"You bet it is."

She stood up and leaned over the table towards him, before gently kissing his right cheek, lingering, giving him enough time to appreciate her soft lips.

As she walked back over to the bar to resume her shift, she turned back around and offered a warm smile. He felt content. The fear he had of dragging Kirsten towards this disaster had faded and he suddenly felt safer and more confident that he could get through this, now that she was in his corner. As with most things of this nature though, he still detected a niggling doubt in the back of his mind, he just hoped he'd made the right call.

CHAPTER TWENTY-TWO

The day had been an emotional rollercoaster, which had taken him to Hell, High Water and the Heavens above. But now he was beginning to fade, exhausted from the various incidents that had taxed his body and mind throughout the day. He'd spent the last few minutes trying to supress an unrelenting yawn, leaving him drained; yearning for his bed and a soft pillow to lay his head upon.

It was 9:30pm and Kirsten still had well over three hours left of her shift. He had tried every trick in the book; a coffee, a splash of cold water on his face from the toilet sink, he'd put some songs on the juke box in the hope they would liven him up, only he was beat. He clung to the bar so not to fall off his stool, desperately trying to appear present each time Kirsten glanced over. He strained to keep his eyes open, however the duration of each passing blink was becoming longer and more difficult to resist.

Now that he'd had a sample, he craved the touch of Kirsten's hands once more. He wanted to be there to walk her home after her shift and reignite their intimacy which was interrupted earlier, he just needed to remain alert enough to do so.

Kirsten made her way over to him during a moment of peace at the bar, which undoubtedly wouldn't last long.

"You must be exhausted," she said.

"Yeah, it's crept up on me all of a sudden. I can't be arsed with work tomorrow. I guess sharing all of that worry with you must have unburdened me or something. I kind of feel as though my mind is a little clearer, like I'm not as uptight now that I've said it out loud to somebody I trust,"

"You know what they say, a problem shared is a problem halved,"

"It certainly is where you're concerned,"

"Why don't you get yourself off, go and get an early night or something? It looks as though you could do with it. Hopefully you'll feel a bit fresher for work tomorrow?" she consoled.

"You're probably right, although I was hanging on so that I was here to walk you home tonight once you'd finished,"

"Hanging on for dear life by the looks of it," she joked. "You're so sweet, Tommy. But don't worry, Uncle Bill will drop me off home and listen, we've got plenty of time to pick up where we left off earlier, yeah?"

She reached across the bar and squeezed his hand affectionately.

"Are you sure?"

"Yes, I'm sure. I want my Tommy on top form, ok? We've got things we need to attend to,"

My Tommy.

A magnetic pull drew him forwards and he suddenly anticipated that this could be their first kiss. Unsure and clumsy as ever, he rose to his feet, leaning over the bar somewhat. He thought as soon as he'd done it that it seemed quite a goofy move and Kirsten's curbed laughter confirmed it, but he'd committed now.

Once she had swallowed the laughter down and composed herself, she stood on her tip toes and she too edged forward to meet him in the middle. Once their eyes were locked, the silliness disappeared. As he absorbed every detail of her beauty, every line, every freckle, he could physically feel his brain pumping endorphins around his central nervous system, creating a sense of invincibility.

"When you're ready, love!" an impatient punter abruptly cried from the opposite end of the bar. He tapped his finger on the rim of his empty tankard, unequivocally unaware that he had just splattered their first, real, romantic moment, before it could even get going.

"I've gotta go," she said apologetically, "I'm sorry. I'll text you later, yeah?"

"No worries, are you sure you don't mind me going?"

"Go on, get out of here,"

As he made his way to the door, he turned his head to glance back towards the bar several times, only to see Kirsten's beaming face staring aimlessly beyond the beer pumps. He couldn't believe that he'd finally let the cat out of the bag regarding his feelings towards her and how unbelievably wonderful it felt that she reciprocated.

He deliberated how much time they'd wasted, sparring with each other, hiding their true feelings and remaining friends, but he reminded himself that all roads had led to here; who knows what would have happened had they rushed it?

The rain was hammering down off the uneven pavement and he began to rue the moment that he'd left home earlier today without a coat. The good thing about a rainy night when walking home in Granville, he thought, was that the streets were likely to be a lot quieter and therefore, he stood less chance of bumping into any trouble.

He heard the squeak of the windscreen wipers behind him, before he detected the sound of an engine. The car crept slowly towards him, edging over to the kerb; its bright headlamps preventing him from seeing the make or model, let alone the driver. He wondered if it was somebody who needed directions, or somebody who had rather more seedy interests that had spotted a coatless young man walking the streets at this hour.

As the car came to a halt and the passenger window began to wind down, he realised who it was: Brightwell.

"Get in, I'll give you a lift home," he demanded.

Tommy grudgingly obeyed, giving in to reason, as the squelch in his trainers told him if he continued walking home in this weather he would potentially arrive with webbed feet. Plus, the added factor of when a policeman who you've ignored all day tells you to do something, you usually do it.

"Cheers," Tommy said, slamming the door closed behind him and immediately benefitting from the gust of warm air currently blasting out of the blowers.

Brightwell immediately took off with speed.

"I've been trying to contact you," he yapped.

"I know, I'm sorry I've not managed to respond," he hesitated, "you wouldn't believe the last twenty-four hours I've had,"

He could feel an ache developing behind his eyes. He rubbed his forehead and gazed out of the rain-speckled window.

"You went to a party, met the O'Cleary brothers, they invited you to watch the football and you obliged, it freaked you out, so you left early. Does that about capture it?"

"Wait, how did you know all of that?"

"It's my job to know,"

Tommy repositioned himself in his seat, shuffling closer to the window and opening up his body. He tightened his grip on the seatbelt across his chest.

"Ok, so what do you need me for?"

"I need details, Tommy. Details. Who was there? What was being discussed?"

Brightwell was rushing his words, spending more time looking anywhere but the road. His eyes bulged almost at ejection point from his skull.

"Well, you know, the usual stuff. Beer, drugs, violence. I'm sure you know more than me about how they operate, it seemed like it was all standard behaviour for them in their world. It was pretty heavy, intimidating if anything,"

"For goodness sake Tommy!" Brightwell yelled, slamming on his brakes to bring the car to a shrieking stop. Tommy nursed his collar bone after it had crushed against the seat-belt.

"What the hell was that about?" he yelled.

Brightwell turned to face him, his lips firmly pursed.

"Wake up and smell the teenage deaths, Tommy!" he bellowed, smacking the steering wheel twice as he did. "There isn't time for your schoolboy dithering. Crikey, if you sit on the fence any more, you'll wake up with splinters in your arse. You're either one of the good guys or you're not?"

Now that Brightwell was facing him and shouting quite belligerently in his direction, Tommy was sure he could detect the smell of alcohol. He was convinced it wasn't from himself, as he'd not had an alcoholic drink since the half-time interval at the football, which was over six hours ago now.

Had he been drinking?

Whether he had, or hadn't, the question Brightwell had posed was a pertinent one. It helped him to simplify his position in this ordeal, which he realised he'd previously been over complicating. He was one of the good guys and there was no way he could turn a blind eye knowing more people could end up dead.

"Well I guess I'm one of the good guys," he muttered.

"Ok, that's good," Brightwell mellowed, starting the car off in motion once more, "so tell me, what did you see and what did you hear?"

"Well there was a lot to take in, I'm not even sure where to start,"

He was distracted. He couldn't shake the alcohol scent, it was strong, like spirit strong.

"What about the party last night?" Brightwell badgered, "there had to be something going on there?"

Tommy surrendered to his curiosity. "Have you been

138

drinking?"

Brightwell nervously put his hand over his mouth, anxiously attempting to smell his own breath. He wriggled in his seat, perhaps realising that his response was a dead giveaway.

He hesitated, "Yes, I went to see an old friend and he poured me a whiskey, that's all. I'm perfectly fine to drive,"

"Hey, listen, most people I know would go to confession stinking of booze, so there's no judgement here,"

"So, where were we? You were saying there was a lot going on?" Brightwell quizzed, keen to push on and blow past the issue of drink-driving.

"I guess all you need to know is that the thing you think is going on between the O'Clearys and the Chemist, is going on for real,"

"How do you know?"

"I heard it, several times in fact,"

"I knew it. Right, I need evidence," Brightwell ordered. There was urgency in his voice.

"No way. No frigging way. I'm done, I nearly got into a heap of shit today and now I'm skulking around like some kind of rat, telling tales to the teacher,"

"Tommy, listen to me. This needs to stop, I can't face telling another parent that their child isn't coming home because of this *Charge*, I just can't. It all needs to end; the Chemist and the O'Clearys. Just keep doing what you're doing, just for a little while longer, please?"

"The only reason I've come this far in the first place is because the universe obviously decided I'd not experienced enough travesty with Smiler – you know him, right?" he ranted, "The bloke whose retirement into the sun I botched up, Granville's most renowned and sadistic criminal, yes him. So, fate just stuck me next to Seb at that party and watched on, laughing as it all unfolded; drugs, deaths and bloody dial-a-threats,"

"Dial-a-threats?" Brightwell deliberated, "Oh I see,

have you heard from that mystery phone again?"

"Yeah, I got another one earlier today. I don't know how it's linked, but it has to be, right?"

"It seems that way, yes. Did either of the O'Cleary brother's mention their dad by the way?"

"He cropped up, but I don't recall anything overly interesting. Darcy mentioned him too, just about a studio he rents out to one of our teachers, which we both found pretty funny,"

"Don't be fooled, he's an evil piece of work," Brightwell warned. "So, do you think you can manage just a little while longer then? To give me a chance to end this, please,"

"I'm not promising anything. I need to figure my own way out of this mess don't forget," he insisted, although he felt resigned to Brightwell's position of authority. "They think I'm one of them now for crying out loud, what am I supposed to do?"

"That's good, that's good. You know, when you're stuck in a dark tunnel and the walls are closing in around you, sometimes the only way out is to keep moving forward,"

"Whatever you say," he said flippantly, as they pulled up outside his house.

"Answer my calls Tommy, I can help you through this, ok?"

He stepped out of the car and softly closed the door behind him. He tapped the roof twice and Brightwell slowly edged his car back into motion with a crank of the gears and a judder, before picking up pace and cruising off down the street. He watched on until all that he could see were two glowing red brake lights piercing through the night's gloom.

CHAPTER TWENTY-THREE

The tinkle of the bell above the door sounded, waking him from his daydream. It had been rather quiet this morning at the Old Mill café. A blustery gale outside perhaps the cause of Granville town centre's bleak atmosphere. Poor weather in the winter was disastrous for trade and today at 11:14am it meant that he'd only had three customers to wait on so far, none of them ordering food and only one stopping long enough to sit down inside and drink her cappuccino, before heading out into the wind again, to be blown to her next stop.

He looked up towards the door to see who the new arrival was; a family of four demanding full English breakfasts with sides of extra toast, juice and hot drinks, he hoped. Unfortunately for Tommy and the café's Sunday takings, it was only Charlie. He whipped off his rubber gloves and discarded the metal Brillo pad into the sink for a rinse, relieved to take a break from scrubbing the oven.

"Alright, mate," Tommy said, "what are you doing here?"

"Tony said for me to come and help you out," Charlie beamed, "you know, get an extra shift in. Just for a few hours, whilst its..."

Charlie looked around at the desolate café.

"Yeah," Tommy said, "it's a slow one today,"

"Oh well, I can keep you company anyway, eh?"

"Sounds good to me, shall I brew up?"

Charlie grinned, "You know me well, my friend."

Tommy flicked on the kettle and reached for the box of tea bags, reflecting upon the fact that he didn't really know Charlie that well at all. They'd worked together several times over the busier summer months of course, but Charlie had very much kept himself to himself and besides, when the sun is shining and the holidaymakers are in town, there's barely a minute to sit down, never mind converse and exchange life stories.

He drove the teaspoon into the mound of sugar, careful not to pick up any of the brown, mushy speckles that had transferred over from somebody, probably their boss Tony, using a wet spoon when making coffee.

"You have two sugars, don't you, Charlie?" he shouted through to the back, before committing to the second spoonful.

"Sure do, mate," he heard Charlie call out, his voice muffled as he tried to remove the hoody over his head.

The kettle whistled to its climax and he cordially poured the piping hot water into the two cups, a slight splatter catching his hand which made him hop and spill some excess onto the worktop.

Disconcertion had a habit of jittering away inside his tummy whenever he was in Charlie's company and today was no different; he was a little older and seemed confident in most situations. He had quite a unique style for a young lad in Granville; converse trainers, drainpipe jeans, checked shirts with band badges sown in. He donned black, thick-rimmed glasses and bit of a messy mop as his hair style. He reckoned the more brutish guys that were Tommy's age would label Charlie a nerd; but he owned it and that made him seem even cooler.

As Tommy added the splash of milk to their cups of tea, the bell above the door rang again. He glanced over his shoulder to see an old couple toddling in through the door, windswept and in need of refreshment.

As he attempted to walk around the counter to greet them, Charlie dashed in front of him, explaining with a smile that he'd see to the customers, whilst Tommy finished their drinks. He watched on in admiration, as Charlie welcomed them with a smile and a joke. He took their coats and ushered them to one of the roomier tables, paying extra attention to the elderly man, who walked with a stick.

After Charlie returned with their order, two regular coffees and two toasted teacakes, Tommy washed out the coffee pot and put on a fresh batch, whilst Charlie got to work on the preparation of the teacakes.

"So, what's been going on, Tommy? Any gossip?" Charlie enthusiastically enquired.

"You know this town, always something going on," he said.

He was wary of not telling the whole world about his current predicament, but mindful that Charlie was being polite and attempting to bond.

"I do, mate. My old man always used to say; there's always a storm in this teacup sized town," Charlie chuckled, "I'll never forget that,"

"I like it, makes so much sense. He's a smart guy your dad,"

"He was," Charlie's cheeks and shoulders dropped slightly, "he passed away about three years ago,"

"Ah man, I'm sorry," Tommy mumbled, kicking himself furiously inside.

"It's cool, we were close, so it knocks me off balance a little whenever I think about him,"

Tommy felt a peculiar envy begin to bubble momentarily, before he quickly shut it down. He had no doubt he would always wonder what could have been with his own

143

dad, but this wasn't about him. Besides, he wasn't sure of the old phrase, which said that it was better to have loved and lost, than never to have loved at all; he would never be able to confirm either way when it came to his father.

"I lost my dad too," Tommy said softly, "but I never really knew him, so I imagine being knocked off balance is perfectly understandable, if you were so close,"

"Yeah, I'm much better with it now. I actually dropped out of university when it happened. Completely lost the plot and crawled into a dark pit," Charlie zoned out for a second. "Sorry, Tommy. We've gone way deep there for a Sunday morning."

A bizarre comfort transcended upon him, recognising that everybody has a story, even cheery Charlie, whose confidence masked a tale of great loss, which obviously affected him deeply. He wondered what he had studied at university and whether dropping out was the reason he worked part-time at the Old Mill. He pondered as to what else could be hiding behind the bubbly exterior of his work colleague.

The grating of the butter knife as it was dragged across the toasted teacake brought him back into the room. Charlie licked the butter knife, prompting Tommy's toes to curl, before he grasped the two mugs of coffee and whisked the order to the awaiting table.

Upon returning behind the counter, with the smile back on his face, Charlie took a healthy sip of his sugary brew. Tommy was intrigued about his university drop out but didn't want to rake up his father's grave any more than he already had.

"What did you get up to yesterday?" Charlie quizzed.

He hesitated, "I went to the Granville footy match,"

"Nice, good result, wasn't it? Who did you go there with?"

"Ha, this is the funny part," Tommy said awkwardly, "do you know Finn and Shay O'Cleary?"

Charlie seemed to stall. His face altered a tad, only

slightly though, it was barely noticeable, but Tommy saw it, like he was trying to hide a niggling discomfort. He watched as Charlie took another sip of his tea and glanced around the room, before clearing his throat.

"Yeah. I mean, yes, I've heard of them. Seen them around and such," he mustered.

"Yeah, well I guess it's hard not to have heard of them," Tommy affirmed, "well, I went to the game with them,"

"I didn't know you hung around with them lot?"

"I don't, I mean, I didn't. It's a long story."

He was looking to shut down the conversation before he said something he shouldn't, he hoped Charlie's uneasiness was a sign that he didn't want to talk about the O'Clearys either. They were violent, bullish characters so it was no surprise to Tommy that people might find it intimidating to even talk about them.

He placed his mug of tea onto the worktop and began to wipe the sides down, sneaking a quick glance out of the corner of his eye back towards Charlie. He still seemed to be stuck, in a trance almost; like a helpless fish awaiting release from a merciless hook.

A shrill *ding* tone and an accompanying *bzz-bzz* from Charlie's mobile phone on top of the microwave signalled that he had received a text message, breaking his apparent, momentary paralysis. He watched him reach for his phone, open the message and once again attempt to suppress some kind of distress. Tommy continued to wipe down the sides, recognising it was none of his business, but his intrigue was scorching hot.

Charlie rubbed the back of his neck, deep in thought. He paced through to the back, then returned moments later with his hoody on and his rucksack over his shoulders.

"Tommy, hold the fort a second mate, I need to nip out,"

"Sure, no problem," he said, his mind racing as to

what had spooked Charlie more, the mention of the O'Clearys or the text message he'd just received.

The familiar jangle of the bell above the door tolled, with a little more ferocity this time. Tommy gazed with wonderment as Charlie scurried out, his bag jamming slightly as he rushed through the open doorway. Tommy relayed a reassuring smile towards the elderly couple, who had looked towards him for answers. Despite his efforts, he imagined his own uncertainty prevented any conviction.

He picked up the damp cloth and returned to the worksurfaces, but his curiosity was strumming a relentless bassline in between his ears.

What was Charlie up to?

A couple of minutes had passed before he surrendered, his inquisitiveness had wrestled its way in and gotten the better of him. He rinsed out the cloth under the hot tap with some disinfectant, then casually strolled out onto the café floor.

As he approached their table, he offered another smile to the customers and asked if everything was ok. The lady was complimentary of his coffee making skills and the gentleman put his thumb up, having just filled his mouth with the last bite of his toasted teacake.

He began to wipe down the red and white chequered plastic cloth on the table closest to the door. Peering out of the window, he craned his neck to get the full 180-degree view up and down the street. There wasn't a soul in sight looking west down Fir Street towards the sea front; it looked miserable out there. He worried for the couple next to him battling their way through these conditions. He turned his head to look up Fir Street and spotted Charlie across the street standing in the doorway of the closed down clothes shop, Berries.

He squinted through the rain speckled window, making sure he carried on simulating the cleaning of the table in front of him. Charlie had checked his phone twice in the last few seconds and taken a quick glanced at his watch too; he seemed shifty. Tommy was on the cusp of returning to the safety of behind the counter, frightened of being rumbled, when another figure joined Charlie in the doorway.

The figure removed his hood to reveal he was wearing a tweed flat cap. They spoke for a few brief moments, before the man with the flat cap on turned to face Charlie, placing his back in the way of Tommy being able to see anything more of their interaction, but if he had to guess, it was a drop-off and in Granville, drop-offs in doorways were ninety-nine times out of ninety-nine related to drugs, money or drugs.

As the man with the cap on walked away down Fir Street towards the promenade, a smirk painted across his smug face, Tommy struggled to swallow down the edge of angst which had risen from the pit of his stomach. He caught a glimpse of who it was; Ryan *the Hat* – associate of the O'Clearys.

He quickly composed himself and raced back behind the counter with his cloth, attending to the sides once more. As the doorbell dinged, he didn't even look up. He just kept wiping, going over the work he'd already done, trying to figure out what world of trouble his friend might be in with the O'Cleary brothers.

It was beginning to feel as though *Charge*, the Chemist and the O'Clearys were like a bacterial infection, multiplying and contaminating anything that moved within their sphere of influence and there wasn't a soul in town forthcoming with an antidote.

CHAPTER TWENTY-FOUR

The week had flown by in an instant. At times, he had struggled to keep track of what day it was, finding himself sounding way beyond his years by asking people; *can you believe its Friday already?*

He sat, or rather slouched, clock watching on one of the comfy chairs in the common room during his free period, his last of the week. Ordinarily he was able to leave college at lunch time on a Friday, due to this perfectly timed free lesson. However, today was different. Today he had to stay behind for a twilight one-to-one tutor session with Miss Cartwright, to catch up on his maths.

Whilst he waited, he reflected upon the past few days, which had played out rather kindly, given the serious circumstances that were festering and what could potentially be at stake.

Things at home had been pretty bog standard; dodging his mum's volatile mood swings, which fluctuated depending on whether she had the funds to score or not, with some brief, yet warm moments with Derek, who for the first time in forever had actually knocked on his bedroom door to see how he was doing.

He was also thankful that he'd managed to coast through the last few days without as much as a murmur from the O'Cleary brothers, in regard to the incident at the match last Saturday. Bizarrely, Finn even nodded over to him across the canteen, on the one and only day he showed up to college; although it didn't look much, he took it to represent a massive stride forward, considering how unwilling Finn had been previously. Whilst he knew that all of this was a charade, he found himself walking a few inches taller after it happened, boosted by the kudos which came courtesy of hanging out with the in-crowd.

Prior to Finn's gesture of acquaintance, he had convinced himself that his ill-timed prying had exposed him last week, that they could see through his pretence and knew that he was an outsider with ulterior motives – but if he was now being acknowledged at college, maybe that wasn't the case after all.

He couldn't help but worry for his work friend, Charlie, though, as the signs seemed to be telling on Sunday. He had replayed the sequence of events several times in his head during the past few days; the shiftiness at the mention of the O'Clearys, the secrecy, the random meet with Ryan *the Hat* in gale force winds, all pointed to Charlie being involved in this treacherous scene. Quite how, he didn't know, and he wasn't sure he wanted to.

Time with Kirsten had been precious, limited to break times and such like and, even in those fleeting moments, it was as if their relationship had already stumbled upon another, magical dimension. Suddenly, talking wasn't just talking and touching wasn't just touching; each split second was now loaded with a flirtatious undercurrent.

He had quietly tended to an ache inside, however, having not seen much of one another in the evenings. Ever since their mutual declaration last week, he yearned to spend some quality time together, but he didn't want to burden her with any kind of guilt, pressure or neediness, especially when her mind was occupied by the relentless dance rehearsals for her role in the upcoming, annual college show.

He pulled out his phone and composed a text message

then hit send:

15:32
"Hey beautiful, hope you've had a nice day,
I'll try and come and see you at work tonight,
I've missed your face this week x"

Each text message they had exchanged, along with a couple of hour-long phone calls late at night, seemed to afford him more than enough fuel to keep the fire burning inside. He only hoped she was experiencing the same.

As he sat there, his mind niggled. Until now, he'd refused to submit to the negativity and self-doubt which had sporadically ghosted in, teasing him with intrusive thoughts; that Kirsten had only said what she had said because she was caught in the moment, or that she pitied him, or that this week was a sign that she wasn't really interested in him on an intimate level after all. He had done his utmost to keep those thoughts at bay, but he was unsure how long he could hold them off.

The bell sounded and the mass exodus commenced, as hundreds of wild-eyed students raced towards the weekend. He opted to stay put and allow the corridors to clear, before making his way to Miss Cartwright's class.

"Come in, Tommy, come in. Sorry to have kept you waiting,"

He'd seen from outside the classroom that Miss Cartwright wasn't responsible for the delay. She had been bombarded with questions from students after the final bell, but he appreciated the apology all the same.

"No problem, Miss. Where shall I sit?"

"Anywhere up at the front will do,"

"Sure,"

He picked a pew on the front row next to her desk and slipped his jacket over the back of the chair. Miss Cartwright was shuffling through a mess of papers on her desk and rummaging around in her top drawer.

"Aha! Found them. So, before we get started, here's the important question," she fanned out what appeared to be two menus, "do you want pizza or cheeseburger?"

"Woah, are you serious?" he buzzed, "You don't have to do that, Miss,"

"Nonsense, it's my treat. Nobody should have to stay behind on a Friday – including me – so we may as well eat fast food whilst we work, what do you say?"

"I say sign me up for Friday tutor sessions every week,"

"Well, let's see how this one goes first shall we?" she chuckled, sarcastically rolling her eyes.

"Ok, cool. And I'm easy on the food front, Miss. You choose something,"

"Well then I say... Pizza."

She quickly phoned through their pizza order; he opted for a pepperoni on a classic crust, whilst Miss Cartwright ordered herself a small Calabrese, which he'd never even heard of, so found himself intrigued as to what it entailed.

There was a comforting and familiar feel to the beginning of the tutor session, almost as though he found himself getting ready to study with a friend. During lessons, Miss Cartwright had a way of being informal and approachable, but the pupils always knew where the boundaries were. This was different, the tension he so often carted round with him had eased and his shoulders were relaxed; it felt safe, which was a rarity when he found himself around adults in educational settings. Perhaps this was all a tactic to get the best out of him. Whatever it was, he believed he could easily get used to it.

Once the order was placed and delivery confirmed for

arrival in around forty-five minutes, Miss Cartwright plopped her phone into her handbag and they got to work on his maths progress, or lack of, would perhaps be more accurate.

It was a painstaking forty-five minutes, with some harsh truths, rumbling bellies and some vulnerability on his part. His mock exam scores were woeful at best and it was quickly apparent that he had a lot of catching up to do. The good news was, that Miss Cartwright seemed to want him to do well, perhaps more than he did himself. She made it clear that she would be with him every step of the way and asked him to see it as a challenge, as opposed to a threat.

The sumptuous aroma from the pizzas wafted under the classroom door seconds before he heard the polite knock. It smelled divine and instantly prompted his taste buds to tingle. Delivering the pizzas was Mrs Maxwell, who worked on the reception of the college and had always offered him a welcoming smile each time he passed her.

Miss Cartwright thanked Mrs Maxwell and divvied up their chosen pizzas as they readied themselves to delve in. He sniggered, as Miss Cartwright tucked a napkin into her white blouse, almost like a baby's bib. He tore away his first slice. The piping hot cheese dangled in every which direction, unwilling to part from its larger form. He managed to navigate the end of the slice into his mouth and took his first bite, as the oil from the pepperoni dribbled back onto the grease stained box; this certainly was a treat for him.

As he savoured each bite of that first slice, Miss Cartwright slid him an old, tattered textbook.

"It doesn't look much; you know how it is around here. But the way I see it, as long as there's a spine and some pages, you've got yourself a book,"

"What's this for?" he asked, covering his mouth to hide the partly chewed crust.

"For you to take home and borrow. Use it to study with, this is all on you now. You know what you need to do,"

"Yes, I know," he mumbled, fidgeting with the remaining crust before casting it to one side.

"Does your mum take an interest in your studies?"

He stuttered, "Erm, not overly. She's more of a figure-it-out-for-yourself kind of parent,"

"Oh, I know the feeling," she assured, before taking a bite from her interesting looking pizza. He presumed it was a spicy one as it had fresh chillies and a fiery looking sausage on top.

"It's been fine. I mean, I made it this far, right?" he faltered.

"What's the matter?" she questioned. Her voice was forgiving and gentle.

"I guess I'm just scared. That I do all of this and still fail,"

"Well that is a common feeling that many people experience. And I've got to tell you, Tommy, there's no escaping the fact that failure is a possibility, one of many might I add. Just for a second though, think about the wild, every species is a genius in some way, right? Ants can carry one hundred times their body weight for example. But if you judge a shark based on its ability to climb a tree, it's going to feel pretty stupid,"

"Ok, that kind of makes sense I guess," he considered.

"If you are the shark, then maths may well be your tree. But it doesn't mean that you're not great at lots of other things,"

He paused for a moment, processing what it was that she was saying. In that moment, he realised that this was probably the most encouraging thing that anybody had ever said to him.

"Wow, thanks Miss. That actually means a lot,"

"Hold on though, mister, it doesn't mean that the shark won't still *try* to climb the tree, ok?"

They giggled in agreement and continued to chomp away at their pizzas. Together they plotted out a study plan for him to follow at home, using the textbook he'd been given, or the computers in the library – when they were working that was. Almost another hour and a half had passed before he realised what time it was.

"Oh shoot Miss, look what time it is. Sorry I've kept you so long,"

"Crikey, look at that its six o'clock. Did you have somewhere to be, Tommy?"

"Not really, I'm going to head home. Might go out later and see my," he hesitated, "well my friend I guess, you?"

"I guess I'll need to burn off all that pizza so I'm heading straight to do back to back Zumba classes, which you know all about having spotted me last week,"

"Yes, of course," he felt his cheeks fill up with a cherry tinge, "well, for what it's worth, Miss, I really appreciate this tonight, it's been mega helpful. Not many adults have gone out of their way to help me in my life, so it means a lot,"

"You're welcome, now you get yourself off to see that friend of yours."

They bid each other farewell and exchanged well wishes for the weekend. He had a spring in his step as he bounced down the corridors towards the main entrance, which would be the only way out at this hour. He began to plot out his evening in his mind; tidy up at home, a quick shower, brush his teeth, get changed and then off to see Kirsten. Even the prospect of propping up the bar and gazing at her all evening triggered all kinds of giddiness.

He stepped out of the college gates and onto the main road to begin his ascent home, placing his earphones in and selecting his favourite good mood soundtrack: *This is the One – The Stone Roses.*

He was just getting into his stride, bordering on playing the air drums with no consideration to his street cred, when a car pulled up next to him. He huffed expecting it to be Brightwell and was ready to remind him of personal space and such, only to be caught off guard by who he saw through the window.

"Hey there, handsome," Darcy shouted, her voice competing with the stereo.

"Oh hey, Darcy," he stammered, crouching down slightly, "how are you?"

"I'm great. Why don't you jump in? I'll give you a ride,"

"Ah that's ok, you don't have to. I don't mind walking,"

"I know I don't have to, I want to. Come on, Tommy, don't shoot me down when I'm out on a whim. What do you say? We'll go for a little drive and catch up,"

To help him with this conundrum, a metaphorical devil resembling Brightwell appeared on one shoulder and an angelic Kirsten appeared on the other, both of whom proved to be anything but helpful. Feeling obliged and quite frankly confused, he climbed in her car and chucked his bag onto the back seat.

What am I doing?

CHAPTER
TWENTY-FIVE

"Where are we going?" he asked, a subtle wobble in his voice, "my house is that way,"

"Would you chill out please, Tommy? Jeez, have you got somewhere you need to be?"

Darcy was direct, confident, yet casual and in control, leaving him unsure of how to handle this situation. He wondered if he was being over cautious and if he should perhaps take a leaf out of her book, but something felt at odds. The churning in his stomach was telling him something.

They passed under the old bridge, which in years gone by had taken the railway line into the centre of Granville, way back when tourism was thriving. Now, it was a part-finished, abandoned attempt at a conversion into a proposed, new dual carriageway. Darcy continued to drive with haste, skipping amber lights and razzing around corners; they were heading towards the outskirts.

"Well, I think my mum will be expecting me, I've not seen her since Wednesday,"

"Oh yeah, where's she been?"

Taking heroin in a flat somewhere…

"She goes out to see her friends sometimes and stays over,"

"See, now we're chatting and getting to know each other, it's not so bad is it?

He nodded. He supposed she was right, maybe there wasn't any harm in getting to know Darcy a little bit. The comment she made at the party last week, about being different and wanting more for herself, had stuck with him and he realised how relatable it was. Maybe she needed a friend, somebody who could take her away from all the incessant violence, crime and tension that must come with being an O'Cleary.

"So, where are you taking me then?" he asked, forcing a little more buoyancy into his words.

"I'm going to take you to where I used to play when I was a kid,"

"Ha! I did not expect that. You are full of surprises, aren't you?"

"Wait until you see it,"

She raced on through yet another questionable amber traffic light and turned the stereo up a few more notches.

They drove for a further two songs before turning into the small car park outside Garfell Lake. Through the gap in the trees, Tommy gazed at the moon shimmering across the still water. It was so quiet out here, which felt alien to him, he almost felt like his ears had closed up and he needed to pop them to release sound.

"Come on let's go and take a walk," Darcy enthused, springing out of the car.

"This was where I used to come and play. We lived out here for a little while around ten years ago, so I'd always come down here," she reminisced, smiling as if she had been transported back to a simpler time. "You see those trees over there, I'd always been running around in there and building dens,"

"That sounds pretty cool. I had a cardboard box to play with ten years ago,"

Uncertainty descended momentarily, before they both burst

out laughing. They shuffled along the path which surrounded the lake, auburn coloured leaves hiding the concrete beneath.

"You make me smile, Tommy Dawson,"

There was an unspoken chemistry developing in the air, it felt unusual, like the most contradicting balance of awkward and pleasant. He cleared his throat.

"You know, I've never been here before,"

"Never?" she gasped.

"Never, never. It's Garfell, only posh people live in Garfell,"

She pushed him away playfully.

"Somebody sounds a little like a reverse snob,"

"What the hell is a reverse snob when it's at home?" he asked, bemused.

"It's like a snob, but instead of the rich dismissing the poor, its," she hesitated.

"The poor dismissing the rich?"

"Yes, that's what I was going to say," she offered, tentatively.

"Well, you might just be right there. If you spend so much time as the muck on somebody's shoe, you start to resent the shoe, if you get me?"

"Yes, that makes sense I guess," she said, warmly. "Right, Tommy. Tell me a bit about your life, where have you come from and where are you going?"

"Ok, I'm starting to feel like I'm on *This is your Life* here," he deflected, but Darcy was serious, she wanted to know. "I guess there's not much to say, I had it pretty rough at home you could say, I found out recently that my dad was killed when I was young, my mum is a user so she's never the most reliable," he stopped for a second, "hold on, why am I telling you all of this, you go now,"

He was blushing, but she didn't seem phased by what he had said, he supposed she of all people understood what dysfunctional felt like.

"What do you want to know? My family are renowned for doing things they shouldn't, I don't like it, but how can I complain? You see that car over there in the car park that brought us here, brand new registration, well that's what happens. You get bought off with gifts in the hope that it will make up for lost time, or the embarrassment when somebody asks – and what does your father do for a living?"

She spoke so honestly yet managed to curb any kind of self-pity, he found it refreshing and so relevant.

"You know that part at the end has bugged me my whole life. I've constantly swerved the question about my mum; if nobody knew, then nobody needed to come and poke their nose in."

There was a brief moment of quiet, both looking at anything but at each other.

"I just want so much more for myself," they both said in sync.

"Oh my god, jinx!" Darcy exclaimed.

She shivered slightly and huddled in a little closer to him. He tried to maintain an acceptable distance, given his feelings for Kirsten, but he felt rude just shrugging her off.

"Come on, let's try and skim these stones off the lake," he suggested.

"Oh, I used to love doing that,"

"Well I've never done it, but how hard can it be?" he said, rapidly realising how naïve he was being and just how tricky skimming stones was in reality.

"Come here," she demanded, shaking her head at his miserable attempts, "let me show you. Relax your knees, turn side on a little bit… that's it, now hold the stone like this,"

He felt her arm rest on his waist, manoeuvring him into position. She placed her second hand on his, guiding the stone into place. He noticed life flood into her eyes and in that moment, he feared that Darcy most definitely had more than friends on her mind.

"Ok, so just like that?" he asked, easing her away from his body ever so delicately.

He released the pebble, whipping his arm as instructed. He stood up and admired his work, gleefully watching on as it bounced off the water a whopping four times in the moonlight, before disappearing into the middle of the lake. As he turned to celebrate with his stone-skimming tutor, he was taken aback as she leaned straight towards him, her pouting lips lingering, looking to land a kiss.

"Woah, Darcy, I don't think that's a good idea," he stuttered slightly, cringing inside at how badly he was probably going to manage this situation.

"What's the matter?" she snapped.

She tucked her hair behind her ears and stepped backwards a pace.

"I just, don't think we should do that,"

"Are you gay or something?"

He was stunned, unsure of what to say to draw this situation to a mutual settlement. He drew a blank, believing that whatever he said next would undoubtedly be the spark required for this to blow up in his face.

"No, I'm not gay, it's just-"

"Oh, I see what's happening,"

"You do?"

"It all makes sense. You're only interested in my brothers. You got a taste of what it's like to be in the gang and now you want more. Typical. I thought you were different, I thought you understood. I thought you were interested in *me*. How could I be so stupid?"

"Darcy, it's not like that-"

"Don't!" she yelled.

The interruption was probably for the best, although it saddened him that she placed her brothers on such a pedestal. He wondered how often she was overlooked in favour of them.

She stormed off towards the car park, carting her embarrassment with her. He detected what sounded like a gentle sob, as he tried to track her through the darkness.

"Darcy, wait, please,"

He stopped as she turned to face him, "Enjoy your walk home, Tommy. I hope my brothers make you happy."

Feeling useless, he watched her leave the place which held so many happy memories for her, crying and agitated because of him. He wanted to tell her that he didn't give two shits about her brothers, he wanted to tell her the truth. She seemed like a genuine person, who deserved better than the hand she'd been dealt, a hand glittered with empty material things and void of any love and attentiveness.

Her headlamps flickered on and the sound of the gravel grinding under her overeager tyres told him that she was not bluffing about the walk home.

He trudged through the soggy leaves and hopped over the railings of the car park. Through the shadowy light he could make out the silhouette of his ruck sack, which she'd had the courtesy to eject from her car before departing.

He scooped it up and began the lengthy trek back to Frampton Road.

CHAPTER TWENTY-SIX

As his icy fingers struggled to grip his house key, he patiently lined it up and slid it into the lock, turning to crank open his front door. The walk home had been bitterly cold, and it had taken him two hours and twenty minutes. It might have been quicker had he not got lost somewhere between Garfell and the marsh; *thank the lord for that bus driver and her directions.*

Time spent battling the winter chill, skulking through areas he was unfamiliar with, had allowed him time to ruminate about Darcy. He hoped she would be ok. In most situations, the thought of upsetting anybody would weigh heavy on him, but upsetting Darcy felt particularly difficult. He wasn't sure whether that was because she seemed like a nice person and somebody who he could relate to, or because of who her brothers were – or maybe a bit of both.

"Hello! Anybody home?" he called out, closing the door behind him and throwing his rucksack onto the stairs.

The sight occupying his front room startled him.

"Kirsten, what are you doing here? Are you smoking?"

Kirsten was propped nervously in the middle of the settee, bouncing her heel. She clutched her midriff with one hand and was stubbing out a cigarette into the ashtray on the coffee table with the other. She wore her work uniform and had her black headband on, keeping her wild hair away from her tear-stained face. Her eyes were bloodshot and glazed, seemingly unable to respond, as she stared vacantly into space.

He spoke again, dropping to his knees next to her.

"What's the matter? Kirsten, what's happened?"

He gently placed his hands around her shoulders and attempted to ease some life into her. She eventually sniffled and wiped her eyes with her sleeve.

"It's your brother," she sobbed, faintly rocking backwards and forwards.

"Derek? What's happened to Derek?"

His chest filled with dread, as his mind raced ahead of real time to a near future with a dozen possibilities.

"He's been rushed to hospital in an ambulance," she paused. "They think he's overdosed,"

"Wait, what? He's clean, you must be mistaken. He's clean,"

"Tommy, I'm sorry. I'm so sorry,"

"No!" he insisted, "You're wrong,"

For the first time, she broke free from her trance and turned to look at him. His eyes flickered around the room as he shook his head vigorously, unwilling to accept what he was hearing as fact. He rose to his feet again, but the walls appeared to be closing in on him; the information repeating over and over in his mind. He was perplexed; *Derek had been doing so well*.

"Tommy, I was there. I was working and I saw him get carried out of the Junction on a stretcher with an oxygen mask on and into an ambulance,"

She let out a painful groan and flung her arms around him, mumbling a repetitive apology through her tears. As tender as her embrace was, he could barely feel it; that familiar smell of mango from her hair and the touch of her soft, fawn skin weren't enough to wake him from this nightmare.

163

"What had he taken, Kirsten?"

"I'm not sure, but I heard somebody gossiping at the bar and they said," she wavered.

"What? They said what?"

"The Chemist strikes again."

Fortunately, the settee was there to catch him, as his legs gave way, causing him to collapse backwards into a paralysed heap. Kirsten was talking to him, perhaps explaining why it was her sat in his front room waiting for him and not his own mum. But her words were muted. He could see her lips move, yet no noise filtered through to his ears.

He didn't need to hear this part anyway; he already knew. His mum was where she usually was during a crisis; either on the missing list and nowhere to be found or passed out in the corner of one of her frequent haunts. Therefore, if his mum was out of the equation, Uncle Bill, as kind as he was, had let Kirsten leave work to come and wait here to be the bearer of the sad news. Or something like that.

He came back into consciousness, "I'm sorry you had to go through this, Kirsten,"

"Oh, you sweet thing, you have nothing to apologise for. I'm right here for you," she said, busying herself, "I tell you what we're going to do, I'm going to ring a taxi, you get yourself changed and get some water or whatever you need, we'll go up to the hospital and everything is going to be fine-"

"Everybody else has died from this kind of situation,"

"We don't know that, Tommy,"

"I do, Brightwell told me," he reached out and grasped her wrist before she could call for the taxi, "Kirsten, I'm scared."

She wrapped her arms around him and squeezed, ensuring that this time he could feel it. Her hands transmitted warmth and care into his body. He wondered what he would do without her.

"I know you are," she comforted, "I'm not going anywhere."

Once their embrace had ran its duration, he paced into the kitchen and poured himself a glass of water from the tap, gulping it down in seconds. He could hear through to the living room that Kirsten was on the phone to the taxi operator and that there was expected to be a short delay on availability. He hovered at the adjoining door and waited patiently for Kirsten to end the call.

"Do you know how it happened?" he asked.

"I saw bits and pieces, but you know how the Junction is on a Friday night,"

"Anything might help, it just doesn't feel right. He was clean. I really started to believe him this time, you know?"

"I know you did," she consoled, placing her hand on his cheek momentarily. "Well, I saw him come in around six with that Jamie Wilcox that he went to school with,"

"Oh yeah, he's not a bad lad Jamie. I think that's who got him into volunteering," he added.

"Yes, well Jamie left about an hour later. Your brother stayed, playing pool with some of the regulars. I glanced over a few times and obviously spoke to him when he came to order his drinks and he seemed really happy and upbeat. Probably the healthiest I've ever seen him, to be honest. Anyway, about half an hour later I was clearing tables and I saw him talking to this bloke in a dark hoody. It looked a bit shifty, but I thought hey, your brother knows some shifty characters – no offence,"

"No, none taken, you're dead right about that. Did you say dark hoody?"

"Yes, I couldn't see his face though as his hood was up. Quite a big bloke. So, after that Derek goes in the toilet and I went back behind the bar. About twenty minutes later he came to order a drink and he looked completely off his head; wide eyes, saliva round his mouth, talking really quickly. Obviously working in the Junction, I've seen my fair share of people under the influence, so I figured he'd taken some coke or whizz or something,"

"Oh man," he moaned, putting his head in his hands.

"Then ten minutes later, there's a big bang by the pool table and a load of commotion. Turns out it was Derek having a seizure and, well, you know the rest."

She reached out and stroked his arm affectionately. He looked into her eyes and saw two great big canyons of pain; he could see that retelling the story was difficult for her. He usually loathed sympathy, but he knew Kirsten's was coming a good place, from the centre of her thoughtful soul and that her sorrow was genuine.

"The dark hoody thing bugs me," he pondered. "The guy who bumped into me at the hospital and planted the phone had a dark hoody on too,"

"I see where you're coming from, but lots of people have dark hoodies, Tommy,"

"It just seems too much of a coincidence. People are out to get me. I don't know why I'm saying people – Smiler is out to get me. And what better way than to send somebody to float the promise of an ultimate high in front of my addict of a brother's face, knowing full well he won't be able to say no, only to watch him collapse and probably die. Somebody gave him the rope and noose, Derek just had to do the rest."

He choked on the last few words, the sensation of tears rising rapidly towards their exit point. Fortunately, the sound of a horn beeping outside pulled him from the spiral of conspiracies and revenge theories, which he was on the cusp of losing himself within.

The taxi was here.

CHAPTER TWENTY-SEVEN

The piercing bleeps of hospital machines swamped Tommy's mind, waking him from his restless doze. His neck ached having been bent out of shape, resting on the arm of a chair in the St James' Hospital ICU waiting room. The screwed-up jumper he'd used as a make-shift pillow hadn't quite stepped up to the mark, leaving creases on his face and a throb behind his forehead.

Looking up at the clock on the wall as it struck 3am, he realised he'd only managed to sleep for around twenty minutes. He straightened up in his chair and attempted to realign his spine, to the sound of a snap, crackle and pop. Through hazy eyes he looked over at Kirsten, as she lay peacefully asleep, despite the uncomfortable surroundings. Even in this turmoil, she brought him a brief second of tranquillity.

The calm was short-lived as the reality of what was going on took over. Lethargically, he climbed to his feet and shuffled over towards the window of the ICU ward again. Almost pressing his nose against the glass, he let out a private whimper, as the unchanged sight of his translucent, unconscious brother stared back at him.

He'd seen Derek unconscious thousands of times before, but never a time that was even remotely close to this. This wasn't a case of pulling his trainers off and rolling him onto his side with a bowl on hand in case he vomited. This was off the scale; the tubes out of his mouth, the heart monitor, the lifeless look which painted his face a ghostly shade of pale.

The distant sounds of footsteps echoing through the hospital halls grew louder. As had been the case when he found himself here a few weeks ago, accompanying Seb, the doctors had been dismissive, unwilling to take a moment to speak to him in the five hours he'd been here, let alone reassure him. He understood they were busy, but that was his brother in there.

The footsteps that arrived in the waiting room were carrying Doctor Knott, who was passing through to check on Derek.

"Doc," Tommy called, "Doc, please. Have you got one minute?"

Knott seemed reluctant, racing to punch in the code to the door and avoid him. The contempt by which he was being treated infuriated him, it was as though he was a leper.

"I don't have time, I'm sorry," Knott deflected, before turning his back.

"Doctor!" Tommy screamed, "That is my brother in there and I am worried sick,"

Knott paused and dropped his head, his thumb hovering over the final digit required to gain entry to the ICU and shut out the inconvenience which littered his waiting room.

To Tommy's surprise, Knott grudgingly stepped away from the door to face him. He rested his back on the wall and removed his glasses, revealing the probable cause of his uptight frown: eyes that were heavy with exhaustion. He gave his temples a firm rub and exhaled frustration from his nose.

"Tommy, is it?" Knott sighed.

"Yes, I'm Derek's younger brother,"

"Your brother is in a coma. He's suffering from hyperpyrexia, which is basically an extremely high fever that we are struggling to control. He is also experiencing cerebral hypoxia, which in plain English is the brain not getting enough oxygen, due to a considerable haemorrhage he experienced during this trauma. There are more tests we are doing as there are more issues we haven't figured out yet. In a nutshell, the drug he took, specifically the amount he took, prompted a seizure so violent that his body has stopped functioning properly. So, if you don't mind, I'd like to stop getting badgered and get back to trying to save your brother's life, so I can return to my other patients, whose life-threatening situations aren't self-inflicted."

Knott span around and burst through the coded door, a look of disdain smeared all over his elitist face. Tommy's insides burned with shame. He stood helpless and impotent, incapable of affecting this situation in any way. Derek's life was in the hands of that doctor. As far as he was concerned though, Knott could look down on him out here all he wanted, as long as he did his job in there with no discrimination.

He turned around to take his seat once more and noticed that Kirsten was awake, with a rather uncomfortable look on her face.

"Sorry, did I wake you by shouting?" he said apologetically, taking the seat next to hers.

"Don't listen to that dick head," she assured.

It was unexpected and prompted him to spit out with laughter.

"Maybe he's right. I don't care, as long as he saves Derek,"

She slipped her hand in his and interlocked their fingers.

"No, Tommy. He couldn't be more wrong. He was so unprofessional then, speaking to you like that was completely out of order. You are worthy of so much more; you're caring, passionate, loyal and smart. And you're not bad to look at either,"

Although he was head was peering down towards his feet, a grin crept across his face; *she knew just what to say*. She

169

unleashed a yawn worthy of a lioness and flopped back into her chair.

"Thank you for staying with me, you really didn't have to," he said.

"Yes, I really did,"

She placed a gentle peck on his cheek, before nestling her head into his shoulder; thick, ringlets of her distinctive, curly hair sprouting all over the place, almost impairing his vision. Time seemed to be going so slow, yet the situation felt as though it was racing away from him, beyond his hopeful grasp.

"What did your mum and dad say about you staying here with me?" he asked.

"My dad is working away," Kirsten explained, "I sent a text message to my mum earlier and she sends her love. She said if you need anything over the coming days, just call round and see her anytime,"

"Thanks, your mum is so thoughtful,"

"She loves you, that's why."

The clinical, antiseptic smell was beginning to irritate him, as though it was coating his skin and licking the back of his throat. Hospitals were unpleasant places at the best of times, but having to sit here, powerless, awaiting a certain tragedy was driving him insane.

They sat in silence for a while as inside his head tossed around one scary thought on top of countless other scary thoughts. He appreciated the safety blanket of which Kirsten's presence provided though; he couldn't bear the thought of sitting here alone.

"I should have told him I was proud of him," he yearned.

"Tommy, don't do this to yourself,"

"He'd been doing so well. I just kept expecting more and more. I didn't stop for one second to recognise how far he'd come and tell him that I was proud of him and it meant so much to have my brother back,"

"Well, you can tell him when he wakes up,"

She caressed his arm supportively, her words doused with hope and positivity. His flood gates were bursting at the seams and he felt an overwhelming urge to continue,

"Maybe if I had done that, if I had told him, he might have thought twice, you know?"

"As blunt as this is going to sound Tommy, your brother is a recovering drug addict, he was drunk and somebody offered him drugs – this is not your fault, please don't torture yourself like this,"

"I guess you're right. I just can't help but feel responsible in some way," he gulped, cracking the knuckles of his fingers and thumbs. "He's taken all kinds of cocktails of drugs over the years – deadly cocktails too – without hardly a scratch. I remember once answering the door to a bloke who had Derek slung over his shoulder in a fireman's lift, passed out. No idea who he was. He'd seen my brother out cold on the bench down by Collingwood Green and when he was unable to wake him, he found our address in Derek's wallet and brought him home. My brother woke up a few hours later and cracked a can open as if nothing had happened. Turns out he'd triple-dropped some 10mg diazepam at his mates house, drank two bottles of cider, then stopped on the bench to smoke a spliff and – and I quote – take in the view, before blacking out,"

He could have told so many reminiscent stories of his brother; some he'd cry at, some he'd laugh and at some he'd cry with laughter. He exhaled a bemused snigger and shook his head, "and now, because somebody has it in for me, he gets stitched up with one bump of this *Charge* stuff and ends up on deaths door. It can't be a coincidence, it just can't,"

"Listen to me," Kirsten asserted, sitting up right, "what happened to your brother is a combination of his own issues and the irresponsible person who is making and selling this horrible, synthetic stuff,"

He had a lightbulb moment, which lifted him for a nanosecond, before crushing him with regret and culpability.

"That's it. That's why I feel guilty. If I'd have said yes to Brightwell straight away, instead of dithering around and trying to protect my own interests and reputation, he might have been able to arrest the Chemist, or at least get *Charge* off the streets. I could have helped him end this and there would have been no need for my brother to be dragged in,"

"But you said yourself, Brightwell was pushy and he made you feel uncomfortable. You listened to your gut, that's perfectly understandable,"

"Yes, and how wrong was my gut?"

"You don't know that, what has happened has happened. You can't rewrite history with shoulda, woulda, coulda. There's nothing you can do, Tommy,"

Kirsten's voice was becoming pitchy and he detected an air of frustration in her words. He couldn't blame her; he knew he was rambling and bordering on self-pity. She was being a good friend, patiently trying to supress any desires to challenge him too strongly and risk upsetting him. He rose to his feet and reached into his pocket to pull out his phone.

"Yeah, well we'll see about that,"

He hit the call button on his phone and paced around the waiting room. The phone rang through to voicemail and he hung up. His agitation intensified, forcing an audible, rumbling growl. He hit the call button again with no hesitation. This time, they answered.

"*Bloody hell, Tommy, do you know what time it is?*" the voice crackled, coughing and spluttering.

"Brightwell," he said, "I'm in. No messing this time. Tell me what I need to do."

CHAPTER TWENTY-EIGHT

"Where the hell have you been?" Tommy yelled, sprinting down the stairs.

His mum looked as though she'd woken up in a coffin. She was almost skeletal; grey complexion, greasy hair, tatty clothes and her bones were almost piercing through her skin. She slammed the door and the vibrations made her jump into the front room. She scavenged around, hunting for something to take the edge off, he presumed.

"Have you seen my cigarettes?" she mustered.

"On the kitchen side. Now any chance you want to answer my question?" he scorned.

The adrenaline pumped around his body, masking the chill that his bare legs were exposed to. He'd jumped out of bed as soon as he heard the front door latch open, so was currently stood wearing only his boxers and a t-shirt, as he confronted his mum.

It was 2pm on Sunday afternoon. Kirsten had gone home from the hospital early yesterday morning and popped back up to see him for an hour yesterday afternoon with a sandwich and some snacks. He stayed up there pacing the waiting room, on his own, until late last night, or perhaps more accurately, until early hours this morning. That was before an empathetic nurse from the ICU ward had offered him a warm cup of coffee and the courtesy of a quick ten-minute chat.

The nurse was the first member of hospital staff in twenty-eight hours that had asked how he was doing. They spoke about Derek and the fact that he had temporarily stabilised, despite heart complications earlier in the day. She took his phone number and advised him to go home to rest, ensuring she would call if anything changed.

Unable to keep his eyes open much longer and feeling conscious of his own odour, he had decided that a shower and some sleep might be helpful for everybody. Upon leaving the hospital at 03:27am, he sent a hopeful text message to Charlie to ask if he could cover his shift at the Old Mill, stating a family emergency as the reason. Charlie had text him back straight away to say it was no problem. He briefly wondered what Charlie was doing up so late, but he didn't have the time or inclination to explore it further; *nothing good,* he presumed.

He'd arrived home to an empty house, seething that his mum still hadn't surfaced. Whilst initially his anger had prevented him from falling to sleep, the overwhelming lack of rest prevailed and he'd conked out until he was woken by his mum stumbling into the house this afternoon, after a four day and night binge.

Her hands rattled whilst lighting her cigarette. The embers crackled amidst the silent stalemate, as she took long, hard drags, as if attempting to suck life back into her soul.

"Well?" he pleaded.

"Oh will you give it a rest, Tommy. There are bigger things going on than your whining at the minute, you're giving me a headache. In fact, scratch that. You're making my headache unbearable. Do we have any aspirin, or headache tablets in?"

"When was the last time you bought any aspirin or headache tablets, Mum?" he gibed. "And anyway, what bigger things? Have you heard about Derek?"

"Of course I have, he's my son. He was here before you,

and he'll be here by my side long after you've pissed off to wherever you keep telling us you're going to," she goaded.

He reviewed his approach. Perhaps poking the bear as she recovered from an intoxicating hibernation wasn't the best choice.

"But, how did you know? I haven't seen you at the hospital, I couldn't get hold of you,"

"Granville Graeme told me yesterday morning,"

"Oh, nice one. And who the frigging hell is Granville Graeme? And did you not think to come and see Derek? Did you not wonder how he was? Did you not wonder how I was?"

"Ah, here he is. You can't resist making this about you can you, Tommy? Whilst my poor first born child is laid up in the hospital as well, shame on you. Well, instead of thinking about ourselves, like you, we said prayers for Derek all day and night,"

"Fat lot praying is going to do," he dismissed.

She scowled, "You wash your mouth out with soap young man,"

"Mum, don't start trying to parent me now, you're seventeen years too late," he said, "and for the record, you're the only one thinking about yourself around here, you're pathetic. And I strongly suggest you start taking this seriously and get up to the hospital, because your poor first born child is staring down the barrel of a gun."

He stormed up the stairs, leaving his harsh truth to scold his mum's conscience. A cauldron of emotion bubbled inside of him: sadness, guilt, anger, frustration, pity, fear. He couldn't sit there and listen to his mum drone on about her deluded perspective of the world right now. She was beyond the reach of logic, floating around in that hazy realm between up and under, drunk and sober, high and low; he had to get out of here.

In a hurry, he threw on some clothes and stuffed what he could in terms of a spare outfit, phone charger a deodorant can and some other hygiene essentials, into his ruck sack.

Whether conscious or not, his brother was in need right now and if his mum was unwilling to pull her head from the sand and be by his side, then he was.

He pulled his bobble hat down a little further so it covered his ears, which had been exposed to the windy chill that bellowed through the streets of Granville. Dusk was chasing away fragments of a yellow-orange hue, as it offered one final burst through patches of cotton cloud that floated aloft of the horizon, ready to depart for the day at any given moment.

He'd walked around aimlessly for a while, waiting for visiting hours to commence at the hospital from 4:30pm. The streets of Granville were hushed at this time on a Sunday, with plenty of time to think.

Familiar thoughts circled, some from the last few weeks and some he'd battled with his whole life. The merry-go-round inside his head eventually settled on his mum and the lingering feeling of regret, after calling her pathetic.

His mum's unique method of parenting had taken many years to accept, but his perception had radically changed the moment he learned of her haunting past. No longer did he see a mum that didn't care, he saw a mum who was trapped in her youth, struggling with her demons and unable to move forward. A mum who was stolen of her childhood innocence by Smiler's evil deceit, who prayed on her vulnerability to exercise his own perverse desires for sex, abuse, power and control. He saw a mum who bottled up that trauma so tight, that avoidance and denial seemed to be the only irrationally logical way to get through the day.

But even taking all of that into consideration, he just could not fathom how she could be so blasé and irresponsible when Derek was clutching to stay alive.

Whilst his mind had been occupied, his feet had taken him on a stroll down to the promenade, where graffiti ridden shutters signalled the out of season gloom had descended upon the town. However, even in the blustery conditions, there were still a couple of desperate vendors, wearing fingerless gloves and empty bum-bags, with their doors open for anyone in need of Granville rock, candy floss or other miscellaneous bric-a-brac. The sight brought new depths to the concept of blind hope; any amount of money to keep the lights switched on.

As he paced back through the town centre, making his way to the hospital to visit Derek, he pulled his phone out to see if anybody had contacted him. No news from the hospital, he supposed, was good news. An attentive text message from Kirsten briefly ignited flutters inside. She was out this afternoon for a Sunday roast dinner with her mum and a distant aunt who was visiting town, but she had still found a quick minute to say she was thinking of him, affectionately signing off her message with several x's.

Since their brief phone call in the early hours on Saturday morning, he hadn't heard a peep from Brightwell. For somebody previously so persistent, he had found this strange and a little annoying, having finally committed to help him bring an end this business with *Charge* and anybody who stood in his way. He guessed he now knew how it felt to have somebody keep you in the dark when you feel at your most desperate.

Shit! Battery dead.

As he was well ahead of time, he decided to stop at the next phone box and give Brightwell a call. He still had his card containing his phone number, so a quick check-in would hopefully put his mind at ease.

He approached the corner of Peter Street and rummaged in his pocket for some change. He opened the door to the phone box, which had been badly vandalised; smashed window, scribbled graffiti, beer cans littering the floor inside and the unmistakeable reek of urine.

He picked up the cracked receiver, the dial tone indicating it was still operational. He pushed a fifty pence piece into the slot and placed Brightwell's card on the ledge underneath, readying himself to dial. But before he did, something caught his eye.

The frame next to the phone designated for advertising had been damaged, scribbled on and had all kinds of call-me-for-a-good-time stickers plastered all over it. But one sticker caught his eye, sending shudders down to his shoes.

A white, shiny sticker was placed smack, bang in the middle, with an unusual logo that could only signify one thing. He looked closer to see the design was a scientist's conical flask filled with bubbling liquid and the letter 'C' splattered across the top.

Was this some kind of promo for the Chemist?

If these stickers had started popping up all over town in phone boxes, on street signs or on the back of toilet doors, the Chemist was no longer an outlaw to be apprehended immediately; instead, he was becoming a celebrity. A celebrity armed with so many promises of unspeakable euphoria, that people were willing to ignore the potential, grave consequences.

He punched in Brightwell's phone number, one silver-squared digit at a time using his index finger. The dial tone turned to ringing and he waited with bated breath.

To his disappointment, the call rang out to voicemail, clouding the glimmer of progress he hoped to make. He left a message requesting a call back and slammed down the receiver, the sound of the telephone swallowing his fifty pence adding an extra layer of frustration. Unleashing a growl of frustration, he stormed out of the phone box to make his way to the hospital.

CHAPTER
TWENTY-NINE

A murky fog had descended during the two hours he'd spent glued to Derek's hospital bed. Its misty bleakness hung ominously, barely aloft of the lampposts, blanketing the Granville skyline. As he absorbed the change in the elements, he almost lost his footing, skidding slightly on the shimmering, black ice, which stealthily lacquered the tarmac outside St James' hospital.

He had arrived at the hospital with rage pulsating through his veins and determination locked between his clenched teeth. He now departed with tear stained cheeks, dragging himself along, deflated and hopeless.

Sharing his personal thoughts and current internal agony with his unconscious brother had been exhausting, amplified further due to the irritating and monotonous bleeps from the multitude of machines that were straining to keep him alive.

He told Derek how sorry he was and how proud he had felt watching him make a go of his life recently. He told him how driven he was to bring the people at fault to justice, by whatever means necessary. He also told him about Kirsten, which is what seemed to be the catalyst for the inevitable outpouring of emotion. He knew how much Derek thought of Kirsten; he'd always rooted for them to get together, way before intimate feelings were ever on Tommy's radar.

Even when Derek was scaling the upper most limits of intoxication, he would always reserve a moment of clarity to try and make an effort, whenever he was in Kirsten's company. Now, he wondered if his brother would ever even get to the chance to hear about how he'd declared his feelings for Kirsten, a step he had encouraged in jest so often.

The fog added a hint of cool moisture to the air, which stung his cheeks as he walked. His insides tightened, the wintery smog dropping before his eyes, as though the sky was falling down on top of him.

He scooted over Finley Drive and turned down Cramley Avenue. He noticed a streetlamp flickering ahead, the flashes of light adding an uncertain tension to his already paranoid state. As he approached, the streetlamp gave out a last gasp blink, condemning all around him to darkness, prompting a sharp flutter beneath his rib cage.

His eyes darted to the right, then to the left. He scanned over his shoulder; there was nobody around, just an empty crisp packet bundling along the middle of the road in the chilly breeze. It was one hundred yards to the next streetlamp, so he continued with haste.

Keep moving!

The headlamps of a car driving towards him illuminated the street temporality, before speeding past. Then another. Then another.

He stepped towards the patch of light which spread across the pavement, bursting from the next lamppost along and let out a sigh of relief. A brief moment of comfort that was cruelly cut short.

A car pulled up alongside him, its diesel engine chugging excessively. The sharp squeak of the window being wound down manually made him cringe.

"Aye aye, it's young Tommy," cackled a voice which was now unmistakable, despite the dimly lit street, "are you coming out to play?"

"Oh, alright Shay," Tommy mumbled, stepping back a stride and placing his hands in his pocket.

Despite Shay's large frame hanging out of the car window, he could still make out the angular silhouette of the driver; it was Finn. There was a third body sat in the shadows of the back seat, but it was anyone's guess who that was.

An unusual sense of hatred consumed him, as though it was doused with fear, despair and resignation, leaving him immobile.

"We're just off to *The Grove* for Sunday night shenanigans," Shay beamed, tapping the side of the car with exuberance, "jump in and join us,"

He wanted to run away as fast as he could. But a mirage of Derek laying in the hospital bed scalded his mind's eye; his pasty complexion, crusty lips, the intrusive pipes and tubes sticking out of every orifice. He heard a whisper deep inside his soul. It was Brightwell; *keep doing what you're doing.*

"Sure, why not?" he said, forcing a spring of cheeriness.

Shay jeered and hopped out of the car, pulling his seat forward to clear the way for him to squeeze into the back. He even spotted a surprising grin from Finn, as he bundled his way onto to the seat behind Shay. He fidgeted, trying to buckle his seatbelt, before letting out a harsh cough that grazed the back of his throat.

"'sup, Tommy?" the third voice said, hazily.

He looked up to see it was Cockett slouched in the seat behind the driver, holding a joint out towards him.

"No thanks, I'm good. My asthma is on the edge at the minute,"

Asthma? I don't even have asthma!

"Let's move, Finn," Shay commanded, slapping the dashboard in front of him, "we've just got to stop and take care of a bit of business along the way, Tommy,"

Tommy gulped, wiping his moist hands across his thighs.

"Cool," he just about mustered, despite his dry, heavy

181

tongue hindering his speech.

The car sped off into the night. Cannabis fumes, loud music and raucous laughter filled the air. A few sets of blurry traffic lights later, Finn cranked the handbrake up after pulling up in the car park of the old, abandoned bus depot on Shelby Road.

The bus depot hadn't been used for years; in its place now stood a building on its knees, barely holding up its flaky, corrugated roof, infected with poisonous asbestos. The boarded-up doors meant that multiple smashed windows provided various access points to whatever the building was needed for on demand; a skag den, a solicitation spot, a playground for the feral and now of course, a place just outside for the O'Clearys to take care of business.

The car park and surrounding areas were desolate tonight, but for a couple of cars left stranded on the road. He noticed upon arrival that one car had no wheels and instead sat on short piles of bricks.

"And now we wait," Finn sighed.

"I'll skin up another zoot then," Cockett gassed, the tip of his previous joint barely extinguished as he tossed it out of the car window.

"What's that smell?" Shay bellowed, "It smells like ammonia or something,"

"What the hell is ammonia?" Finn yapped.

"Cat piss," Cockett said, his eyes heavy, almost closing.

Tommy stuttered, "It's a toxin, you find it in bleach or mould or... cat piss yeah,"

"Woo," Shay jibed, "Mr. Ammonia over here,"

"Well, there's mould right there on the back seat," Finn said, a mischievous smirk cracking his otherwise glum face, "just where you're sat, Tommy,"

Oh, great.

"How's it going with you and our Darcy then?" Shay

queried.

He froze, wondering if she had told her brothers about their falling out. And if she had, he was desperate to know how much she had said.

"Yeah, good thanks. You know how it is,"

"I think I can hear wedding bells," Shay teased.

He found himself torn between continuing the charade that they were dating, something that the O'Clearys had dreamt up, or whether to try and softly diffuse the hearsay before it got out of hand and they called in the wedding planner.

"Well I don't know about that, we're good mates that's all,"

"Whatever you say Casanova. Just don't go hurting our baby sis... or else."

Shay's words were matched with a firm, unwavering scowl from Finn through the rear-view mirror. Tommy swallowed the unruly pressure being applied, nervously breaking eye contact to stare out of the window.

As Cockett neared completion of his masterpiece, a set of headlamps caught their attention. The bright lights pulled into the car park, stopping dead on the opposite side. He could just about see the beginning of the registration and that the make of car was an *Audi*. But the combination of darkness, mist and Finn's muck ridden windscreen made visibility of anything else near to impossible.

The lights flashed twice.

"Show time," Shay said, stepping out of the car and yanking a bag from the footwell. He slung it over his shoulder before adding, "keep the engine running little brother."

Shay slammed the door shut and marched over towards the mysterious car.

"What are we doing here?" Tommy quizzed, his eyes straining to see what was happening.

"What have I told you about you and your questions?" snapped Finn.

"We're making an exchange with the Chemist,"

"Cockett!" Finn yelled.

"What? Give the kid a break, man," Cockett breezed, "You've been riding him hard, Finn. It's time to chill out, he's cool. Aren't you, Tommy?"

"Yeah, I guess,"

Suddenly the faint but familiar sound of a siren grew increasingly louder. A flicker of blue could be seen up high, swirling across the reflective windows of the office blocks a few streets away.

Oh bugger, the police!

"Keep your cool," Finn said, calmly.

He flicked off the car lights and Tommy noticed the *Audi* do the same, almost simultaneously. In a flash the siren became more than a faraway noise and some distant blue shadows on a wall; a police van appeared, screeching around the corner and onto the road which stretched across the front front of the bus depot car park.

Tommy could feel his heart gallop, gaining in speed and velocity, in keeping with a locomotive steam engine locked on an unfinished track, possibly about to plunge into the heart of an unforgiving ravine.

He held his breath, alarmed by Cockett's relaxed aura.

The police van was almost at the entrance to the car park; siren whirring and worping, gears crunching and grinding, engine roaring and raging. He closed one eye, gripping his door handle so tight that the perspiration on his palm squelched, as adrenaline thumped against his ear drums.

Seconds stuttered by until he was able to let out an almighty sigh of relief, gawping with shallow breaths as the police van zoomed on by; *yet another crisis to attend to within the Granville community.*

Finn cackled wickedly, whilst Cockett rolled his thumb over his lighter three times, before the grating flint finally caused a spark to light his pristinely formed spliff.

"Close one, eh?" Cockett said, tapping him on the shoulder reassuringly.

"Here we go," Finn asserted, readying himself in his seat.

Peering around the front seat and through the dirty front windscreen, Tommy could see Shay making his way back to the car. The tiny, amber glow of his cigarette was just about detectable through the gloom, as he took a final drag before discarding it with a flick of his fingers.

Once the surge of danger had settled to a more manageable level, it dawned upon Tommy that he had just been part of a drug deal and that the drug was most probably *Charge*; the same drug that had put his brother in a hospital bed battling for his life.

He was twisted with conflicting emotions. His body wanted to explode with infuriating anger and vengeance. His trembling bones told him he was fearful and trapped and to hide. His head was telling him to be smart and play the long game as Brightwell would want - *wherever he was*. He knew he was more likely to end up in a hospital bed next to his brother if he dared to cause a scene here.

Shay jumped in the car, his bag in tow, before Finn sped off towards their destination; Sunday night shenanigans at *The Grove*.

CHAPTER THIRTY

The atmosphere in *The Grove* was bouncing, even on a Sunday. He supposed it didn't really matter what day it was, if you didn't have to get up for school, college or work in the morning, as was the case with most the people in here. Whilst it had its obvious and serious risks, there was no escaping that crime paid well, especially drugs, so it was no wonder to Tommy that a large proportion of Granville's youth pursued it as their career of choice. Although ironically, there was no amount of choice involved at all; it was a case of a lack of other options.

Repetitive ringing lingered inside his ears, as the DJ played a variety of loud, high tempo tunes, not your average easy listening which might be associated with a weekend wind down. Folk danced on the tables, carefree and happy, or so it seemed.

After several drinks, none of which he had to pay for, a stint of painstaking karaoke and a bar brawl resulting in two men and a woman being escorted from the premises, he had decided it was time to make his exit. Shay and Finn were preoccupied with endless chat and boisterous camaraderie now, or so it appeared. All that he needed to do, was figure out a way to skulk out of the door unseen, so not to be denied his departure.

As he finished his pint of lager, he felt a buzz inside of his pocket. He pulled out his phone and saw a text from his work friend, Charlie:

21:20

"Tommy, just locking up. I've got
your wages, can we meet?"

He contemplated why Charlie would only just be locking up the café at this time, but that thought quickly dispersed in favour of getting his hands on his fortnightly wage
packet, which would be depleted having only worked one
shift, but every penny counted.

He composed a message to reply with:

21:21

"Great. I'm actually in town
now, where shall I meet you?"

21:24

"Meet me at the corner by Mojo's
Burgers. Let's go nxt door 2 Edward's."

Edward's Lounge was Granville's attempt at quirki-
ness, with retro arcade machines and 9-ball pool tables. It was
a regular haunt for those who weren't yet old enough to be allowed into drinking establishments and unfortunate enough
not to carry the genes to look even around the age of eighteen,
but who still wanted that feel of going out and socialising in
a place that arguably resembled a bar in the town centre; the
music, the layout, the ambience.

Tommy was pleased, he now had a legitimate cause
to leave his gang of frenemies, in case he got accosted on the
way out. Fortunately, he didn't need it. He waited until Finn
had disappeared yet again to the toilet with *Tortoise* Pete
and Pullit, and with Shay now cornering another victim and

chewing their ear off with his relentless stories, the coast was clear for him to sneak towards the door and make his exit.

The walk to Mojo's was barely three minutes, Granville was handy like that he supposed. A small town centre meant that everything was always in close proximity, something one could feel extra benefit from on wintery nights like tonight. The downside to a small town of course, is not being able to move a muscle without somebody knowing about it.

The streets and cut throughs were quiet tonight, contrasting to the party atmosphere he'd left behind in *The Grove*. He was thankful for the space to think, still struggling with the conflicting thoughts he had around spending time with the O'Clearys, as though they were best buddies. It just didn't feel right. Plus, the added disappointment that he could now add *accessory to a drug deal* within the experience column of his CV.

As he strolled down Docker Way, subtle yet soothing tones eased his tension somewhat. He smiled, chucking thirty pence into an empty guitar case as he passed through, the busker playing one of his favourite songs perched in the back doorway of the Mayflower restaurant: *Step On My Old Size Nines – The Stereophonics*.

Turning the corner, he approached Mojo's, the smell of greasy burgers and fried onions whistling their way up his nose. He then saw the unmistakeable image of Charlie; drainpipe jeans, a Parker coat, with his ever-present rucksack strapped to his back. Tommy watched as he flicked a cigarette onto the floor, the golden embers spiralling through the shadowy night, before he extinguished its life with the sole of his Converse trainer.

"Here he is," Charlie yelled.

"Thanks for texting about my wages, mate. I'm skint,"

"No worries at all," Charlie passed him one of the familiar small, brown envelopes which contained their wages in cash. "Come on let's go to Edward's, it's freezing. I phoned up before I left the café and reserved us a pool table,"

"Are you sure you want humiliating after a long shift?"

The few beers he'd sunk this evening had triggered his competitive side, but Charlie laughed and took it in good spirit.

"Now, now, young Tommy, we'll see about that,"

They picked up the pace towards Edward's Lounge, which was down at the quieter end of Brook Street.

"How was it today?" Tommy asked.

"Ok this morning," Charlie sighed, "but mind-numbingly quiet this afternoon,"

"Nightmare. How come you stayed open so late then?"

Charlie hesitated and appeared flustered all of a sudden.

"Erm, Tony wanted me to give everywhere a deep clean, you know how grim the place can get,"

"Ok, cool," Tommy mustered, sensing that something seemed a little off, he was just unsure as to what.

They approached Edward's Lounge to be greeted by none other than Barry the doorman, from the Junction pub, lighting up the street with his bright orange, high visibility bouncer jacket and trademark smile.

"Evening, Tommy," he said.

"Hello Barry, what brings you up here?"

"A bit of a crisis to be honest with you, Tommy," he explained, "another kid has OD'd on that *Charge* stuff and they're in a bad way. So, basically our gaffer has been given orders to put a doorman on every pub, club, bar and social venue across Granville, until this is squashed. And we're on a strict search-before-entry policy,"

"Jeez, another person? That stuff is lethal," Tommy responded, feeling a little desolate.

"I know," Barry sighed, "and listen, I'm sorry to hear about your brother. He's a good kid, I hope he pulls through,"

"Thanks Baz, that means a lot,"

"Hey, I mean it. Now what is it tonight, few games of pool?"

"It's going to be a masterclass, that's what," Tommy boasted, attempting to walk in through the glass doors.

"I'm sorry, but rules are rules lads," Barry put his huge hand out in front of him apologetically, "I'm going to have to search everyone who comes in tonight, that includes you two,"

"Don't worry," said Tommy, stepping to the side co-operatively and raising his arms, "we get it, don't we, Charlie?"

When Charlie didn't respond, Tommy turned to see what was going on, but his work friend didn't look too good. The colour had drained from his cheeks. His knuckles appeared white, almost splitting through the skin, as he tightened the grip on each of the straps of his rucksack. Tommy was confused, as Charlie then took a couple of shuffled steps backwards and began stammering to get his words out.

"Sorry, Tommy," he eventually mumbled, scratching his jawline and struggling to make eye contact, "I've just remembered, I've got somewhere I need to be,"

Before he could respond, Charlie was already frantically pacing his way back down Brook Street. He was at a loss for words momentarily, before finally the cogs managed to start turning.

"Are you ok, Charlie?" he called out after him.

Charlie cocked his head over his shoulder, not stopping for a second, "I'm fine, honest. I'll see you next week at work. Sorry again,"

First a secret meeting with Ryan *the Hat*, now running for the hills at the prospect of a door search for *Charge*. Something wasn't lining up straight with Charlie, his actions had started to arouse Tommy's scepticism and he didn't like what it was telling him.

"Well, I guess I won't be coming in to play pool after all," he sighed.

"You don't need me to tell you what spooked your mate, do you?" Barry insinuated, with a concerned expression.

"Yeah, I think I know exactly what spooked him, that's what worries me,"

"Just be careful, Tommy,"

"Yeah, I think I might need to be,"

"You look after yourself now, ok?" Barry comforted, with a parting fist bump, as per his usual style.

"See ya, Barry," he said, forcing a smile, despite his mind pulling him towards cynical, sinister thoughts, "good to see you."

CHAPTER
THIRTY-ONE

After grudgingly fraternising with the enemy for a few hours on Sunday night at *The Grove*, on top of the bizarre turn of events with Charlie outside Edward's Lounge, an overwhelming sense of guilt and worry had consumed him. He was beginning to lose himself in this myriad of heroes and villains; he no longer felt clear on what was right and what was wrong.

This, coupled with the mild trace of a hangover, meant that he chose to skip college on Monday morning and instead take advantage of the quieter visiting hours at the hospital. He spent time with Derek and tried to make sense of his role in this terrifying circus, perhaps at times even justifying his actions to his unresponsive older brother.

By the time Tuesday's registration came around, he had some explaining to stumble through with his form tutor regarding his no show the previous day. Upon hearing about his unfortunate family situation, he appreciated that his tutor did seem to allow empathy to lead the conversation, which afforded Tommy some breathing room.

It didn't last long however, as Miss Cartwright was less forgiving given that he'd skipped her double maths lesson. In order to keep on track with their plan, she had sanctioned him to complete an hour's mandatory study session after college, on a day of his choice this week.

He'd decided upon today, Wednesday, as Kirsten had dance rehearsals and he didn't really want to go home right away, given that he and his mum still weren't seeing eye to eye at the minute.

He zipped his jacket up tight to his chin as he left college, the sky blackening by the second. He reflected upon the study session and realised it wasn't as bad as he had anticipated. Miss Cartwright had left him some work to do, as she had other commitments, so he scribbled his way through it at his own pace. Mr Gibbons had sat at the front of the class appearing to be more interested in reading his *Guns and Ammo* magazine, than taking any notice of what Tommy and his fellow detainees were doing.

When the clock struck 4:45pm, Mr Gibbons had waved them off in less than enthused fashion and so the five culprits of sloppiness bolted for the exit towards their freedom.

He arrived home unsure of how he had got there. He'd spent the bulk of the journey internally, pacing around his own mind, blindly trusting that one foot would step in front of the other and safely take him to where he needed to go. To his conscience it had almost been like instant teleportation from college to his front door, yet his sub-conscience had journeyed far and wide. Past, present and future. Up, down and all around.

An unusual yet subtle aroma of winter spices greeted him as he entered his house, shutting out the bitter chill which had followed him home. As his nose followed this peculiarly pleasant scent into the living room, he slowly digested what lay before his discombobulated eyes. He was left gobsmacked to find a tidy lounge, cleaned and dusted, with a scented candle on display, its glow holding centre stage upon the wooden coffee table.

There were no empty bottles cast aside, no mountain of cigarette butts and ash, no unopened mail, no stale smells and perhaps more surprisingly, no mum growling at him.

He heard a shuffle coming from the kitchen.

"Hi, son,"

There was pain, humiliation and vulnerability in his mum's quivering voice. Having spent so long as the recipient of her scornful quips, it felt strange to walk into the house without the need for his guard to be firmly locked into place.

"Hey, Mum. What's all this?"

She tucked a stray strand of hair behind her ear. He noticed it had been washed, brushed and half tied up. She was dressed; a long, tartan over shirt with a black vest top underneath, some clean jeans and a pair of slippers on her feet. Her sleeves were rolled up, her cheeks flushed.

"Well, I think it's well overdue that I had a little clean and tidy up around here, don't you?"

"Yeah, I mean, it looks great,"

"Thank you," she said, humbly, "how was college?"

Wow! Stop the press...

"It was ok, thanks. I'm still struggling with my maths, but my teacher is helping me,"

"Oh, I didn't know you were struggling, why didn't you say anything?"

"Ah, well I guess it never really came up,"

His mum coiled up, cringing with embarrassment he presumed. That wasn't his intention, but he wasn't going to pander to protect her from his harsh, daily reality that she had not only been oblivious to for so long, but also a colluder in its reign.

"I'm sorry, Tommy," she mumbled, before turning back into the kitchen and slipping her hands into some yellow, rubber gloves.

He wasn't sure what had instigated this apparent revival, or at least what appeared to be the early stages of one, but he wasn't about to complain.

He wondered if it had anything to do with Derek. He hoped it did, as that would mean deep inside, underneath the disturbing trauma and self-destructive behaviour, there was still the faint pump of a mother's heart.

He heard the quiet crackle of the radio as his mum turned the dial in search of a station. She settled of *Radio Seaside*.

"Oh, I love this one," she said to herself, humming the unmistakable melody of *Step into Christmas* by *Elton John*.

"I'm sure they start playing these songs earlier and earlier," he shouted back into the kitchen.

His mum laughed, "I know, it was only Halloween last week,"

He didn't have the heart to tell her it was actually over a month ago. He just wanted to revel in this moment of calm and normality.

As the sound of Christmas faded out, being replaced by an all too familiar modern pop hit, a knock sounded at the front door. He leapt to his feet and darted across the living room to answer. Turning the stiff Yale lock, he yanked the door open towards him and peered through the gap.

"Mind if I come in?" Kirsten gasped, pushing her way past him before he could muster a response. She seemed to be scampering for breath; exuberant, almost wired even.

"Hey, are you ok?" he asked, bemused.

"I don't know," she wheezed, "I've ran over here so let me just catch my breath,"

"Are you not supposed to be at rehearsals?"

"Yeah, but something more important came up,"

"Hi Kirsten," Theresa called, interrupting from the kitchen, "would you like a brew?"

"Hey Mrs D, a tea would be nice please," Kirsten panted. He caught confusion trickle across her face for a split second, he presumed due to the personality transplant his mum had undertaken.

"Do we have milk in, Mum?"

"Yes, I called at the shops earlier today after I went to the hospital to see Derek," she said, scrubbing the kitchen sides down as she spoke.

He smiled, his ears picking up the gentle flow of life trickling back into his mum's soul from a distance.

"Tommy, we need to talk. This is mega," Kirsten exclaimed.

She now had his undivided attention. The breathlessness had him intrigued, the fact she had missed rehearsals had him surprised, now her serious tone jangled his nerves, making him concerned.

"Let's go upstairs," he suggested.

"I'll just grab my cup of tea off your mum."

The steaming cup of tea arrived promptly a minute or so later. Tommy offered to carry it up the narrow staircase, recognising that Kirsten had her bag on her shoulder and a plastic wallet in her hand containing a document of some sort.

Once the tea was safely placed onto his bedside table, they crashed onto his bed, eagerly facing one another. He felt his eyes bulging and his hands were restless, desperate to know what was so urgent, yet fearful for what she might reveal.

"What's going on with your mum by the way?" she asked.

"Kirsten! What is it?"

"Sorry, yes, that can wait,"

Kirsten took a deep breath and momentarily closed her eyes, gently pushing her hair away from her forehead before she began.

"So, I started doing some digging on my laptop, during my free period today. I was trying to see if I could fill in any gaps about this whole Chemist conundrum you've been sucked into. To cut a long story short, I entered some of the key names into a search engine on the internet and as I scrolled, I stumbled upon this,"

She reached for the mysterious piece of paper inside the plastic wallet.

"It didn't sit right with me how pushy he was being, and I think this might explain it," she added.

"Who?" he fired back, his stomach cramping.

"Brightwell," she said, turning over the piece of paper and dropping it into his lap.

He picked it up and slowly brought it closer to his face, almost until it was touching his nose, his eyes scanning every detail as fast as they could.

It was a print-out of a newspaper article dated around about ten years prior; the headline read: *Girl, aged 5, dies in Granville Blaze.*

He read the article carefully. Once he finished, he looked up at Kirsten, "I can't believe Brightwell lost his daughter," he wobbled.

"Poor girl. Poor guy," she said, sadness pooling at the base of her eyelashes.

"No wonder he seems lost,"

"It gets worse," said Kirsten, her words prickling the hairs across his upper back.

"Of course it does. It always gets worse," he said, resigned.

"Now read this article,"

She passed him another newspaper print out, he snatched it uncharacteristically, rushing to see what it said.

He felt his mouth drop open, followed by a delayed explosion inside his chest. A thousand thoughts bashed and bruised his brain in an instant. He struggled to comprehend what he was reading and what it meant for him; he was in the middle of a tragic story with revenge still to be served.

He read the last paragraph again. Then again out loud.

"Despite condemning evidence, a strong alibi acquitted the main suspect, Stephen O'Cleary, of the petrol bomb attack on the property of Mr Brightwell and his family, causing the death of 5-year-old, Ellie." He looked up at Kirsten, "You've got to be kidding me?"

CHAPTER
THIRTY TWO

"So, this explains it," he blasted, pacing around his bedroom, which at five paces wide didn't really provide him with anywhere near the adequate stomping ground he needed right now.

"Explains why he's been so pushy you mean?" Kirsten probed.

"Yeah. Pushy, obsessive, inappropriate. I had a hunch that he had a grudge, that part seems so obvious now looking back. I just never would have thought it would be because of something like this," he contemplated momentarily, "I can't say I blame him; it's unthinkable what's happened to him and his family,"

He paused and took a fleeting glance at the articles once more, before slapping the pieces of paper against his face in frustration.

"What are we going to do?" she asked.

He dropped back down into a slump on the bed and put his head in his hands. Kirsten shuffled over to him and placed her arm around his shoulders, rubbing tentatively backwards and forwards.

"I think I need to speak to him and find out if he can keep me safe first and foremost. He's been making decisions and plotting schemes that have put me in real bleedin' danger, when he's probably not even thinking straight. He could be blinded by the purest strain of revenge there can possibly be. I mean, when he's telling me to get in there with the O'Clearys, is he considering the collateral damage, or does he even care for that matter?"

"Tommy, look at me," she commanded, oozing reassurance, "of course he cares. He's one of the good guys, remember? This is going to be ok, lets phone him and see what's going on,"

"You're right," he conceded, recognising that aimlessly squawking wasn't getting him anywhere.

He picked up his mobile phone, searched for Brightwell's number and hit call. His hands were trembling slightly, making navigating through his phone a trickier task than usual.

He let out a heavy sigh as the call went straight to voicemail. He tried again, but the same disheartening outcome greeted him. He noticed he'd started to nibble at his nails, a habit he thought he'd left behind him pre-teens. Deflation was about to take over once more.

"Why don't you try the station?" Kirsten suggested, hopefully.

"Great idea. I've got his card somewhere,"

He jumped to his feet and began rooting around in his top drawer for Brightwell's card, amidst old batteries, copper coins, pens and a range of other random things that he'd probably never use again, but somehow found them too difficult to part with.

He then remembered it was in his coat pocket, having tried to use it to call him from the phone box on Sunday. Upon finding the business card, he cracked a smile and punched in the telephone number for the police station, entering Brightwell's unique extension number on cue.

"It's ringing," he said.

A female operator answered. Tommy cleared his throat to speak.

"Hi, may I speak to Detective Brightwell, please?"

"What's it regarding, please sir?" the operator responded, assertively.

"It's to do with one of his open cases that I am involved in,"

"I'm sorry sir, Detective Brightwell isn't here at the moment," she hesitated, "and he isn't working any open cases,"

The strain from his bewildered eyebrows twisted the frown lines across his forehead in all kinds of different directions, as he struggled to comprehend what he had been told.

"That doesn't make any sense. I need to speak to him urgently,"

"I'm sorry, but Detective Brightwell is on a period of administrative leave. I can pass you on to one of his colleagues if that would help?"

What the hell?

Covering the mouthpiece of the phone with his hand, he frantically tried to mouth the jaw-dropping revelation of Brightwell's enforced absence to Kirsten, who appeared to be struggling interpreting his mimes.

"Look," he continued on the phone, "I'm sorry, but I am in way too deep here; this is serious, serious stuff. I'm only seventeen. Brightwell has been my contact; I don't know what to do. I'm far too involved with this case; I don't feel safe. I'm too close to it," Tommy pleaded.

"Yes, well, you're not the only one from what I can gather,"

"What's that supposed to mean?"

"I'm sorry, I shouldn't have said anything. Detective Brightwell isn't around. I can put you in touch with another detective or otherwise I'm afraid I can't help you,"

"Well, then I guess you can't help me. Thank you for your time."

He ended the call and threw his phone onto the bed.

"What's happened?" Kirsten quizzed, grasping at his

wrists to keep him still for a moment. Her confused facial expression matched the alarm he detected in her voice.

He exhaled strongly, "Apparently, Brightwell is on administrative leave and isn't working cases at the moment. I'm right in thinking that this means he's suspended, yeah?"

"I think so, yes," Kirsten surmised. "That is so strange. I mean, what does this mean for you now?"

"I've no idea,"

"It's ok. We'll figure this out,"

"There was something else," he pondered, attempting to vigorously rub some much needed wisdom through his skull and into his brain, "when I mentioned that I was too close to the case, she said I wasn't the only one. Now, I'm no Sherlock Holmes, but something isn't sitting right here,"

He began pacing the floor again, as if his carpet wasn't thread bare enough.

He continued, "I get that he's got a personal vendetta against the O'Clearys, jeez who wouldn't have with that godawful tragedy that happened to him and his family? But now it's obviously stretched beyond the professional boundaries or whatever they call it. So, somebody at work must have found out, dobbed him in and he gets put on leave. I can't believe he didn't tell me he's been suspended and still sent me out there with those lunatics; he told me to keep doing what I was doing, bold as brass. Anything could have happened to me,"

"That is a pretty shady move," Kirsten agreed, "but thankfully you're safe; that's the important thing in all of this,"

"I guess you're right," he said.

"Hey, I know I'm right, I always am, aren't I?" she gushed, cheekily, before holding her arms out to offer him a hug. He smirked. Yet as quickly as he stepped into her embrace, he stepped out again.

"Do you think he's been getting me to work this whole Chemist angle off the record so he can have a pop at Stephen O'Cleary?"

"Shiiiit!" Kirsten blurted, extending her vowel considerably as a chord seemed to strike, "Maybe that's it. I mean you said yourself, his eagerness made you feel uncomfortable. Now we know a bit more it seems to make sense as to why he was so fixated on the O'Clearys,"

"I'll tell you one thing; he got me into this mess, now he's damn well going to have to get me out of it."

He scooped his phone up off the bed and tried to call Brightwell's mobile number again, only this time it rang. His eyes widened upon hearing the dial tone and he nodded towards Kirsten to let her know this could be the breakthrough. It continued to ring. He was on the cusp of hanging up, when the dial tone ceased, and somebody answered. A bolt of trepidation surged through his body.

"Hello, Tommy," Brightwell said.

CHAPTER THIRTY-THREE

As Tommy approached the McDonald's on the Pembrook Retail Park, he realised how thankful he was that Brightwell had suggested this as their meeting point; somewhere public. To him, the bright lights of the infamous Golden Arches signified safety, happiness and, most importantly, hordes of people at 7pm on a Thursday.

It wasn't that he didn't trust Brightwell, at least he hoped he still did. But he'd been burned before, by the most fireproof person he could have ever imagined: Jack. He had flashbacks to that fateful night visiting the gym unbeknown what was waiting for him. He ignored the uncertainty and scepticism which had niggled him back then; he wasn't about to repeat history.

He believed his murmuring suspicions were of course founded in learning of the horrifying back story that Kirsten had discovered and the added dimension that Brightwell's compromised emotions had led to his suspension, which he'd failed to mention as yet. He was beginning to recognise how desperate Brightwell must be and he knew all too well that desperate people are willing to carry out desperate acts.

When they spoke on the phone last night, he thought Brightwell had seemed cool and composed, so he didn't want to rattle his cage by firing relentless questions at him. He didn't know where to even start about the death of his daughter. Instead, Tommy had just requested that they meet up to discuss the O'Clearys. After all, he still needed Brightwell's help to climb out of this spider's web he found himself tangled up in; the last thing he wanted to do was spook him.

A fluttering heartbeat and a jangle of nerves irritated him, as the speech he had prepared on the walk over here seemed to be completely erased from his conscience. It was like GCSE time all over again, only this time it wasn't maths equations and an exam hall he was walking into, it was to confront a policeman about a potentially life altering issue. In case his assertive approach to question why Brightwell had been hiding the suspension from him didn't go to plan, he knew that he had some information about the O'Clearys to share – the drug exchange for a start – and he also had the threatening text messages to fall back on from the mysterious phone, which he had brought with him. He also wondered if Brightwell had even heard about Derek's situation.

The automatic door juddered open as he arrived. He was immediately struck with the distinctive whiff of McDonald's fast food; juicy cheeseburgers and salty fries, making his belly grumble. His hands tingled and turned a mild shade of pink, once the contrasting cold was greeted by warm blowers above the door.

Laughter filled the air as children chased each other round, innocently playing with action figures that had been plucked from their Happy Meal moments earlier.

Through the crowded foyer area, he spotted Brightwell enthusiastically wave over to him from one of the booths situated by the window. As he approached, he saw a cup of coffee on the table with the lid, two open sugar packets and a wooden stirrer discarded onto a napkin. There was also another drinks cup sat on the table.

"Here, Tommy, sit down. I took a wild guess and got you a strawberry milkshake," Brightwell announced animatedly.

"Thank you," he replied, sliding into the seat opposite. "Good guess by the way,"

It was strange to see Brightwell out of his more formal attire of suit jackets and pants. Granted, he hadn't always looked the smartest, with a loose tie or an untucked shirt, but seeing him in jeans and a hoody humanised him somewhat. He was unsure if it was really his dresswear that did that, or whether it was now secretly knowing how tortured he must be, every single day, after suffering such heartbreak.

He took a sip of his milkshake, straining to get the cold, thick mixture into his mouth through the narrow straw. He thought about what to say, how to even begin the conversation. Words gathered towards the tip of his tongue, but none seemed forthcoming in forming a spoken sentence.

"Listen, before we start," Brightwell began, relieving Tommy temporarily, "there's something I think I should tell you,"

He noticed Brightwell fiddling with the wooden stirrer in his hands as he took a few seconds to compose himself. Whilst Tommy came here to confront him, he now felt uncomfortable – guilty almost – for doubting the detective's intentions, when here he was, potentially about to declare his suspension and not to mention possibly share something deeply personal and no doubt emotionally distressing.

Brightwell cleared his throat, "About ten years ago, I lost my daughter in a fire. I say a fire, it was a petrol bomb attack on my house. My baby girl got trapped in her bedroom and I couldn't save her. Nobody could." His eyes filled like lagoons of raw emotion, as though his tragic loss occurred ten minutes ago, as opposed to ten years. "Anyway, I'd recently blown a case wide open, it was before I made detective when I was still a bobby; loads of contraband was seized, they reckoned it was quarter of a million pounds worth of illegal cigarettes and tobacco; it was back in the day when runs to Europe was a big money earner. Turns out it lost Stephen O'Cleary and some other people a lot of money. Cut a long story short, he got nicked. He was bang to rights, he had form for petrol bombs and all that stuff, we had evidence, but a witness came forward late on and gave a rock-solid alibi. Case was overthrown, he got away with it and I've never been able to forget it."

Tommy suddenly became very aware that this was all supposed to be brand new information, not something he had read in an archived newspaper article the previous evening. He was trying to seem shocked, empathetic and casual all at the same time. He was conscious about everything; where to place his hands, where to look, whether to take another sip of his drink. His heart went out to Brightwell, he seemed so sad.

"Ah man, I'm so sorry to hear that. Must be awful," he said.

"Thank you. But life goes on, I guess," Brightwell snuffled, "anyway, the reason I'm telling you all of this is because this whole thing with the O'Clearys has stirred up some bitter feelings for me. I've perhaps crossed the line of objectivity that's required as a police detective," he paused awkwardly, "So, I've been suspended."

Thoughts again shot to appearing surprised at this apparent new revelation.

"Oh. Ok," he said, waiting an appropriate amount of time for it to seem like he was digesting this information for the first time. "And where does that leave us then? I'm worried for my safety now that I'm hooked in with the O'Cleary brothers to be honest, and Darcy isn't exactly my biggest fan either,"

"I know, I know. You've got to trust me though, Tommy. We're almost there, you've done more than you could ever know. Keep doing what you're doing. We'd have been nowhere without you. I've got people inside the team working this case, friends of mine; Ellie's godfather to be precise. I'm keeping things moving from a distance, just because the bosses don't think I can do my job, doesn't mean I can't chip in from afar. Just a little while longer and you'll be free and that horrible *Charge* stuff will be off the streets, as well as the bastard O'Clearys,"

Despite being roused by Brightwell's rallying call, he couldn't help but feel as though his role in proceedings was being a tad over-exaggerated. He wasn't sure what he'd actually done, other than confirm that the Chemist and the O'Clearys were in cahoots.

"Just doing my bit," he mustered.

"You had me worried you weren't going to commit to helping at the start of all this," Brightwell confessed.

He thought for a moment; *why did I commit?* Then he remembered Seb lying there in the hospital bed, he thought about the threat of Smiler from those unexplained yet agonising text messages and of course, he now had his brother's life in the balance as extra motivation.

"Do you know who the Chemist is or how Smiler is connected?" he asked, unable to resist delving deeper into the hive of danger, regardless of the fear which followed him around.

"We think so," he said, "but it's best if you don't,"

"Ok, if you say so,"

Brightwell snapped the wooden stirrer in two and dropped it into his empty coffee cup.

"It's warm in here isn't it?" he said, zipping down his hoody a little, "I'm just going to nip to the toilet,"

As Brightwell slipped out of the booth and turned to head to the toilets, Tommy saw something which caught his attention. He recognised the brand logo on the shoulder of the black hoody that Brightwell was wearing, but he couldn't quite place it. It was a luminous crow emblem, an unusual label that he'd spotted somewhere prior.

Oh my god, I've seen that before!

His eyes were flickering yet fixed on Brightwell's back as he trudged off to the toilets through a small crowd of people, almost in slow motion. He'd seen that exact sight before and as it registered where and when, and perhaps more poignantly what that meant, a shiver of ball-bursting fear rushed from his toes right the way up to his ears.

He stuffed his hand into his pocket and retrieved the mystery phone that the hooded man planted on his possession during his hospital visit, when he attempted to see Seb. He stared at the phone, then took one last look up at Brightwell's dark hoody with the unique crow emblem, before it disappeared behind the toilet door. There was no mistaking where he'd seen it before.

Surely not? Brightwell was behind the text messages all along?

He began to flap, his heart was ready to burst out of his chest, his mind frantic, his eyes looking around the room for a way out. He struggled contemplating why Brightwell would do such a thing and what he could possibly have to gain from tricking him into believing Smiler was still haunting him. Then his words from a moment earlier hurried to the forefront of his mind; *you had me worried you weren't going to commit.*

He slid out of the booth and darted towards the exit. He couldn't believe that Brightwell would be so callous. He knew he was desperate, but this was beyond a mere bending of the rules. He had cruelly toyed with his emotions; it prompted awful flashbacks and the unnecessary revisiting of some horrendous trauma, not to mention living for weeks on end not knowing when somebody might tap him on the shoulder and send him to meet his maker. All so he would pledge to help him close a case and gain closure on his own personal cause; both things that had started as nothing to do with him, yet he now found himself trapped within, beyond reprieve.

At the exit, a silent force stopped him in his tracks; he had to be sure. He opened the phone and started to type out a text message:

19:22pm

"Hello,"

He waited by the door; eyes fixed on the entrance to the toilets waiting to release the message at just the right time. The door opened and he caught a glimpse of Bright-well's face through the glass panel and hesitantly pressed send.

As Brightwell closed the toilet door behind him and glanced over towards the now empty table, his hand moved towards his pocket. He looked down and pulled out a phone. Tommy's heart exploded; his faith in mankind taking yet another shattering. Brightwell appeared to be unlocking the phone, when suddenly he looked startled. Tommy watched as the detective's eyes zipped around the room. Then, their stare eventually met.

Brightwell yelped what sounded like *Wait!* But Tommy had already bolted out of the sliding doors. He dodged a couple holding hands who told him to *Watch it!* He turned to look over his shoulder, only to see Brightwell hunting him down. As he turned back to face in the direction he was running, a white car screeched up in front of him and let out a whopping honk of its horn. He slapped both of his hands on the bonnet keeping him upright, before waving to indicate he was sorry. As the car sped off, Brightwell had almost caught up to him. They were locked in a stand-off, around five metres apart.

"How could you?" he screamed.

"Tommy, please, I can explain,"

"I don't even want to hear it, you tricked me!"

"I know," Brightwell conceded, his tone softening, "I know. And I am so ashamed of myself for that. I am truly sorry for putting you through it,"

"Do you have any idea what I've been going through? I've been fretting about Smiler ever since that day that *you* planted that phone on me. I've been hanging around with thugs worrying if I'm going to be beaten up or forced to take drugs. My brother is lying in-"

He stopped; his whole body prickled, culminating at the top of his spine in an overwhelming feeling of astonishment. He tried to speak but no words would come out. He felt tears fill up his eyes and freefall down his cheeks, yet his face remained completely still, staring at Brightwell, not wanting to believe what his thoughts were telling him. He backed away a few paces.

"You?" he said pointing his finger, "You did that to my brother? You gave him *Charge*, didn't you? You knew he would take it; you knew what it would do to him and you knew that I would do anything to avenge him. That's how you made sure I would fully commit to your cause, you absolute psycho,"

"Tommy, please, I swear-"

"No! Keep away!" he yelled, drawing attention from passers-by heading towards their fix of unhealthy yumminess, or shooting to catch the 19:35 movie at the *Odeon* cinema, "You stay away from me!"

Leaving Brightwell glued to the tarmac, he raced away into the night towards home. He didn't stop running until he reached the corner of his street, before his legs gave way and he slumped against the wall of, the currently unoccupied, number forty-two. An unrelenting outpouring of tears, emotion and snot descended upon his jacket. He wiped his eyes and nose with his sleeve, only for it to be replaced by more seconds later.

He couldn't believe how he'd been played. In that moment, having spent so many years battling against self-pity, he finally yielded and allowed it to consume him.

CHAPTER THIRTY-FOUR

Following a few minutes without tears or snot, he gave his face one last wipe and dragged himself to his feet. He shuffled down the round past the never-ending block of Accrington brick terraced houses towards home, neck slouched, carting the weight of his world on top of his exhausted, fragile shoulders.

He entered his house, only to be greeted by yet more disappointment. He sighed and shook his head, before letting out an ironic chuckle, delirium overriding his short-circuiting emotions.

In stark contrast to the previous evening of candles and cleanliness, the living room appeared as though a bomb had exploded in there. The house was in darkness, with visibility only possible due to the kindness of the streetlamps and the stark moonlight bursting through the tattered blinds clinging to the kitchen window. There were empty cans and bottles discarded on the floor, the stale odour of cigarettes had returned, cushions were cast aside and, the cherry on the cake, what appeared to be a blackened teaspoon sat on top of the remains of some tin foil on the coffee table.

He flicked the light switch, however there was no response. He walked into the kitchen and the same happened again.

No electric, great.

As the thoughts of a warm shower and an early night dissolved, he dashed up the stairs to fill his ruck sack with yet another supply of spare clothes and essentials, straining his eyes in the corners of the house that the external light sources failed to stretch to.

He bundled downstairs and into the kitchen to pour himself a glass of water. Upon passing the fridge, he noticed a piece of paper pinned up by the chipped Newquay magnet, a gift which Jack had brought him back home, following his holiday there, perhaps seven or so years ago.

He snatched the paper away from the fridge and held it up at the back window towards the moonlight; it was a note. He took a sip of his water and attempted to process what it said.

Sorry, Tommy.

Now on the one hand he felt this was typical of his mum. Typical that she would give up at the first sign of a craving or any remote difficultly and race back to her selfish ways. Typical that she would leave the house like this. Typical that she would be so thoughtless with regards to her actions.

Sorry. Sorry for what? Sorry for the state of our home. Sorry for being a woeful mother. Sorry for being a heroin addict and an alcoholic who burdens everybody around her. Sorry that I can't help you with Derek. Sorry that I won't be coming back. Which was it?

He felt his nemesis, self-pity, gurgling at the back of his throat, waiting for another chance to pounce and smother him. But he composed himself and took a deep breath, suppressing those defeatist thoughts to focus on the one positive; it was the first time she had ever left him a note.

He turned the page over and scribbled his response, pinning it back in the same place using the magnet he was so fond of. He picked up his bag and headed for the door, slamming it behind him, before breathing in the freezing cold air until it burned his lungs. He marched up Frampton Road with only one destination in mind.

"Come in, of course," Mrs Cole said, turning side on and ushering him into the house and out of the misery.

"I'm sorry to turn up unannounced," he bumbled, "is Kirsten home?"

"Don't you worry, love," she comforted, "Kirsten's upstairs. And even if she wasn't, you're welcome round here anytime,"

Mrs Cole radiated love and warmth, a characteristic that was rare in his world. As usual, the heating was blasting out to almost uncomfortable temperatures, but he wasn't going to complain. Placing his bag by the telephone table in the hall, he continued through to the lounge, where a roaring fire greeted him and a cosy ambience that he wished he could curl up in and hibernate; hiding from the impending terror, which seemed to have an unrelenting tracking device on him.

He was left by himself as Mrs Cole pottered her way into the kitchen to do the dishes. He always found he breathed a little easier in Kirsten's house whenever Mr Cole was working away on the oil rigs. Not because he didn't like him, for the most part he did, and he most certainly had maximum respect for him. It was perhaps more related to not wanting to screw up in front of him that made him feel uneasy and, ironically, probably more likely to screw up, especially given his blossoming feelings for his first-born daughter.

"Hey, you," Kirsten piped.

She waltzed into the lounge, finishing off tying her hair up on top of her head in a bun, and plonked herself on the couch next to him.

"Hey," he said.

"I didn't know you were coming around; I would have got changed out of my casuals if I did," she joked, yet her blushing cheeks told him that maybe some forewarning might have been preferred.

"I'm sorry, I should have sent a text on my way," he apologised, before lowering his voice a notch, "and you look beautiful by the way,"

The thing he needed most arrived right on cue, as Kirsten's beaming smile illuminated the room, even more so than the glowing fire before them. She manoeuvred herself effortlessly into a comfier position. He spotted that her leg was now resting on top of his, something that his pulse had picked up on too.

"You don't have to whisper," she goaded, "my dad's not here,"

They burst out laughing, but his chuckle dried up way before Kirsten's.

She spoke again, "What's the matter? You've got that haunted look all over your face, what's happened? How did it go with Brightwell?"

"Ah man, where to even begin…"

He proceeded to tell Kirsten what had happened with Brightwell at their McDonald's meet, including the part about him actually declaring his suspension after all, before he'd even needed to tell him what they had found in the newspaper. Plus, the fact he held Tommy in such high regard for the input he'd had on the Chemist-O'Cleary case, which Kirsten agreed seemed a little over the top. Then of course he revealed, with devastation, the crushing news about the phone, the text messages and Derek's overdose, which were attributed to Brightwell in his deceitful revenge scheme, to lure him into helping put Stephen O'Cleary behind bars. Before the final piece of this evening's jigsaw, the state of his house when he arrived back home after sprinting all the way, his mum's rapid return to chaos and not forgetting the lack of electric – so business as usual.

"What. The. Fudge?" she cried out in disbelief, her eyes confuzzled as she struggled to comprehend the latest developments.

"I know, its heavy, right?" he added.

"Ok, first thing is first, you can have a shower here," she asserted.

"I don't want to impose,"

Whilst he really did want to impose, he tussled with his foolish pride, still lugging around with him the complex of not wanting to be looked upon as *poor Tommy*.

"You're not imposing. Believe it or not, I actually like having you around," Kirsten teased, jabbing him spiritedly in the leg.

He smiled and placed his hand on her knee, a gesture he hoped would indicate to her how much this moment meant to him. Their eyes locked in an intimate gaze. He noticed her subtly moisten her plump lips and then gently grasp her bottom one with her teeth, mischief suddenly painting her perfect complexion. He quickly looked down to see if his heart was visibly pumping out of his chest, but his exterior seemed able to conceal his animated emotions. Yet internally he was on fire, his vital organs doing somersaults.

She sat up and moved closer towards him. He inelegantly repositioned himself too and their noses almost touched.

This is it.

The sound of Mrs Cole walking in the room humming a classic *Beatles* tune, prompted him to jump awkwardly and bump heads with Kirsten.

"Ouch! Sorry," he gasped.

Kirsten rolled back onto the sofa and giggled profusely, hugging her midriff and flopping her legs back onto his lap.

"What are you two kids laughing at?" Mrs Cole said innocently, holding a tray in her hands.

"Oh nothing, Mum," Kirsten smirked, managing to catch a breath in between her chuckling. "Is it alright if Tommy takes a shower?"

"Only if its ok with you, Mrs Cole?" he interjected, almost like an involuntary spasm.

"Of course he can," Mrs Cole said kindly, glancing over towards the clock on the fireplace "it's getting late, you can stay over if you like?"

He flashed a peak across the couch towards Kirsten, who had a cunning grin on her face. He looked back to Mrs Cole.

"Are you sure you don't mind?"

"No, its fine. Kirsten will set the spare room up for you. Now stop apologising and make yourself at home," she put down the tray which contained a plate of chocolate biscuits and two fresh cups of tea, before retreating back to the kitchen, "and for the millionth time – call me Judy!"

Excitedly, he reached over towards the tray and picked up one of the cups of tea. He passed it over to Kirsten carefully, before returning to claim his own, along with one of the chocolate biscuits to dunk.

"I can't believe Brightwell was behind those threats all along and he had you believing it was Smiler," Kirsten said, a more serious tone returning to the room.

"I know," he huffed, "It's almost like everyone in my life isn't who they say they are, or they turn out to be a let-down, or both,"

"Not everybody," she assured, "but yeah, Brightwell really has played a stinker here. And to do that to Derek too, jeez talk about calculated. Did he admit it?"

"He didn't need to, he had the same hoody on, and it was written all over his smarmy, scheming little face,"

"What a swine," Kirsten slammed with venom, her ferocious loyalty coming out to play. She took a sip of her drink, before continuing her rant, "And he says he knows who the Chemist is, but won't tell you?"

"Yeah, that's the bit that scares me. He says he does, but crikey, who knows? How do I know he's not the bleedin' Chemist the way he's been going about things?"

"Don't say that, could you imagine? Sending you on a wild goose chase so he could keep an eye on you, whilst he cooks up *Charge* in his garage,"

There was jest in her voice, but he struggled to lighten up enough and laugh.

"That's the thing, with how everything panned out with Smiler last year, I *could* imagine. Nothing would surprise me anymore,"

They paused briefly in a moment of reflection. Unsurprisingly, he had a hunch that they both had their own demons to slay, casting back to that frightful turn of events. He knew his troubles were there for all to see, but Kirsten never really talked about her experience of those excruciating few weeks of cat and mouse with Smiler. She was tied up, hit round the face and had repeatedly put her life in danger. But she never mentioned it. He presumed it was because she felt her trauma didn't compare to his, or something like that, which made his heart ache. He couldn't bear to think she could be struggling in silence. Then a reoccurring thought punched him in the gut; everyone he got close to seemed to get hurt.

"Is this all my fault?" he asked, with unashamed tears brimming at the surface of his clouded eyes.

"Don't be daft," she comforted, "Please, Tommy, you've got to listen to me on this one. None of this is your fault. Smiler, Brightwell, the Chemist, *Charge*, Seb, Darcy O'Cleary, her bloody brothers, your brother, your mum; not one single thing there is your fault. You've done your best to do the right thing at every step of the way, so don't look for blame when it's not there. If you look hard enough, you can convince yourself to take responsibility for just about anything,"

"Thank you," he sniffled.

"Are you going to be ok?" she asked, softly.

"I really don't know. I mean, does all this mean that Smiler isn't even in the picture? Has he disappeared for good? Or is he still watching from afar, in the darkness just waiting for a moment to strike? And what am I supposed to do about Brightwell, or the O'Clearys for that matter? I can't exactly go to the police, can I? I'm just so scared and confused,"

"Aw, Tommy," she placed her cup of tea onto a coaster on the side and switched positions on the couch again, this time swinging her legs down to the other end and nestling her head into his rib cage. He placed his arm over her shoulder and gently caressed her waist. "We'll figure this out," she rallied, gently tapping his chest, "Remember, you're not on your own."

CHAPTER
THIRTY-FIVE

He slid his door key into the lock at home, before closing his eyes and saying a little prayer. He wasn't religious by any stretch, if anything he was a little sceptical of the whole thing. But he did believe in a higher power of some sort, the fact he was still alive told him somebody must be looking down on him from time to time. Well now he was calling upon whoever it was, to give him the guidance and strength to deal with whatever was facing him behind the door.

Despite waking up in the comfort of the Cole residence and having Kirsten's company for breakfast, the first breakfast he'd eaten in weeks that wasn't a cheap chocolate bar, the day had quickly turned sour. He couldn't escape thoughts of Brightwell and cynical ideas of the whole town being corrupt, and any person born from their mother potentially being culpable. He bumped in to Finn O'Cleary at break time who, in typical fashion, ordered him to meet up with the gang tonight at *The Grove*; he'd nodded in agreement at the time, but secretly he had plans to avoid that at all costs, perhaps with a sudden breakout of the flu, or a sickness bug, or a migraine or whatever other illnesses were currently doing the rounds.

He had dashed to see Derek after college. Having some alone time with his brother was nice and peaceful to begin with, but an overwhelming sense of the reality they found themselves in had smashed into him like a truck; his brother was likely to die, any day now, just like the rest of the victims of a *Charge* overdose.

Derek had defied the doctors so far with his fighting spirit, something that Tommy thought he'd smoked away into non-existence over the years, but he was still hanging in there, clawing at every single breath he took. Day by day this had triggered sparks of hope for Tommy; *maybe he will come around.*

But whilst visiting earlier, his hopes were slashed back down to their very roots, as his brother had another seizure. It occurred in the midst of updating an unconscious Derek on the latest happenings in this twisted tale of ever-devouring deceit. The sight of his poor older brother helplessly thrashing around, whilst practically chained to the bed with wires and tubes, had knocked him sick to the pit of his stomach. The nurses had barked at him to leave the room, but he just stood there; frozen, helpless, guilt-ridden.

On the walk home he couldn't get that image out of his mind. He missed Derek so much, more than he ever would have imagined. He thought back to times gone by, when he had wished the skies would fall down on his mum and brother; when they had messed up, or left him in a pickle, or embarrassed him, or let him down over and over again. His chest had filled with regret and it was yet to drain away.

Please come home Derek.

He pushed open the door and his heart lifted slightly. It was the smell that hit him first; it was a fragrant lavender today. The door opened smoothly, no junk mail, take away menus or free local papers to bulldoze through behind it. He went to close the door behind him, but his attention strayed as he noted the cleanliness had returned and he couldn't hide the grin that crawled from ear to ear. Another candle was flickering upon the coffee table, omitting scented goodness into the usually ghastly polluted air. His mum had never fluctuated from bad to good to bad to good so quickly before; *maybe she really did want to change?*

"We're in here love," his mum's familiar voice shouted.

Who's we?

He dropped his bag on the floor and hesitantly walked into the kitchen area, at which point his chin plummeted to the ground.

What was she doing here?

"Hi, Tommy," Miss Cartwright cooed, propped against the kitchen worktop, nursing a mug of coffee.

"Hello, Miss," he mumbled, "what are you doing here?"

"Ha!" his mum cackled, "I told you his face would be a picture, didn't I?"

They both chuckled, like a pair of familiar acquaintances. His whole body stiffened up.

"You certainly did, Theresa." Miss Cartwright confirmed. "Well, Tommy, I'm here because firstly I wanted to see how you were getting on with our study plan, seeing as you don't come to see me anymore,"

"Miss, its barely been a week since we sat down and wrote the thing, give me chance," he shunned.

"Don't be cheeky, Tommy," his mum interrupted, flashing one of her infamous dagger glances his way, "your lovely teacher has come all this way to see how you're doing,"

"Thanks, Theresa, but its fine, honestly," Miss Cartwright explained.

"Ok, well then, I guess I'm doing good," he snapped, "thanks, bye."

He felt a rush of scorching redness fill his face. On one count he was so relieved his mum had cleaned up and she was actually having a good day, which up until two days ago he was beginning to think he'd never experience again. But he still felt so embarrassed, ashamed and uncomfortable at having a teacher visit his house.

"That's good to hear," she continued casually, "I've

also come here to meet your mum,"

"Oh, isn't that nice, Tommy?" his mum gushed.

He offered a sarcastic smirk, still unimpressed by this invasion of his own, private base camp.

"Yes," Miss Cartwright continued, "I'm a big believer that students should be supported at home, as much as they are in college,"

His stomach tightened as he clenched his teeth almost to the point of shattering them. He noticed his mum had become a little less composed too, fidgeting with the last remaining ring on her finger, the rest of which had been sold or pawned over the years and never retrieved. Her eyes had set off, darting around the room, as though seeking something out – probably her cigarettes.

"No problem with that here, hey Tommy?" his mum stammered.

"Is that right, Theresa?" Miss Cartwright asserted, "because from what I can tell, you're not doing anywhere near enough to support this boy through his day to day life, never mind his education,"

Woah, that was harsh.

"Ok, Miss, I think that will do," he clambered. "We're fine here, I'm studying, it's all good,"

He attempted to shepherd Miss Cartwright out of the kitchen, but she wasn't budging anywhere.

"No, it isn't," she demanded. "You're a waste of space, Mrs Dawson,"

His mum's eyes transformed in an instant; however good today had been for her, it was now over. Bitter, twisted and angry Mum was emerging, the one he knew so well, blazing with fire out of the flowery meadow she had managed to occupy, trouble-free, for the short amount of time Miss Cartwright had been here. And for once, he didn't blame her.

"What have you been saying?" his mum barked at him, "What lies have you been spilling at that college to this trollop you needy little swine?"

"Mum, I swear, I-"

"Leave it Tommy," Miss Cartwright commanded, "you think I can't make my own mind up, Theresa? Your son is so blinded by loyalty to you he thinks that even with your flaws, that you still love him and you do your best,"

Miss Cartwright was irate, almost frothing at the mouth. This was the most surreal thing he'd ever experienced; he was aghast.

What was she trying to do?

"You don't know shit about me or my life," his mum defended, reaching for a cigarette out of the pack and heading towards the fridge.

"Actually, I know just about everything there is to know about your life,"

He stepped back in complete shock as his mum and his maths teacher went toe-to-toe. He was unsure what Miss Cartwright's aims and objectives were here, it seemed as though she was trying to make things better for him, but by badgering and baiting his mum this way, she obviously didn't know the situation as much as she was making out.

His mum poured herself a pint glass of white wine and took two defiant gulps, almost draining the vessel of its contents.

"Try me," she provoked, beginning to swagger around the place, in the way he was so used to.

"You blame the world for your problems. You had something bad happen to you when you were younger, I don't know what, but you use that to escape responsibility for anything and anyone, including your kids. Am I getting close? You're too busy getting smacked up off your chops to notice the smart and beautiful young man that is dragging himself up in front of your scornful eyes,"

Her words stung, stirring an innate protective instinct deep inside of him. He knew what she was saying was accurate, scarily accurate if the truth be told, he'd told himself the same thing time and time again; his mum was a wreck, but she was *his* wreck. For Miss Cartwright to have the audacity to enter his home and attempt to belittle and destroy his mum this way, especially on one of her good days, was something he couldn't stand by and watch.

"You teachers think you know everything, ha! Try living in the real world, Hun," his mum dismissed.

"You mean the real world where you get given up for adoption? Where you free-fall through the care system, stopping at every hell hole along the way; living with abusive foster carers, crying yourself to sleep in violent residential homes and finding yourself almost on the brink of homelessness by the age of thirteen? You mean that world?"

He was flabbergasted, this whole situation had obviously touched an extremely sensitive nerve for Miss Cartwright. And whilst he felt anger towards her and her actions, he secretly nursed an even greater, if paradoxical, respect than before for his teacher. Having gone through all of that and still making it out alive was impressive, never mind becoming a successful teacher.

"Bullshit," his mum said flippantly, drawing her cigarette and letting the ash crumble to the floor.

"Typical response for somebody unwilling to accept reality,"

"Woah, woah," Tommy called, stepping forward into the middle of the conflict, his bias always swaying to protect his mum, "time-out guys. Miss, I'm guessing you mean well, although your methods are a little strange. You've said some really hurtful things, things that are private for me and my mum. I think it's time to go, don't you?"

"Oh no, I'm just getting started, Tommy,"

Miss Cartwright seemed different. Her glamorous poise had dissipated, being replaced by an aggressive demeanour and a snarl to match.

"Don't come in here, preaching to me about how to be a mother, ok?" his mum snapped back, as he watched on, hesitant to try and intervene again. "We've had a tough ride, alright, but we're muddling through. Now if you don't mind, I don't know who the hell you are, but can you leave my house, before I get somebody to make you leave?"

She took a purposeful drag of her cigarette that radiated arrogance. Ordinarily, when he was on the receiving end of this attitude, he would be tearing his hair out. But now, he was strangely basking in his mum's boldness.

"I'm not finished. All your life you've only cared about yourself, regardless of who gets hurt along the way. Go on, tell me I'm wrong,"

Right, this is getting beyond the joke now.

"Miss, please, just leave, this isn't helping!" he exclaimed.

"Yeah, get the hell out of my house" his mum added, "I don't know who the heck you think you are, you crazy bitch,"

"What's the matter, Theresa?" Miss Cartwright mocked, slamming her mug on the kitchen side, her eyes now wild, "Don't you recognise your own daughter?"

CHAPTER THIRTY-SIX

"Pardon?" he asked timidly, breaking the never-ending silence which had fallen upon his home.

He'd subconsciously moved closer to his mum and now had his arm out in front of her. They'd retreated a few paces until their backs were pressed against the sink, which sat before the kitchen window.

Miss Cartwright had transformed into a tiger that was stalking its prey, confident and dominant, prowling the centre of the room.

"Go on, tell him," she said, goading his mum. Her eyes were incensed, bulging to the point of explosion; he'd not seen her blink for what seemed an eternity.

"Tell me what?" he gibed, "You're off the scale loopy, Miss. Get the hell out of our house, now!"

He turned to glance at his mum for backup, but she appeared to be frozen, cowering almost, entrenched in fear. Her usual complexion was pale at the best of times, not seeing the sunshine that much will do that to a person, but she had turned an odd, pasty shade of yellow. Her blueish lips were wobbling as if she wanted to speak, but no words were coming out.

Miss Cartwright was pacing up and down now, revelling in this perverse situation of control and scaremongering.

"Mum, tell me what? Why's she saying she's your daughter?" he asked gently, turning to place both hands on his mum's shoulders in comfort.

"Is it really you?" his mum asked in disbelief.

"I won't say it again. Tell him."

Finally, his mum cleared her throat, "Tommy, there's something I need to tell you,"

"Come on," Miss Cartwright rolled her eyes, "we haven't got all day,"

"Shush!" he snapped. "Let her speak,"

"When I was younger," his mum hesitated, "I erm, well, the stuff you know about Jim Carruthers, or should I say Smiler, and what he did with those kids," she sobbed.

"Mum, its ok. I know,"

He wrapped his arms around her and squeezed as tight as he could do, without fracturing her brittle frame.

"You know? Since when?"

"He told me. The night he tied us up and was trying to beat information out of us, he told me. He told me you were his first victim. He lauded it up in front of me, like you were some kind of trophy,"

"Oh, Tommy. I am so sorry,"

"Don't you dare apologise for the actions of that evil psychopath," he demanded.

She placed her hand on his cheek, "I can't believe you knew, and you just carried it around with you, you brave boy,"

"You're the brave one," he declared.

Miss Cartwright was agitated, growing impatient, "Oh please, will you just get on with it. I'm about to vomit,"

Ignoring Miss Cartwright's quip, his mum continued, "Well, what you won't know, is that a few of months after I'd realised that I was in an abusive relationship with him, I found out I was pregnant,"

Tommy's body grew numb. He couldn't believe what he was

hearing. Based on what he understood, his poor mother had been through such a horrendous experience, and he was now finding out he'd only known the half of it.

She continued, "I'd received multiple death threats by this point, you know, to keep me quiet about the abuse that went on. He had moved on to exploiting some other poor lasses by this point, I had nowhere to turn. I felt ashamed, guilty and powerless – I still do. I felt so stupid, I just thought I had stomach ache and had put a bit of weight on. Until I went to see a doctor and he told me. I was fifteen and scared for my life. I couldn't be a mother, there was no way. I couldn't face a daily reminder of that sadistic bastard and what he'd done to me,"

His eyes filled with tears as his mum struggled to recall the god-forbidden events from her childhood.

"Before I knew it, I was giving birth. I gave the baby up for adoption straight away; I didn't even find out the sex. As far as I saw it, the less I knew, the less it would hurt and the less he could ever find out. I didn't want that twisted son of a bitch getting anywhere near an innocent baby,"

She broke down sobbing, slamming her forehead into his chest. He shushed and told her it was going to be ok. He lied. He didn't know what was going to happen, but right now, he needed to comfort her and buy some time to process what was going on.

I can't believe I've got a sister.

"Erm, hello," Miss Cartwright shrieked. "That *twisted son of a bitch* is my father and my saving grace. He's the reason I'm alive. As far as I'm concerned, you're the horrible human being in this story,"

"How can you say that?" he baffled, turning to face Miss Cartwright, his mum continuing to wail with emotion.

"This stupid, selfish cow threw me into the system without a second thought," she screamed, aggressively pointing at his mum. He stepped across to shield her from the latest instalment of verbal abuse. "I wanted to die so many times during my childhood, and all the while I wondered why on earth my mummy gave me up,"

"I'm sorry, I'm so sorry," his mum pleaded, her voice quivering with acceptance, as the weight of responsibility took its toll, "there's not a day goes by I didn't think about what I had done, I swear," she paused and wiped her eyes, "and every single time I did, I knew I'd made the right choice,"

"You bitch. You still maintain you did the right thing? Unbelievable. And taking me home with you to raise me as your daughter and be part of a family would just be too unthinkable, would it?"

"Yes, it would!" his mum screeched, "With Jim Carruthers lurking in the picture, anything would have been better than him,"

"Oh really? The same Jim Carruthers who tracked me down and found me? Who took me out of the care system and placed me with my Uncle Hugh and Auntie Doll. The same man who came to see me once a week, at least, without fail from the moment he plucked me from hell, to the day I graduated university – which he supported and encouraged me to go to, by the way,"

"You don't know the things he's done," his mum trembled.

"Tommy, go and shut the curtains in the front room," Miss Cartwright summoned coldly, reaching for her handbag, "we're going to be here a while,"

Fear rattled his bones, painfully crushing him into submission, as he saw what his teacher slowly withdrew from her bag. Her face was joyously crazy; somehow, she had begun to enjoy this. He watched as she licked her lips, holding up the blade, light shimmering from its reflection. She wrapped her fingers comfortably around the black handle of the large kitchen knife and let it flop down by her side, as though it was a mere extension of her right arm.

There was hesitation in his movements, reluctant to leave his mum in the kitchen by herself, but Miss Cartwright spoke again, and this time she meant it.

"Now."

"Ok, ok. I'll shut them,"

Shuffling into the front room towards the lounge window, he carefully began to draw the curtains, starting with the left-hand side. Feeling completely at a loss, he scrambled to regain his composure. Miss Cartwright was ready to lose it all here, there was no way back from this.

Think, Tommy. Think!

Out of the corner of his eye, he spotted that he hadn't closed the front door when he'd first arrived home. There was a cool draft, but the way things were heating up in the kitchen, it had gone unnoticed. He was about to stretch his arm out of the lounge towards the door and close it, but a flashing thought stopped him. Maybe if he left it ajar, somebody might pass and hear the commotion.

Eagerly glancing back into the kitchen, he saw Miss Cartwright circling his mum, teasing her with the knife, the image of a classic bully. All those years of suppressed pain and unanswered questions were about to burst out into an act of rage, and it seemed as though there was nothing he could do about it. He thought about making a run for it, fleeing out of the open door. But how could he leave his mum?

As he moved across the front window towards the right-hand curtain, he spotted a fancy car outside. Fancy cars weren't often seen on Frampton Road and if there were, they were usually cutting through, not parked up. This one caught his eye immediately; it was shiny, new and expensive.

Logic told him that the car belonged to Miss Cartwright; college teaching must pay rather well after all. Then he took a closer look and spotted the make of the car. It seemed familiar, the model, the colour, the registration. Inside, anxious pennies were dropping everywhere, as if somebody had up-ended a cash register filled with the currency of his deepest fears. The car was an *Audi* and he'd seen it before.

Surely not?

CHAPTER THIRTY-SEVEN

"What did you study at university?" he quizzed, slowly making his way back into the kitchen, reluctantly returning to the hostility.

"Ah, that's sweet," Miss Cartwright patronised, "a little bit of brother and sister bonding already?"

"If you say so,"

"I have a master's degree in pharmacology and my teaching qualification is in mathematics,"

Holy moly, it is her!

His stomach churned leaving an unbearable queasiness lodged at the back of his tongue. A thousand thoughts and endless what-ifs sprung to life, messing with his conscience. This didn't seem real, or possible for that matter. It didn't make sense. She had been so nice and supportive; she had wanted him to succeed. And now within the space of fifteen minutes she had become his evil stepsister, sent to Granville to continue her dad's despicable business.

He tried to collect himself, wiping his perspiring palms on his jeans, "Oh, that sounds difficult. Teaching pay well does it?"

"Why, are you finally thinking about a career, Tommy?" she teased.

"I might be,"

"Tommy, what's going on?" his mum whispered, clutching at his arm, "I'm scared,"

"What your son has shrewdly figured out *Mother*," Miss Cartwright blasted, "is what I'm really doing here in Granville, haven't you Tommy?"

"Well, I don't know about that," he said, "I never really figured this mystery so-called-genius would be a girl to be honest, or that my teacher would be happy killing kids as a little earner on the side line,"

"Don't try me, Tommy. When you can kick-ass as much as I can, gender and age are irrelevant,"

Her words were venomous, he imagined she'd been beat down so much as a kid, that one day she eventually fought back, and she probably hadn't stopped fighting since. *Abusive foster carers and violent residential homes*. It was no wonder she saw blurred lines when it came to the treatment of others.

"Look, what do you want?" he asked, as his mum shrank behind him even more, almost attaching herself to him. If it was possible, his mum was another twist in the tale away from climbing inside his skin and using it as a protective cloak.

Despite his front, his apparent assertiveness was out of his control, he felt detached from his actions in a surreal dissociating moment. In truth, he was shuddering to his core, switching glances between Miss Cartwright and the blade, which she was toying with deliberately. But his mum was scared and at risk, so instinct must have taken the wheel.

"This is going to sound a little crazy," Miss Cartwright laughed.

"From you? Surely not?" he ridiculed, before tasting instant regret.

"Don't be a dick," she growled. "I want you to leave with me. Start over,"

He spat out an over-exuberant laugh, which made his mum

jump.

"Is that why you paid extra attention to me at college? What planet are you on, seriously?"

"Hear me out, I know it sounds mental. Me being in your house with a knife probably doesn't help," she gushed, creepily.

"Oh, so you do realise what's going on here and how frigging psychotic it is? Because for a second, it sounded as though you didn't,"

"You need saving, Tommy. Just the way I did. I can see it so clearly; this place is no good for you. You'll die before you've even reached your prime,"

He screwed his face up and offered another imploring glimpse at the knife.

Was that a threat?

"Ok, maybe not physically," she continued, her eyes and tone softening, "but mentally and spiritually. I can offer you a new life, I've got money and opportunity. We're blood, you and me. We're like two peas in a pod, you're bright and intelligent, you just need somebody to look out for you, instead you've got this waste of oxygen here,"

She flicked the knife towards his mum and her bitter scowl returned.

He was utterly dumbfounded at what she was suggesting, it was borderline fanatical; wanting blood to spill one minute, and keen to play happy families the next.

"So, you wanted to what? Recruit me at college? Come here and kidnap me? Expect me to go willingly? Kill my mum? What?"

"I came here, to try and open your eyes," poison had returned to her tone as she visibly became frustrated, "I wanted you to see that I can offer you something that our stupid mother can't. She's had seventeen years to prove herself to you and you're still wavering. Of course, I didn't want to kill her initially. I hoped you would see the light and come peacefully. I might have to now though. I've already got that retarded brother of yours out of the picture,"

"Wait, what?" he said, stepping forward aggressively.

"Woah, easy boy," she mocked, raising the knife and stopping him in his tracks. "Yes that's right. Ah, poor Derek was easy work. I only had to send one of my boys in to see him and it was like taking candy from a baby. Actually, no. He said it was easier than that. One vague promise of the thrill of a lifetime and he was off to the toilets as quick as a greyhound, bless him."

"Why would you do that?" he cried.

"Because he was a distraction. He's the same as her, empty promises of getting better, they were only ever going to let you down and hurt you,"

"You horrible, horrible woman!" his mum screeched, finding her voice.

"Theresa, nice of you to join us," Miss Cartwright played, sarcastically, "we were just talking about how messed up your kids are, great job, you go girl,"

"So, it was you who stitched Derek up? Not Brightwell?"

"Brightwell?" she exclaimed, "that silly police detective who doesn't know his arse from his elbow? Oh please, that guy is so blinded chasing a fool's errand, he doesn't know what day it is. Obviously, it was me. I did it for us Tommy, so we could break away and be happy as brother and sister, taking on the world together,"

Her voice had turned hopeful and obsessive and it was beginning to freak him out. Panic quickened his pulse, throbbing at the pressure points around his body. Images of Derek, suffering on his own at the hospital, flashed before his eyes. The distant sound of occasional cars drifting past his inconspicuous house, oblivious to the vindictive actions going on in inside, amplified the panic; there was no way out.

Grasping his mum's hand in his, her cold, clammy and lifeless skin contrasting against his warm, moist palms, he took a rebellious stand.

"You're not going to get away with this," he vowed defiantly, frustration crippling his inner rage, leaving him feeling helpless and weak.

"Ha, sure," she chuckled, "I'll take it as a no then, you don't fancy a better life?"

"I'd rather burn in hell," he voiced, frothing through gritted teeth, still wary of the ever-moving knife.

"Well you can say hello to your brother, then can't you? Because you just made a big mistake crossing me, Tommy. I tried to save you; I tried my best. I even kept my dad away from you, whilst I undertook this operation. But you know what, you've made it perfectly clear that you don't want anything to do with me. So, that puts you in the same category as *her*,"

Tears began to sting his eyes after her callous remark about Derek, leaving him questioning whether she knew something that he didn't. She had fire in her eyes, yet ice running through her veins.

"So that's it is it?" he barked, shielding his mum a little more. "Your dad sent you to Granville to do his dirty work, did he? Sounds like real hero,"

At that point, his vision was drawn through the kitchen doorway and the lounge, towards the front door. He saw the flicker of some hair peeking outside the door frame, which just as quickly popped back into hiding at the base of the stairs; somebody was in the house. Tommy hoped to all and sundry that it was somebody able to assist him and his mum but, knowing his luck, it was more likely somebody to lend a helping hand to Miss Cartwright, an O'Cleary perhaps.

Keeping his eyes fixed on his newfound stepsister, he did his utmost not to spook her.

"Deary me, how wrong you are, little brother," she mocked, "He sent me? No, no, no. I approached him. I came up with the chemical compound for *Charge* around the same time you botched his retirement plans to escape into the sun. I've always been a believer in fate, and this miracle drug was a sign from the Lord himself,"

"Satan, more like," he coughed.

"Very funny, Tommy. Anyway, I took this idea to him, I told him it was my gift, call it a homage to his services, payback for everything he'd done for me," she emphasised, ogling at his mum. "He tried to talk me out of it, but this time I insisted. And I told him that I was going to be the one to deliver upon the potential power of *Charge*. I was going to be the one who returned the grip of this stinking town to its rightful Master,"

"He is a disgusting paedophile!" his mum yelled.

Miss Cartwright slammed the point of the knife into the kitchen worktop with destructive force, splitting it right to the edge. He gulped, the reality of the situation registering now more than ever.

"He is my father, and he is a good man," she said, irate and dishevelled, "We're each other's everything. He saved me from an unthinkable life, like an angel sent from above, and in return he says I have brought him a happiness he never thought existed; I am his pride and joy,"

As she was drifting into the fantasies of her own warped existence, he spotted that the hair had appeared again, creeping around the lounge door frame, only this time it was accompanied by eyes, a nose and eventually a full profile. Tommy's heart bounced as he recognised who it was.

The face brought his index finger up to his mouth and indicated for Tommy and his mum, both of whom were facing in that direction, to be quiet. Tommy tried to stay focussed and keep Miss Cartwright from turning around. Adrenaline pumped through his body like a siren, a siren indicating that help was on its way; help in the form of Brightwell.

He kept his eyes on Miss Cartwright, he would need to entertain her now, to give Brightwell a chance at sneaking further into the house unnoticed. He knew that she was far from finished in glorifying her master plan in front of them, so it shouldn't be too difficult.

"So, basically this whole *Charge* thing was your idea, but you needed daddy's permission?" he antagonised.

"It was my idea, my plan and I only needed *my* permission," she thundered. "My dad put me in touch with a few people, that's all."

"You mean like the O'Clearys?"

"You catch on fast," she smirked, "plus an old contact of his at the college to get me on the payroll there and ensure I was teaching your classes, no questions asked. I meant what I said earlier, I genuinely wanted to give you a way out, a fresh start,"

"Jesus, this town knocks me sick the amount of corruption that goes on," he preached.

"Face facts, Tommy. The town and its people do what needs to be done to survive. There are no rights and wrongs, there's just what is. You passed on a ticket out of here, remember?"

"Screw you!" he bellowed. "What about all the people that have died from taking *Charge*? Those poor kids, gone before they've even had a chance,"

"They had a chance," she growled, "they had more of a chance than I ever had, and they still decided to take drugs and be stupid. Is that really my fault?"

"I can't believe what I'm hearing, you absolute psychopath. You and your dad deserve each other,"

"I know we do, thank you, that's really sweet,"

Her condescending tone infuriated him.

She continued, "So, once I had my contacts in place, all that was left for me to do, was settle into my new home, meet my new acquaintances and get to work. And that is when the Chemist was born."

CHAPTER THIRTY-EIGHT

The rain had started to shatter against the kitchen window, wind swirling aggressively as the deep rumbling of a thunderstorm was groaning in the distance. The tense atmosphere inside the house mirrored the outside elements, as Miss Cartwright continued to ramp up the stakes, wafting the knife erratically up inside his personal space. She had stepped in close now, increasing the intimidation. The blade had been so near to his face, he could see his own reflection in it.

"Drop the knife," Brightwell called out.

She didn't even flinch. A calculated smirk branded her ice-cold expression, as she slowly turned away from Tommy and his mum to face Detective Brightwell, finally lowering the knife by her side.

"Well, well, well, if it isn't Detective Brightwell," she charmed. "Why don't you come into the kitchen and join the party?"

Brightwell was tense, crouched almost, as he slowly crept his way forward.

"We can sort this out," he implored, "you just need to put the knife down on the floor,"

"I guess you can find your arse from your elbow after all," she dismissed sarcastically.

"Well if that's the case, this must be my arse and surprise surprise, there's a giant pain in it,"

"Please, less of the dramatics Detective,"

She rolled her eyes with sass and bizarrely started picking at her nails with the twelve-inch carving knife, as though this was just your average Friday evening get together.

"Tommy's right, you can't get away with this. It doesn't end well, I know it and you know it," he pleaded.

Brightwell had his hands out in front of him, palms facing outwards. Crossing his feet carefully, he traversed around the edge of the small kitchen, squaring Miss Cartwright up, relieving Tommy and his mum of the intense smothering that had preceded.

"Don't play the innocent hero act with me," Miss Cartwright demanded, suggestively.

"Tommy," Brightwell said, not breaking eye contact with his target, "are you ok?"

"Not exactly, but I'm glad to see you,"

"Understandable. Theresa, how are you doing?"

His mum couldn't muster the words to answer, as she trembled, her eyes locked on the flailing knife which commanded so much caution.

Tommy could sense what Brightwell was doing, perhaps trying to bring calmness and stability back to the room, but he'd feel a lot calmer once the knife was removed from Miss Cartwright's vengeful grasp. Despite his attempts at projecting composure and the addition of the wintery conditions outside, Brightwell was sweating profusely in this pressure cooker environment; a grey shirt wasn't the most flattering when attempting to save the day.

"Miss, it's over now," Tommy said softly, "the police will be storming through that door any minute. I know you must be angry with the world bu-"

"There's only one person who I'm angry with Tommy, and that is *her*,"

Miss Cartwright became animated once again, stepping into the centre of the room, an attempt at regaining the initiative he supposed, despite the numbers being against her.

She continued, "and for your information, the police will be doing no such thing. This guy is a joke, a loser. They kept him around out of pity, just waiting for the right time to cut him loose. He's not even on duty, so how do you suppose the cavalry will know which door to storm through?"

Silence pierced his ear drums as he yearned for Brightwell to give him a sign that he wasn't their one and only shot at getting out of this. But he remained portrait still, no signs, no tells.

"Who says they're not already here?" Tommy chanced.

"Because they don't trust his judgement, retribution is a bitch for that. They knew he couldn't move on after what happened, so they seized their chance to give him the boot when he started operating outside of the law, to get what he had yearned for all this time. I mean, who can blame him? Hell, he's not the only one to carry a grudge, is he?" she cackled, "Am I right, *Mother*?"

The three of them began to fan out a little, his mum eventually finding the strength to pull away from his protection and hobble a couple of steps to the left towards Brightwell. Miss Cartwright was now the one surrounded, like a caged animal that had tasted the wild, being told that play-time is over.

The tide was turning. Whilst Tommy had to remind himself to breathe, he recognised that the pendulum of control had started to swing their way. Miss Cartwright's face told the story; from considered and dominant, to desperate and dangerous in the space of a couple of minutes. She flashed the knife out erratically towards his mum, then towards him, but missed by a foot or so. Sweat now matted her hair and mascara had smudged across her cheeks; she looked a mess.

"You need to put the knife down," Brightwell spoke firmly, "It's over,"

"It's over, when I say it's over,"

She unleashed a terrifying screech and lunged desperately towards his mum, the knife pointing directly at her stomach. The sound of a tear made Tommy's heart stop, but it became rapidly apparent that his mum had managed to jump out of the way as she bundled into him, returning to the safety of his touch; it was her trailing cardigan which took the hit.

Whilst his mum had escaped on that occasion, her course of evasion had now put her and Tommy in unescapable danger. They were trapped, squashed into the corner of the adjoining worktops, the sink on one side, the kettle and the tea, coffee and empty sugar jars on the other side and the unpredictability of a treacherous Miss Cartwright in front of them.

A disturbing feeling compounded him, as he watched his supposed stepsister pant perversely before him; they were cornered, and she knew it. She lifted the knife and clutched at the blade, ridding it of the stray, black fibres that had caught from her previous swing at his mum's cardigan. The sharp blade nicked her palm ever so slightly, prompting a trickle of crimson blood to be released. Her wicked grin now projected arousal, as she licked her hand clean and prepared herself to strike again, only this time there was no way out.

An image of Brightwell's mouth shouting and screaming blurred into the background. All around him had turned deathly silent as his eyes homed in on Miss Cartwright's face; the purest rage bubbling beyond her pupils, her cheeks were puffy and red, her growling expression told him she was committed to this.

She drew the knife back ready to shunt her arm forwards and condemn whoever got in the way. Tommy grabbed his mum close to his body and span around. Closing his eyes, he turned his back towards the incoming knife, shielding his mum tightly against his chest in an act which epitomised their relationship and the arguable role reversal which had taken place time and time again throughout his life. He was the protector; his mum was the defenceless. The difference on this occasion, it might be for the very last time. There was no thought, no logic, no decision that took place. He just did it.

His narrow existence flashed before his eyes, along with the million lives he was yet to live. In his mind's eye appeared Kirsten's beauty and a surreal peacefulness transcended. After what felt like a minute, but was perhaps more like a second, the sound of a dull thud caused him to open one eye, then the other, and turn around, remarkably unscathed.

What lay before him triggered a potent cocktail of emotion, which he wasn't expecting. His mum let out a horrified gasp, placing her hands nervously over her mouth as tears of relief and sadness trickled down her face, climbing onto her fingers.

Miss Cartwright was sprawled ungainly across the kitchen floor, appearing unconscious. A river of claret blood began to flow steadily from her crown, smearing the formally white, now muck-stained lino. It took Brightwell a few seconds to snap free from the traumatised trance which seemed to have a grip of him momentarily, before he dropped to his knees in search of a pulse.

Whipping his mobile phone out of his pocket, he frantically hit the keypad before nestling the phone in between his ear and his shoulder, continuing to check for Miss Cartwright's vital signs.

"This is Detective Brightwell, badge number DC 743W. I need an ambulance right now to number ten Frampton Road. I've got an unconscious female, aged between thirty and thirty-five, serious blunt force trauma to the head, bleeding from the wound, pulse is extremely weak. Now!" He ended the call and dropped his phone by his side. He placed his ear by Miss Cartwright's mouth, before delivering desperate chest compressions. "Tommy, can you pass me that towel, please?"

"Sure," he said, reaching for the tea towel immediately and throwing it across the kitchen. His body parts were moving, but he couldn't feel a thing; he was numb. "Can I do anything?"

"Just give me some space and keep a look out for the ambulance," Brightwell panted. "Maybe take your mum through there to the lounge, yeah?"

"Yes, I will do," he hesitated, "are you ok? What happened?"

"Not now, please," Brightwell gasped, his breath shortening with every vigorous thump he inflicted upon her chest, not pausing for even a second to look up at Tommy or his mum as they tiptoed out of the kitchen.

A sudden crack of lightning split the sky in two and illuminated the whole house; the thunderstorm had arrived, its anger grumbled as it sent torpedoes of rain crashing towards Granville, with Tommy's house audibly feeling the wrath.

Despite the biblical conditions outside, he exhaled a confused sigh of relief as he moved into the lounge with his mum, teeth chattering and hands rattling. He had survived, they both had. Yet he couldn't help but feel a hollow emptiness inside. Maybe despondency, maybe guilt, maybe grief. Whilst he and his mum would live to see another day, in the other room lay his long-lost sister, now potentially dead and Detective Brightwell gasping for breath, with blood on his hands, quite literally.

CHAPTER THIRTY-NINE

The last few days had presented Tommy with a void, an inability to think or feel, or sleep for that matter. A conflict of thoughts and feelings had consumed not just him, but his mum too. He'd noticed she'd been neither her usual chaotic self, nor her newer-found clean and considerate attempt at playing mum; she'd been vacant.

Receiving confirmation that Miss Cartwright had died was a jagged pill to swallow; feeling relieved that your sister had passed away was such a contradiction, so he couldn't even begin to imagine how his mum was processing her interpretation of what had gone on; the guilt, the shame, the reprieve. When Brightwell visited yesterday evening to break the news, his stay was brief, but he informed them that Jane, Miss Cartwright's real name, had passed away soon after she arrived at the hospital. Tommy had a million questions tripping over themselves on the tip of his tongue, but he refrained from airing them, unsure if he was ready to converse with Brightwell on that level, just yet.

The Chemist had gone, but he couldn't shake the feeling that this wasn't over; the O'Clearys were a forceful entity that weren't going away with and of course Derek's fate remained unknown, yet it was noticeably becoming increasingly darker. He was wrong about Brightwell gunning for Derek in pursuit of his services, but he had still tricked him with the phone and, despite saving their lives, Tommy was lost in a vacuum of betrayal.

Lifting the bucket up to the kitchen sink and emptying the murky, blood-ridden liquid down the drain, he turned on the tap to replenish with fresh, hot, soapy water, readying himself to continue scrubbing away the last remaining trace of Jane's blood, smeared across the lino floor.

It had taken him until today, Monday – three days after the incident, to pluck up the courage and get it cleaned up. His mum had tried to give it a once over with a damp cloth the very same night, but crime scene investigation team had stopped her in her tracks, before her delirium wore off and she left the house without telling Tommy where she was going, only returning earlier this morning.

"Bring me that vodka through here, Tommy," his mum called from the front room.

He huffed, whipping off the rubber gloves, which were littered with holes, so he may as well not have worn them in the first place.

"Really, mum?" he challenged, popping his head into the lounge, "It's one thirty in the afternoon, you've already had three,"

"Don't start with the lectures, I need to take the edge off. The images of her lying there are driving me insane,"

Whilst he could have continued the debate, he recognised it was futile. His mum was so far set in her ways and besides, how could he argue with her stance? She'd found out the daughter she had given up for adoption, the pregnancy being the result of her sexual abuse as a teenager, had tracked her down and tried to kill her, but instead wound up dead in her kitchen. I think every judge in the country would side with granting permission for an afternoon drink or two to take the edge off.

Even if he loathed his mum's approach, it's how she had learned to cope with problems and right now they were all that was operational of the family unit, they needed stability, not rifts over pointless tittle tattle.

"Ok, Mum. Coming right up,"

"Thanks, son,"

She smiled and readjusted her dressing gown, settling back down for her dose of daytime television.

He toddled back into the kitchen and set about fixing his mum up with a vodka and water, a bland beverage perhaps, but more flavoursome mixers were thin on the ground.

A thunderous bang-bang-bang sounded at the door, causing him to almost choke on apprehension.

"I'll get it," his mum offered, uncharacteristically.

He slowly made his way towards the kitchen doorway, and peered his head around ever so subtly, enough to give him a chance at hearing who it was that was almost breaking down the hatches. His mum released the latch and pulled open the door a fraction.

"Is Tommy home?" the voice boomed directly.

He recognised it instantly; *it was Shay O'Cleary!*

"Who wants to know?" his mum remarked, folding her arms.

Their voices were muffled but he could just about make out what they were saying.

"A mate. Now is he in, or do I have to come inside and take a look?"

"You'll do no such thing," his mum ordered. He was now suddenly thankful for the generous helping of vodka that she had consumed pre-noon, as it brought out her valiant side.

"Look, I don't want this to get messy," Shay's voice was growing in volume and tenacity, "so if he's in there, just tell him to come to the door and nobody needs to get hurt, ok?"

"He's at college," his mum sneered, "where he should be. Now if you don't mind, can you get away from my house?"

Tommy peered around the door enough to see the back of his mum, yet still remain out of sight of Shay. She calmly reached inside her dressing gown pocket and withdrew what could only be a cigarette. From what he could tell, it looked as though she was popping it in her mouth and lighting it, as he'd seen her do a million times before.

"Well when he gets back, you tell him I need to see him, right?"

Another voice projected into the scenario, a voice that Tommy couldn't quite place, "Oi, what's going on? She asked you leave pal, now move on,"

"Alright, tough guy," Shay remarked, a subtle shift in volume suggesting he had backed off a little. "Let's just hope I don't bump into either of you or your precious son anytime soon, I don't know, say somewhere a little less public?"

Shay's fading cackle sent chills down Tommy's spine, as he puzzled over who the intervening voice belonged to out on the street.

After inviting the unknown voice in for a cup of tea and closing the door, his mum teased, "It's alright, you can come out now,"

Tommy crept around the corner into the lounge to see his brother's old friend Dorian standing there, in his fatigues, rucksack in tow. Without giving it a second thought, he raced over and threw both arms around him.

"Woah," Dorian said, dropping his bag, "good to see you too, Tom,"

He felt his cheeks flush, "Sorry, just glad to see a friendly face, that's all,"

"Yeah, I can tell," Dorian smirked, patting him firmly on the back before stepping away to give his mum a hug and a peck on the cheek.

"Dorian, what on earth are you doing here?" his mum cooed. "It's so lovely to see you, they must be feeding you well there, you look smashing,"

"Thanks Theresa," he said, his eyes dropping a fraction, "I'm here to see Derek. I got special leave from my squadron leader as soon as I found out,"

"Aw you've always been such a good friend," his mum

said, bending to flick the ash of her cigarette into the ashtray on the coffee table, "I wish he would have listened to you a bit more often, he might have been off saving the world in the RAF now too, instead of where he is,"

"What's happened to him exactly? I've only heard bits a pieces, but you know what the Granville rumour mill is like, it's about as accurate as Piss-Pot Pete playing darts down at the Junction,"

"*Charge*," Tommy declared, "that's what happened,"

"Is that stuff as bad as everybody is saying then?"

"My brother is one of many that have ended up over-dosing. The rest of them, that we know of, have died,"

"Crikey." Dorian scratched his head momentarily, appearing to be searching his conscience for something. "Last time I spoke to him, it sounded like he was doing really well, he was so upbeat,"

"He was," his mum interjected, "wasn't he, Tommy?"

"Yeah, for sure," he insisted. "Look, it's a long story Dorian, why don't you have a brew before you go up to the hospital and we'll fill you in. I'll come with you later, if you like? I can show you what ward he's on,"

"Seems like a great idea to me, visiting hours up there aren't for another couple of hours anyway. Plus, I'm absolutely parched. Get that kettle on, Tommy,"

Dorian offered a cheeky grin and a snigger. Tommy had no objection to Dorian's demands; he'd do almost anything to make him feel at home. His mum was right, he'd been such a good friend to Derek all through growing up together, into their twenties even. He was almost like one of the family and Tommy missed not having him around anymore, now he was working away with the RAF. He was somebody who knew all the complicated intricacies of his family, warts and all, and that brought an indescribable comfort with it.

"You better sit down," Tommy advised, "because this is one big, crazy, rollercoaster ride that you will struggle to believe,"

"Sounds ominous," Dorian chortled. "Please can I bump a ciggy, Theresa? I don't know, just when I thought Granville couldn't get any worse, eh?"

CHAPTER FORTY

Seeing Dorian's reaction to Derek's unconsciousness in the hospital bed earlier, had triggered yet another surge of emotion, just as he was starting to think he had no more tears left. He realised in that moment that he'd become numb during his latest visits to see his brother; his eyes had become accustomed to seeing Derek in this state, his brain blasé when assessing the severity of the circumstances. Yet witnessing the visible heartbreak, the tears and the helplessness within Dorian, reminded him how tragic this situation really was.

He watched as Dorian kissed his brother affectionately on the forehead and listened as he told him with a wobbling voice that he would return the following day to visit again. He and Dorian left the ward together, before going their separate ways upon departing from the main hospital entrance. Dorian had said he needed to go home and shower and besides, he had his own place he needed to be this evening: Kirsten's house.

The coffee was too hot to drink at the moment. It was the third time he'd anxiously tried to take a sip, only this time the piping liquid burned his lips as he attempted to slurp. He carefully placed it back onto the coaster on Kirsten's bed side table, awaiting her response.

"It sounds absolutely awful, Tommy," she eased, gently stroking his forearm.

"It was. It was horrifying," he said, gazing into the space in front of him. "The look in her eyes, her anger, she was riddled with pain. I know it sounds daft, but I felt sorry for her,"

"I can imagine. It's because you're a caring person, that's why,"

"She was my sister," he paused. "I can't believe I've got a sister. Or had a sister. I feel so guilty. And I thought I'd had it rough,"

"I know, I know," Kirsten nodded sympathetically, now squeezing his hand. "You've got to remember that she wasn't well though, Tommy. She was poorly, she tried to kill you, your mum and Derek. You couldn't do anything to prevent this, she was practically grooming you,"

"I guess you're right. I know it's crazy, but deep down I think she cared for me. Yes, it was on a completely bizarre level, but I believed her when she said she wanted to help me. And she also said it was her that had kept Smiler at bay all this time, to protect me,"

"Really?" Kirsten asked.

"Yeah, she told me. I don't know how long that will stand for now though, once he learns of her little accident in my kitchen,"

"Try and not worry," she comforted, before adding, "I know that's easier said than done mind,"

"Well word must have spread already, as Shay O'Cleary was battering my door down earlier looking for me,"

"No way? What did he say?"

"My mum said I wasn't home, but he wasn't happy. He had a real menacing tone. Threw a couple of flippant threats our way too," he paused for a moment. "I'm screwed,"

"Bloody hell. So, what actually happened with Miss, I mean your sister, then? Did Brightwell shed any light?"

"He was a bit vague," he said, "but from what I can gather, once he saw she was going to drive the knife towards me and my mum, Brightwell grabbed hold of her hair and yanked her backwards. She fell and smacked her head right off the end corner of the kitchen worktop. She was out cold, blood pissing out of her skull and that was that. He scrambled to save her life, he did his best, even I could see that. But it was too late, by the time they'd got her to the hospital she'd passed."

He felt further deflation as he broke down the incident yet again, reliving the minor details to their gruesome extent. When images of the scene were creeping around inside his head, keeping him awake the last few nights, it seemed to be another world away, as though his brain had fabricated it, but saying it out loud reminded him how very real it was.

"Well thank heavens he did," Kirsten exclaimed.

Her response startled him a little and shook him free from the misery within which he was wallowing. He looked up to see her smiling at him. She reached up and tenderly stroked his face, before running her fingers through his wavy hair, which was already due another trim.

"I'm glad I've got you," he said, his heart waking up with a mellow fuss.

"Me too,"

Suddenly the deafening shatter of glass shook the whole house and jolted them both to their feet. It was quickly followed by a second, smashing sound and then a piercing shriek from downstairs.

"What was that?" Kirsten choked.

He gulped, "I don't know, but it didn't sound good,"

They both raced towards the bedroom door as the screaming continued from the floor below; it was Kirsten's mum and she sounded distressed. As Kirsten yanked open the door, the acrid smell of burning hit them instantly; there was a fire in the house.

"Mum!" Kirsten cried out, galloping towards the top of the stairs.

"Down here, Kirsten!" Mrs Cole screamed, pausing to make way for a harsh cough. "There's a fire, we need to get out,"

Kirsten began to bundle her way down the stairs, yet Tommy found himself pausing, frozen almost, glued to the carpet which hugged the top step, attempting to process what his eyes were seeing. Already, he could see that the whole of the downstairs was cloudy with thick smoke; the haunting image of Mrs Cole crouching over the telephone table in the hall, desperately attempting to cover her mouth, just about visible. The amber flames had already begun to dance their way out of the lounge, presumably where the fire had originated. Flakes of wallpaper and furniture were rapidly turning to ash, ready to invade the lungs of anybody caught in its path.

This can't be real!

"Tommy! Come on!" Kirsten yelled up the stairs towards him, as she whipped her mum's arm around her shoulder to prop her up.

He quickly got his motor running and fumbled his way down towards them.

"What happened?" he asked, urgently.

Mrs Cole attempted to speak, but her breathlessness was restricting the fluidity of her speech. Her cheeks were shiny and raw in appearance, with black smudging from the carbon smog smeared across her face. A charred smell came from her clothes as they omitted yet more smoky fumes, signalling she had been exposed to the fury of the fire up close.

She took a deep breath, "The front room window... a brick... petrol bomb," before her neck gave up and her head dropped with the swift onset of exhaustion.

The temperature inside the house had almost instantly reached an unbearable level. The hot air scorched his skin, as he came to terms with the fact that this was a deliberate attack, and that he was probably the intended target.

Petrol bomb, the mark of an O'Cleary.

There was no time for deliberation, but he already felt a murmuring of guilt for drawing such a horrific and cowardly act of evil towards Kirsten and her family home.

"Come on," he yapped, "let's get out of here,"

Mrs Cole's eyes were suddenly injected with sheer panic, as she whipped her head back up to face him. She mouthed a word, but he couldn't tell what it was. He glanced at Kirsten as she too now appeared to be weakening. He attempted to usher them both towards the front door, pulling his t-shirt up over his mouth and encouraging them to crouch as low as they could, but Mrs Cole began to convulse in dispute. She opened her mouth again to speak.

"Where's Daisy?" she croaked.

"My sister!" Kirsten screamed, "I thought she was staying at her friend's house tonight?

"No, she's in her room,"

After shaking her head, the whites of Mrs Cole's eyes rolled into view and she became lifeless, slumping into Kirsten, who battled to keep her upright.

"Oh no!" Kirsten trembled.

Horror stained her face like nothing he'd ever seen before, her soul compromised, as she attempted to communicate above the roaring fire and through the murky air. She glanced at the front door, then up the stairs towards the swirling smoke, now engulfing any sign of life from the landing light. Her eyes were screaming at him, he knew what he had to do.

"Take your mum out to the front of the house and stay away from the windows," he ordered. "I will get Daisy,"

"You know which one her room is?"

"Yes,"

"Tommy, I won't be able to live with-"

"Just go, now!" he barked.

He clutched at a bobble hat from the coat rack, held it up to his face and stuffed his mouth and nose inside it, before sprinting up the stairs two steps at a time. As he approached over halfway, he took one last glance over his shoulder and watched Kirsten drag her mum out of the front door, hounded by hellish flames, which now charged into the hallway.

The blaze was yet to climb up the stairs to the landing, but the smoke up there was pitch black and the fumes were debilitating. He cowered down onto all fours and shuffled his way towards Daisy's bedroom, guided by the faint yelp which came from behind her door.

"Daisy!" he shouted, in as friendly and calm a manner as he could muster. "It's Tommy. Everything is going to be ok. But I need you to focus, ok?"

"I want my Mummy," she cried.

"I know you do, darling. And that's exactly who I am going to take you to. But there's a fire, ok? I need you to get a blanket, or something, to put over your mouth, can you do that for me?"

A heinous cough interrupted his instructions to Daisy. It felt as though his lungs were ablaze and that somebody had taken to his windpipe with a band sander.

"Tommy, I'm scared,"

Even with a door in the way, Daisy's voice was so innocent and pure.

"It's going to be ok," he assured, trying to compose himself, but his head was feeling lighter by the second and he was no longer sure if his legs could do what he needed them to do. "When I open this door, it's going to be very hot and very smoky, ok? But don't panic. I need you to crouch down as low as you can, and we are going to head straight down the stairs, towards the front door to see your mummy and your sister. Are you ready?"

He braced himself.

"Yeah," she whimpered.

"Ready, steady, go!"

He pushed open the door as quickly as he could and

peered into the smoulder, which lightly lingered across the bedroom, compared with the rest of the house. A silhouette of Daisy standing there in her pyjamas, with a blanket hanging by her side, buoyed his heart, giving him a much-needed boost of energy and hope. He gestured towards her, indicating that she needed to put the blanket over her mouth. He took her hand and crouched down low, leading the way back out into the cauldron.

As they scampered their way down the stairs, the flames awaiting them at the bottom, now dangerously licking the walls, the distant sound of sirens tickled his ears. The front door seemed so close, yet drawing each and every breath felt like running a marathon. An uncomfortable warmth burned under his clothes; he wondered if he was going to make it to safety before combusting.

Daisy had made it this far, but he suddenly realised he was dragging her more than she was moving herself. She had become limp, floppy almost. He hoisted her up, one arm under her back and one arm under her knees, preparing to carry her the rest of the way, through a corridor of unforgiving smoke and fire.

He staggered a few yards, his legs heavy and jelly-like, as he tightened his grip on Daisy, who by this time appeared to have passed-out. He could feel sweat pouring down his face, the smoke stinging his eyes, the heat torching his face, the fumes poisoning his body. The toughest part of this journey was still to come; getting past the doorway to the lounge, which was the source of the fire by the looks of things, as huge flames were bursting out at short and explosive intervals.

Images of people flashed all around him, unable to tell if they were real or hallucinations, mere figments of his imagination. He saw his mum stood by the front door waving at him, only it wasn't his mum of today, it was a version of his mum from the future; clean and sober. He smiled as he saw his old mentor, Jack, who seemed to be characteristically barking orders at him; *One more round, kid!* And then he saw a huge yellow helmet standing in the open front doorway, having been hammered down by some kind of contraption.

Hazily recognising that the yellow helmet belonged to a fire fighter and that the image was indeed as real as the blaze which surrounded him, relief momentarily surged, but it was short lived. His legs gave way a few metres short of his escape and he crashed to the floor, losing his grip of Daisy in the process.

He strained his eyes but was unable to keep them open long enough to take in what happened next. The last image he was able to capture was a framed photograph, hanging on the wall above him, of Kirsten, Daisy and Mr and Mrs Cole, all smiling on holiday as one big, happy family, before everything turned black.

CHAPTER
FORTY-ONE

The sun warmed his face and the sand lightly scratched in between his toes. Confusion was quickly replaced with peacefulness as he found himself following in the footsteps of a tall, familiar, but, as yet, unidentifiable figure. He trailed a few paces behind on the sand dunes; the bright sunshine causing a shadow leaving him unsure of who it was he was following; he knew he felt safe though. He could hear the seagulls squawking and children laughing. He looked down, his feet looked so tiny, but he was in a daze, blinded by a warmness which felt alien to him.

As they reached the summit of the particular dune he found himself on, he was able to look out upon a rare, tranquil view of the Irish sea, peaceful and still. It became apparent to him that he'd been in this exact spot before.

"What do you reckon, son?" the voice of the man spoke, soothing him.

He looked up to see his dad standing over him. He was screaming with joy inside, yet no words would come out, his jaw stuck together with tar. Joy quickly turned to frustration, as he realised that this had happened before, and he was simply reliving a suppressed yet skewed memory.

Was this a dream?

He was two years old when his dad was cruelly taken

from him, yet in this mirage he must have been six or seven, maybe even eight. As he gazed at his youthful hands, he could still feel the heat from the fire at the Cole residence tingling his skin, despite it now feeling like it happened a million miles away.

"This can't be real, can it?" he asked.

His dad laughed, placing a hand on his shoulder, "No. I always knew you'd be a smart boy. I'm proud of you, Tommy,"

"It's nice here with you. I wish I could stay,"

"I would love nothing more. But we don't make the rules, son,"

"Who does? I need more time with you,"

His dad's mouth continued to talk but his voice had been replaced by a deafening, repetitive beeping sound. He tried to protest, but as he did, the dream became even more distorted and the beeps intensified.

He was waking up.

But where am I?

He felt his eyes begin to flicker, allowing a different kind of light to blind him momentarily, only this time it was the artificial lighting of a hospital ward. The beeps were now present, he could hear them clearly and match them to their origin, the machine towering over him as he lay uncomfortably in a hospital bed.

He'd never dreamt of his father so vividly before and he yearned to return, closing his eyes tightly, but as was the case with dreams, he knew it was impossible to re-enter the same realm now that he had awoken. Then he heard a voice which enabled him to find reason to stay here in the real world and open his eyes.

"Tommy, can you hear me?" Kirsten scrambled, grasping his hand in hers.

"Argh," he rasped, the cannula in the back of his hand causing a sharp pain to shoot up his arm. His lips were crispy and his throat hoarse.

"Oh my goodness, I'm so sorry,"

"It's ok," he reassured, before coughing abundantly. Once his breath calmed and his confusion settled, he was able to continue, "what happened?"

"There was a fire. At my house. You were our hero," she gushed, "that's what happened,"

"Oh yeah, it's coming back to me. How's your sister?"

"She's going to be fine, thanks to you,"

"And your mum?"

"Also fine, she's with my sister now, they're getting discharged soon. But I wanted to stay here until you woke,"

They smiled at one another, the romantic tension building, wrapping itself around his heart and applying gentle pressure. Kirsten had the same clothes on from the fire, her face was still smudged with smoke and yet she'd never looked so pretty. He sensed that she might have wanted to kiss him in that moment, but the ward was busy, and he was kind of glad about that. He'd envisioned their first kiss to be perfect several times over, and not once was he cooped up on a hospital bed with flaky lips, undoubted bad breath and a dozen strangers watching.

"What have they said about me, am I ok?"

"The doctor seems to think you'll be ok too, thank God. They just need to monitor you for smoke and carbon monoxide inhalation, or something like that,"

"Jeez, I smell like a barbecue. Why's this in my hand?" he asked, ogling at the cannula.

"They needed to give you fluids, I think, or pain relief. You had me worried, you big, daft sod,"

Tears formed in Kirsten's eyes, glossing their beauty.

"I'm sure I'll live," he jested.

"You better had, who knows when I'm going to need a superhero again,"

His laughter was cut short by the realisation of why the fire started in the first place. He painfully readjusted himself on the bed, pulling himself upright. Kirsten jumped to her feet to help rearrange the pillow behind him.

"It's all my fault, Kirst',"

"Don't do this, Tommy," she said, stroking his forehead, "we've been over this whole blaming yourself thing. I won't stand for it,"

"I know, but for goodness sake, they could have killed you. And your family,"

"And you. You're a victim in this remember, please don't feel responsible,"

She filled up a cup of water, using the jug which sat on a swivel table next to his bed and brought the straw up close to his mouth, encouraging him to take a sip. They both sniggered, awkwardly.

"Well, it looks like nobody is safe whilst the O'Clearys are still at large," he surmised, resting back into his pillow.

A familiar voice interrupted, "Actually, that's not exactly true,"

It was Brightwell. He approached the bed sporting a cautious grin. He looked smart; clean shaven, tie and jacket and a look of a man who had started to take himself seriously again. A slight tinge of pink in his cheeks and a stumble of his words indicated he might be feeling a little sheepish.

"Tell me something good, please," Tommy pleaded.

"I will, two lots of good news actually. But first, here's some get-well-soon presents," he held out a box of chocolates and a toy fire fighter's badge, before adding, "too early to joke?"

Both Tommy and Kirsten couldn't help but giggle.

"Thank you," Tommy coughed, "but I'm still not sure where I stand with you. You played a horrible trick, Detective,"

Brightwell looked down at his freshly shined shoes. He placed the gifts on the end of the bed and pinched the bridge of his nose.

"Tommy, from the bottom of my heart, I am truly sorry for what I did. It was careless, vindictive,"

"Manipulative," Kirsten interjected, crossing her arms purposefully.

"Yes, manipulative. I still can't believe I did what I did with that phone, I'm ashamed. I don't want to make excuses, but if I can offer any kind of rationale, however wrong, it would be that I have been out of my mind for ten years chasing that bastard for what he did to me, what he took from me. I was blinded by an opportunity for justice and revenge and for a moment I completely lost myself in it. Your sister was right, I am a fool,"

"What happened to you was horrible, Detective," Kirsten consoled, dropping her fiercely loyal stance for a moment and unfolding her arms, "but having said that, you had Tommy and I fearing for our lives. Again. You're supposed to be somebody we can trust,"

"You can. I mean, you could do, and you still can. I messed up big time,"

"What Smiler did to us, that will never leave me," Kirsten revealed, perching on the edge of her seat, "It haunts my dreams to this day,"

This was the most Tommy had ever heard Kirsten open-up with regards to her feelings about Smiler. She seemed vulnerable, yet strong in the same breath. He wanted to jump up and throw his arms around her. And if it wasn't for his wheezing, the tubes tangling him to the bed and the slightly revealing hospital robe, he might have done.

"I understand. And I've no excuse. I can only say I'm sorry, I guess I didn't think it would get so out of hand. I thought it would give you a nudge, not submerge you into this catastrophe. I thought if you believed Smiler was back and involved, you'd want to see the back of him and that would be an incentive towards helping me. I didn't think of the repercussions,"

"Well, your plan worked," Tommy sighed.

"Ashamedly it did. But I swear I didn't do anything to hurt Derek,"

"I know. It was my lovely stepsister, she told me gleefully. I think she was actually expecting me to be grateful in her warped version of reality,"

"I'm sorry about your sister too. I didn't mean any real harm to come to her, I just wanted to protect you and your mum. It was a reflex,"

"Oh I know that, I appreciate you coming to the rescue. Lord knows what would have happened. I think it's safe to say she was a bit of a fruitcake,"

"She may well have been. She was still your sister though, that's big news to discover. So, take it easy on yourself, ok? It might be a confusing thing to get your head around,"

"I guess. I mean, I do feel a bit weird about it all. I just keep reminding myself of what she'd done, what she'd created and cascaded. I can't believe that she was the Chemist this whole time. She basically sent death disguised as Christmas into the lives of Granville's youth, and for what? Money, greed, control? I don't know,"

"Well, I guess we never will, and we never need to know either," Kirsten added.

"Plus, she wanted to kill my mum, there's no doubt in my mind,"

"That's the way I saw it," Brightwell affirmed.

"Speaking of my mum, where is she?"

"She was here for a bit earlier," Kirsten said, craning to take a look around the ward, "but I've not seen her for an hour or so,"

"I have," Brightwell acknowledged, "but I'll get to that in a minute. I said I had some good news, didn't I?"

"Now you've got my interest," stated Tommy.

"Me too," Kirsten added, excitedly.

Brightwell paused, as Tommy felt apprehension bubble up again inside his tummy. He moved over towards the curtain and wrapped it around Tommy's bed, sealing the three of them in a cove of privacy.

"We've got them,"

"Who?" Tommy quizzed, before nursing another shooting pain, this time in his chest.

"The O'Clearys."

CHAPTER FORTY-TWO

"Which ones? How?" Tommy spluttered.

"All of them," Brightwell confirmed, a wry smile creeping its way into view.

The relief which channelled its way through Tommy's body felt more comforting than any medication which the doctors and nurses at St. James' hospital could administer. He sat back for a moment, letting his head rest on the pillow and gazed up at the ceiling. He tried to comprehend what this meant, but he couldn't relax without more details.

"I need to know more, if you don't mind?" he asked.

"I think that's the least I can do, don't you?" Brightwell charmed. "What you don't know Tommy, is that ever since you started knocking around with the O'Clearys, I've had you followed. Some of my colleagues aren't too fond of kids dying from ropey drugs either, so as soon as we knew we had a shot, we took the necessary precautions to put a tail on you, wherever you went. That's why I knew you were in trouble at home when the Chemist made an appearance. My colleague called me, and I came straight away, even though I was suspended,"

"Ah that's so creepy to think I was being followed. I didn't see anyone, ever," he said, surprised.

"That must mean they're good at their job," Brightwell beamed proudly. "Now, what you were somehow able to do is get in the right place at the right time on more than one occasion. I've worked with guys for ten years who could only dream of catching the breaks you did during their undercover detail. You got involved in some real key moments that got us solid photographic evidence of drug distribution, loan sharking-"

"Distribution?" he quizzed, "you were there for the drop at the bus depot?"

"I wasn't personally, but my mate D.I. Terry Jones was. Do you remember seeing a car with bricks instead of wheels?"

He thought for a moment. "Yeah, I do actually,"

"That my friend is the oldest trick in the book for a stake out and a few sneaky photographs. Nobody ever suspects the banger with no wheels,"

"I didn't have a clue," he marvelled, "although to be fair, I was more worried about where the hell they were taking me to notice much else,"

"We'd had tip offs before about drug drops down at that location at certain times, but it was nothing concrete, so we were never afforded the resources. So as soon as you were initiated and gave me some solid intel', we set up a camp just in case,"

"I don't know whether to feel relieved or violated," Tommy jibed.

"Just be happy. Tracking you was also the reason we were able to call the fire brigade so quickly after the attack on Kirsten's house. We were also able to hunt down the perpetrator fleeing from the scene of the crime and boy did he lead us straight to the pot of gold. He's in custody singing like a canary, dropping the names of big players that we can take down, all to cut a deal for himself. Criminals, eh? More loyalty amongst a bunch of rats,"

"So, what now?" Kirsten asked.

"We've already raided the studio above *The Grove* earlier this evening after we caught Mr. Petrol Bomb. Basically, we've got everything we need to put away Finn, Shay and Stephen O'Cleary for a good few years. And, as upsetting as the scenario was, we don't have to worry about the Chemist finding another distributer for *Charge*. Sorry again, Tommy,"

"Hey, no, you're in the business of stopping bad things happening to good people. It sounds like a win to me,"

"I appreciate that," Brightwell sighed, "I'm still hopeful I can reignite my daughter's case and stick some more evidence on Stephen O'Cleary. We're waiting on confirmation, but the suspicions point to the same type of petrol bomb, a *Molotov Cocktail,* used in both attacks. With this, plus the bloke in custody's testimony, we might have half a chance."

Kirsten rose to her feet and stepped towards Detective Brightwell, before throwing her arms around him in typical fashion, offering a comforting embrace.

"Sorry, I tend to hug people in delicate moments. Ask Tommy,"

"She does," Tommy confirmed affectionately.

Kirsten continued, "Thank you Detective, and I know we disagreed on your approach at times, but I really appreciate you shutting all of this mess down," she paused. "I truly hope you find peace and closure with your daughter."

She turned back towards her chair and flashed a peaceful smile towards Tommy. A niggling thought surfaced at that moment.

"Brightwell, can I ask you a question," he asked.

"Sure,"

"My friend from work, Charlie. He'd been acting very strange recently. Was he involved in any way?"

Brightwell placed both of his hands on the metal frame of the bed and leant over slightly, sighing in the process.

"The thing is, Tommy," he began, "there are literally hundreds and hundreds of people taking this drug around the town, we can't keep tabs on them all. I suspect your mate is a little goldfish in a lake full of piranhas. Whether that be that he likes using *Charge* every now and again, or he moves a bit of it around at the lower levels, or he's in a bit deeper for some more serious cash. But nothing he's doing is anywhere near the radar that we're looking at with guys like the O'Clearys and the Chemist,"

"I understand," Tommy said, "he's a nice lad you see, I would hate to think of him messed up in all of that,"

"Most people are nice, Tommy. It makes our job even harder, trust me."

A nurse popped her head around the corner of the curtain and asked if everything was ok, before requesting permission to interrupt and check Tommy's blood pressure, wheeling the appropriate machine in behind her. The three of them looked around awkwardly as she worked through the procedure. He guessed that both Brightwell and Kirsten felt the same reluctance as he did, opting for silence over continuing their conversation with the nurse in their presence.

The nurse left seeming happy with the readings and once both she and the trolley were out of sight, Tommy broke the silence.

"You said you had two bits of good news, what was the other?"

A huge grin painted Brightwell's face as he prepared himself to answer.

"It's your brother, Derek. He's awake."

As he approached the private room which had housed his brother for the last few weeks, where he'd spent so much of his time feeling hopeless, enraged and heartbroken, he stopped just shy of entering to observe the sight that lay before him. A familiar song crackled from the speakers which transmitted St James' hospital radio at varying points during the day: *Come Back to What You Know – Embrace.*

Peeking through the toughened glass window, he watched on with contentment, as his mum and brother exchanged infectious laughter. He saw his mum holding Derek's hand in hers, with an expression of gratitude that had been missing throughout his entire life. His brother was cracking jokes as usual and lay in the hospital bed as though he'd just woken up after a night on the tiles. He could feel his eyes brimming with the sting of happy tears.

He braced himself, quickly wiped under his cheeks with the knuckle of his index finger, before walking through the door to join them.

I'm coming back to what I know.

"Bloody Nora!" Derek hollered, "what's happened to you? You look dreadful,"

Tommy chuckled, wiping a persistent tear away with his sleeve, "You're one to talk,"

"Nice gown bro," Derek joked, "it suits you, brings out your eyes,"

The three of them burst out laughing, counterbalancing the raw emotion that was fizzing inside of him.

"I've missed you, bro'" Tommy wobbled.

Derek held out his arms, "Get over here, Tom'."

Without needing to be asked twice, Tommy galloped over to his brother's bed and almost dived onto him. They'd never been the most affectionate family, but this had been exceptional circumstances. He thought he'd lost his brother for good and, judging by the buckets of tears currently streaming down his mum's face as she joined in the family hug, he wasn't the only one.

Whilst the last few weeks had been testing in more ways than one, it had given Tommy some hard thinking time; a period of reflection that had taken him to the pits of despair and back again. He'd spent so long resenting his mum and his brother, resisting what they stood for and searching beyond the horizon for what else might be out there, he'd lost himself in complacency, he'd underestimated what was really important, or rather who was really important.

At this moment, he accepted that his mum and brother were more than likely going to mess up, everybody does, even himself, even Detective Brightwell. But what mattered most was this embrace right now; they had each other and everybody was still breathing.

CHAPTER FORTY-THREE

The bright twinkle of multi coloured Christmas lights, which decorated the houses facing Collingwood Green, contrasted against the impenetrable, murky clouds. Dusk was rapidly descending upon Granville, as Tommy and Kirsten strolled, side by side, along the leafy path towards the noise of distant traffic.

Kirsten's chin was nuzzled into an oversized camel scarf, her curly hair spiralling out of the matching woolly hat. They'd spent the last twenty minutes walking and talking, smiling and laughing, not really discussing anything in particular, yet he couldn't shake the excitable nerves which jangled around his belly.

The unspoken chemistry had been screaming, their eyes catching one another peeking, as though their hidden intentions were taboo. Any of his awkward attempts at conversation had been politely entertained by Kirsten, but the promise in her eyes said more.

He was still in a phase of having to pinch himself whenever he was in Kirsten's company, ever since their feelings were blurted into the open. She was a straight up ten out of ten, a diamond inside and out; he'd never believed he was good enough, but she seemed to see it another way.

They nudged along, with periodic stints of holding

hands and not. It felt the easiest kind of uneasiness he'd ever experienced. As they reached the main road, leaving one of the town's more picturesque green spaces in their tracks, they crossed over and made the short walk towards Tommy's house, with the neighbourhood changing from Beverley Hills to Beirut within a matter of yards.

As they turned onto Frampton Road, a familiar car pulled up; *it was Darcy O'Cleary.*

"Oh no," he sighed, flashing an anxious glance towards Kirsten.

"Don't worry, I'm here," she said.

Darcy eased her way out of her car and gently closed the door, the engine still running and the radio uncharacteristically low in volume.

"I was just on my way to your house, glad I bumped into you first," Darcy said sheepishly.

"Oh really?" Tommy mustered.

"Sorry to interrupt," she said, offering a sincere smile Kirsten's way, "do you mind if we have a quick word, Tommy?"

This is bizarre...

He nodded, following her the fifteen or so paces she trotted for some privacy.

"I'm not really sure what to say," he offered apologetically.

"You don't have to say anything," she sighed. "I came to clear the air, to tell you there's no hard feelings,"

His neuro pathways began scrapping with one another to try and decode the possible hidden meaning in what was being said.

She continued, "I always knew they were up to no good. Yeah, threats and violence came with the territory I guess, and obviously I knew selling a bit of gear paid for some fancy cars and nice holidays and it never really crossed my conscience. The less I knew the better, right? But if they've done half of what they're being accused of; knowingly pushing lethal drugs, killing people, teenagers, my friends, that Detective's daughter, that poor little girl," she paused, choking on tears, her wavering pride the only thing preventing the dam from bursting open.

He reached out his hand and rested it on her shoulder, "Hey, are you ok?"

"I will be," she sniffled, "it's a lot to take in,"

"I bet. I've had some pretty big revelations myself," he said.

"I've heard. I swear I didn't know," she protested.

"Don't worry about it, it's all been a bit messy. I've done things I regret throughout this, getting involved, pretending to people, that's not usually me. I'm sorry if I hurt you,"

"I know, that's why I came to bury the hatchet. Do me a favour though, yeah?

"If I can, I will,"

"Be careful. Look, I get it, you were the cheese that was placed in the trap to catch a rat, whether you knew about it or not. And this time you're ok, you've come out the other side, which I'm relieved about believe it or not. Are you sure you can always trust the trap to come through though? Because one day it might malfunction, and the cheese is going to get gobbled up by any number of nasty rodents out there. You're a good guy, Tommy, and it looks to me like you've got yourself a lovely girl," she flashed another acknowledging smile over at Kirsten, who was watching on with bated breath.

"I appreciate that, I've every intention of staying well away from anything like this ever again, trust me,"

"I hope so,"

"And listen," he added, "you're a great girl, you know that, right?"

"I'm slowly learning, but it's going to take me a while. I've basically found out all the men in my life are absolute scum bags, so it's probably going to take some serious therapy to iron out those knots," she giggled, as endearing snot bubbled at the end of her nose, before embarrassment took over.

"What's your plan?" he asked, moving the subject on and giving her time to wipe it away with her sleeve.

"Me and my mum are moving out of town. Fresh start. Turns out my mum has been embezzling cash out from under my dad's nose for years, plotting our escape from his tyranny. There's loads I could tell you that I've found out, but its best left unsaid. The main thing is me and my mum can move on and we've got a bit of money for independence and a clean slate,"

"I'd love to say I'm happy for you, but you know what I mean,"

"I do," she said, before rising onto her tiptoes and giving him a peck on the cheek. "Goodbye, Tommy,"

"Bye, Darcy."

She walked back to her car and offered a parting wave to Kirsten, who of course politely returned the gesture with her own. She hopped in her car, punched her seatbelt into the socket and sped off up Frampton Road towards her new beginning.

"Well that was unexpected," Kirsten comforted, siding up next to him.

"Yeah, very," he marvelled, admiring Darcy's gesture, whilst acknowledging how much peace of mind that it would bring him knowing that there were no hard feelings.

They continued the walk up Tommy's street towards his house, with Kirsten having slipped her arm through his, linking them in body and in spirit. They bid farewell to another short, winter's day as the quick succession of flickering streetlamps indicated that it was now officially evening.

"Wait," Kirsten said abruptly, stopping in her tracks just before Tommy's residence.

"What's up?" he asked, turning back to face her.

"Nothing's up, I just," she stopped, slipped her hand in his and, despite the December chill, he felt an instant warmth through to his soul. She continued, "I've been wanting to do something for a long time, and I've decided that no-body else is going to get in the way,"

She pulled him forwards gently. Her lips were pursed, plump and glossy from her strawberry balm. Their eyes now locked, unafraid as intentions were no longer hidden. They both felt this, he could see that now. His pulse throbbed against his ear drums, almost leaving him deaf, but he didn't care.

Leaning in towards him, she closed her eyes and their lips finally met in a moment of purity. Adrenaline raced, shooting to all four corners of his being, as previously unchar-tered emotions detonated inside of him. Her scarf tickled underneath his chin, as she lifted her hand and gently placed it on his chest.

Another pinch yourself moment.

Their lips eventually unlocked after a prolonged ex-change of raw electricity. He knew right there in that mo-ment that he loved her, there was no doubt in his mind. A love shy home had always left him wondering if he would ever truly find it for himself and if he did, he questioned how on earth he would know what it felt like. But now he knew. It felt like somebody reaching inside of his chest and cradling his heart with unadulterated acceptance.

He looked into her eyes, preparing himself to say those precious three words, when Kirsten's expression sud-denly changed. She appeared serious, concerned even, as he no longer held her gaze, instead she looked right through him.

"Kirsten?" he panicked, paranoid that his kiss hadn't lived up to expectations.

Her lips were frozen momentarily, before she man-aged to speak, "Look,"

She pointed behind him, towards his house. He turned in an instant and saw a sight that reignited an unwelcome, yet familiar, feel of terror and panic. The front door of his house had been branded with red spray paint; the iconic smiley face was back. A message had been sent loud and clear

and there was no mistaking that red paint spelled danger.
He swallowed hard, "This isn't over, is it?"

GET IN TOUCH

You can keep in touch with author, Nathan Parker,
via his social media accounts below:

Facebook page: Parker Book
Instagram: @parker_book
Twitter: @parker_book

Or for event bookings, school visits, authors
talks, please email:

parker_book@outlook.com

If you enjoyed this book, please
spare a few minutes to review.

Thank you!

ABOUT THE AUTHOR

Nathan Parker

Nathan Parker is a professional Youth Worker, with various experiences in schools, the community, substance misuse and mental health, spanning 12 years. He has recently decided to transition to part-time hours, to pursue his writing career, including visits to schools to work on literacy with young people, particulalry those who are disadvantaged.

Nathan's first novel, The Disappearance of Timothy Dawson (Book 1 in the Granville Series) was shortlisted for the Lancashire Book of the Year 2019.

His writing style incorporates real life challenges and adversity into gripping and mysterious plots.

Printed in Great Britain
by Amazon